She yearned to learn his ways....

"*Wiwasteka*, my beautiful woman ..."

She opened her eyes and gazed deeply into his. He thought her beautiful. She had wanted this, to see his desire. She had waited patiently for him, knowing what would happen once he saw her. She had scrubbed her skin until it tingled and then dried herself with fur. A mixture of pulverized columbine seeds and water perfumed her entire body. For what had seemed like an eternity she'd brushed her hair until it shone. She'd waited, letting the warmth of the sun shining from the opening above finger her naked body, preparing herself for his return.

His voice soft, deep and sensual licked her skin like the heat of a flame. "I burn hot for you," he whispered against her ear.

"And I for you."

"Listen to the language of my heart." He placed her hand against his bare chest. She could feel its rapid thumping.

"My heart, too, speaks your language." She brought his hand to her breast.

Slowly, seductively, his gaze slid downward over her body—a gaze as soft as a caress. The air around them seemed electrified. She drew in a shuddering breath. The fresh scent of pine and mountain mahogany leaves that lay scattered around them, filled her lungs.

He leaned closer, wrapped his arms around her waist and drew her near. She encircled his neck with her arms. His leather loincloth pressed against her hips. His chest crushed her breasts.

"*Winyan. Tanyán yahí yélo.*"

Their lips only inches apart, she could taste his hot, hypnotic whispers upon her mouth. The need to touch him, to feel him touch her was insatiable.

She stared deeply into his eyes, magnificent dark eyes, warm with desire. "I do not understand your words."

"Woman," he repeated. "I am glad you came."

A
Find
Through
Time

Marianne Petit

New Leaf ✧ Illinois

This is a work of fiction. Names, characters, places and incidences are either a product of the author's imagination or used fictitiously. Any similarity to actual organizations and persons, living or deceased, is entirely coincidental.

A New Leaf Book
Published by WigWam Publishing Co.
P.O. Box 6992
Villa Park, IL 60181
http://www.newleafbooks.net

Second edition 2001

Printed in the U.S.A.

*This book is dedicated in loving memory to
my father, Frenchie, whose love of history
rubbed off on me.*

A special thank you to Sylvia, my mentor and teacher, for all those hours of editing and rereads; to Lisa and all my critique partners, especially Vickie who helped me with the Lakota language.

And finally, from the bottom of my heart, I thank my sons, Robert and Nick, who put up with my constant computer work; and my husband, Steve, my best friend, whose encouragement, love and faith in me is the driving force behind my inspiration.

The old ones say that dreams are but visions into other worlds....

PROLOGUE

*T*he whip bit down upon his back, flicking layer upon layer of swollen flesh from his body, yet the Sioux warrior held himself erect. To show his weakness would be more unforgiving than the white man's piece of rawhide that seared his skin like white-hot lightning.

Sweat pooled on the bridge of his nose and upper lip. He dug his fingernails into his palms. Curse the blue clad soldiers who stood around waiting, watching. Pressed up against the pole, splinters worked their way into his chest. The rope around his wrists cut deeply. It mattered not. He had withstood the pain of many a dance to the sun, had gone many days without food or water on his vision quests. He must fight, stand tall.

Again the whip unfurled its teeth upon him. Soon his strength would give out and his enemies would have the satisfaction of seeing him fall, but until then he was going to make *Wakan Tanka*, the Great Spirit, proud.

"Tell them! Where is Sitting Bull?" The words spoken in his Lakota tongue by the Crow scout seemed many moons away.

"Traitor! White man's dog!" He glared with hatred at the enemy before him. "One day this Sioux warrior will have his revenge and you will find your scalp hanging high before my lodging."

His gaze shifted to the one with the hair of the sun. "Hanging beside his." He spat the words this time in the white man's tongue so that Yellow Hair Custer would understand.

"*Hey-ay-hee-ee*, hear my call. This is my promise."

"Hit him again," he heard the white general order.

"Fool," the Crow scout whispered near the warrior's face. "I gave you a chance, a chance to end this pain but you refused."

"You my enemy, enemy of my people, answerable to the white man, it would please you to see me shame myself by taking my own life." The warrior spat. "That is what I think of you and your offer."

Furious the Crow scout swiped his face, raised the whip in his hand and stepped around the pole.

Pain shot across the warrior's back. "My sister's injustice will be..." His jaw tightened in anticipation of yet another jolt of pain. Again the whip unfurled its biting tongue. "... revenged." His eyelids dropped and he struggled to open them. His vision blurred. The light of day seemed to fade. The fiery blaze on his back spread rapidly, devouring him in its jaws.

Then just before he felt himself journey into that dark place in his mind, where the shadowed path led to light, he raised his gaze to the sky. Slowly the clouds began to shift and change form. The ghostly image of a white wolf with pale blue eyes stared back at him, hauntingly.

His lids dropped shut. And in his mind's eye, from the darkness that surrounded him there came a song, and a woman journeyed down from the land above....

ONE

*T*he skull sat on the table challenging her to put all the pieces of the puzzle together. There was something mysterious about that skull. Not that it looked any different from all the rest she had examined over the years. Yet, how else could she explain the way it had seemed to call out to her from its grave beneath the ground?

Clay in hand, Gabrielle Camden began the long, exciting procedure of reconstructing the face. To actually bring a find to life, to be able to look into that image and unlock a part of the past, made being a forensic artist all worthwhile.

Starting at the forehead she carefully placed a piece of tan clay from the tissue marker of the left temple, to the parallel white peg of the right temple. With nimble fingers she smoothed and shaped the clay to fit perfectly, cutting off the extra pieces that weren't necessary to the contour of the skull. She continued in this manner until she had the entire facial line in place, then sat back and studied her work.

Tiny goose bumps pricked her arm, just as before when she first discovered the skull. Nothing had prepared them—or her—for the likes of NAF, the acronym they gave their Native American Find. Or should she say *her* find?

On a whim she had decided to stop by the dig site to see if anything new had been found. She'd come to the top of the hill overlooking the winding river, when the feeling had slammed into her like a giant wave. The pull so strong and intense, she'd known without a doubt if she followed her feet to the spot beside the river and dug beneath the entwined roots of the big cottonwood tree, NAF would be there waiting.

When they'd finally found it, seven feet under, she couldn't believe she was seeing correctly. When she'd managed to stop her hands from shaking and held the skull in her open palms, she had felt a connection to that skull the likes of which she'd never known before.

A strange familiarity. Which, of course, was absurd.

Disturbed by her thoughts, Gabrielle picked up her caliper and measured the gum line for the depth of the teeth and size, then laid the

1

fork-shaped instrument back down on the table.

She glanced up as George Stevens pushed aside the tent flap. Thirty-five years of age, her boss' nephew, he had the IQ of a twelve-year-old, which made some of her coworkers uncomfortable. She wasn't one of them. A kind and considerate man, George followed the digs from site to site, doing odd jobs. He was a hard worker, and she liked having him around.

"George, hand me that long piece of clay." She pointed to the end of the table.

He handed her a tan strip. She placed the narrow piece across and under the skull's mouth, then used her fingers to mold and shape the area until satisfied with the lips she had created. A large square chunk and the front, left side, was smoothed down into place from the cheekbone marker to the marker on the jawbone.

"There's someone outside waiting for you," George announced.

"Could you just tell whoever it is that I'm not here?" She'd been interrupted four times and it wasn't even eleven o'clock. Why couldn't she ever finish a project in peace? Working in a tent at the site was like being in the middle of a parade with a headache.

George hurried over to the tent flap and peaked through a slit in the opening. "It's that reporter, Roy Prescott," he whispered loud enough to wake the dead.

"Oh, no. Not now." Last time Prescott paid her a visit it felt as though he were photographing her with his eyes, instead of the camera in his hand.

George leaned over her workbench and gave her a silly smirk. "He brings flowers."

"You know that's just a bribe. You'd think he'd get the message that he's not wanted here." Her brow furrowed. "Reporters aren't allowed near the site." She had to admire his driving persistence though.

"He likes you," George teased.

"You remember what happened last time, don't you?"

"Yeah." He frowned. "You want me to get rid of him?"

Anticipation and aggravation churned in her stomach. "Yes."

As George turned to leave, the phone rang. Exasperated, she flung up her hands, reached down and picked up the line. What she wouldn't give to be left alone.

"Hello? Mother? Hi. I can barely hear you. This cellular isn't working well."

"Did you get the blouse I sent over to you?" her mother repeated.

"Yes, Mother. I got it. Thanks. It's beautiful." Gabrielle glanced down at the fancy blue silk blouse she'd unwrapped earlier. Another birthday present never to be worn. She flicked the tissue paper over the shirt. They were never going to think alike. With both of them being in the same field of work you'd think they'd agree on something.

"What?" She drew her attention back to her mother's voice at the end of the line.

"I said, the color goes well with your eyes, doesn't it?"

"Yes, it matches perfectly." She drummed her fingers on the table. Her neck and chest tensed.

"Are you coming to dinner Saturday? I'm inviting a few people over."

"Gee. No. Sorry, I can't." *Liar.* Gabrielle sniffed with haughty denial. Somehow she never measured up to Mother's expectations. Willimina, the university's prized archeologist. Head of the department, topnotch, best of the bunch, she'd always been too busy for the likes of her.

Gabrielle snapped open the book about the Battle of Little Big Horn that lay on the table. Not a single solider had survived that day in 1876, including Jackson Wilfred, her great-great-grandfather. Sadness overcame her. She would have liked to have met the strong-looking man whose picture lay nestled between the pages of the family photo album.

"You didn't come last time either," Willimina said.

Gabrielle exhaled. "Yes, mother, I know I missed the last dinner party."

"So cancel your plans and come."

"I can't. I've got way too much work."

Scanning down the page she noticed the list of Native Americans killed was far shorter than the hundreds of cavalrymen killed that day. Approximately thirty-two Indian casualties. It seemed the Indians had fared better, but it could hardly be called a victory.

Her mother's voice still rang in her ear. "You really need to get out more. Date. Meet a nice man."

Gabrielle's stomach contracted into a tight ball. "Mother, I'm not interested in dating."

"Look, I'm not getting any younger."

Here it comes. She rolled her gaze to the ceiling and mouthed her mother's next words.

"I'd like to have a grandchild before I die."

"Yes, I know." *A thousand times over.* The paper beneath her fingertips crimped as she flicked to the next page. A picture of a Native American camp spanned the two pages. Life had to have been a lot less complicated then.

"So find a nice guy and settle down." Her mother's nasal voice pounded her brain.

Gabrielle pinched the bridge of her nose. Her temples began to throb. "How many times do we have to go over this?" She struggled to control her voice from quavering.

"Look. You're not the first woman to be left at the altar. Granted the guy was a jerk but, get on with your life. You're not a little girl anymore." Willimina's patronizing tone brought a lump to her throat.

The pain of the day three years ago still hurt more than she cared to admit, and now thanks to her mother, all the hurtful memories came pouring back. Gripping the phone with a tight fist, she swallowed dryly and took a deep calming breath. "Mother, I've got—"

"To get on with your life. I agree. So get a date and come over."

Disappointment, resentment, burned her chest. The walls of her small tent seemed to close in, suffocating her. "I've got to hang up now. I have a lot of work still ahead of me."

Dead silence.

"Well ..." Her mother sighed. "I understand. Perhaps next time?"

"Next time."

"Take care dear."

"Bye."

Funny, how retirement changed a person. With a twinge of guilt, Gabrielle hit the shut off button on her cellular. Now Mother had plenty of time.

Only thing was—she didn't.

What she wouldn't have given as a child just to have spent some time with her mother, play games, listen to stories like other children. Thank God for Jeffery. He'd been more than her tutor. He'd been her only friend; had filled a void in a lonely child's life. He'd made living from one site to another almost fun.

At the age of thirteen, when her father had left, had her mother taken the time to comfort her? No. And her wedding day, she had suffered alone in a brittle silence that had hardened her heart against men; all men, whose reaction when it came to their feelings was to run away.

An acute sense of loss weighted her shoulders. She straightened. Willimina wasn't going to make her feel—

George swung open the tent flap interrupting her thoughts. "Sorry." He raised his hands in defeat. "No go. He won't leave until he talks to you. Go talk to him. He's nice."

She sighed. "Doesn't that guy ever give up?" Maybe it was her imagination, but he seemed to be hanging around a little more than usual.

George shrugged and held out his hand.

"Oh, all right." She grabbed the flowers and marched outside.

Blond-haired, brown-eyed Roy Prescott possessed a ruggedness and vital power that seemed to reach out and grab her. His chiseled face, bronzed by the sun, held a certain sensuality. Immaculately dressed in tight, new blue jeans and a crisp black shirt, he held his slender but strong physique tall with confidence.

She cast her eyes to the ground before her, keenly aware of her own dusty boots and soiled, creased shorts. Her stomach lurched. What was it about him that constantly made her feel like an adolescent schoolgirl with a crush? Damn. She glanced back up. Why did he have to be so good looking? And since when did his hair get long enough to tie back?

The sun glistened off a long silver feather hanging from his ear. Though the earring didn't quite fit her old image of him, it couldn't detract from his overwhelming masculinity. And that smile. Her heart pounded foolishly. What the hell was the matter with her? Had she completely lost it? She wasn't interested in dating. Not him, not anyone. She pushed a strand of dark hair from her eye, squared her shoulders and handed him the bouquet.

"Here. I can't accept these. Thanks anyway."

His stance solid, he crossed his muscular tan arms in front of his chest, refusing the flowers. The set of his chin suggested a stubborn streak. He wasn't going to give in too easily.

"Please. Take them."

"Now Gabby, it's a peace offering. Surely you can't turn that down?" His attitude of self-command unnerved her.

"Mr. Prescott—"

Reluctantly, he grabbed the bouquet. "Don't you think we should be on a first name basis by now? After all, it's not like we just met. What is it, six months now that I've been hounding you?" He frowned. "Hell, I know more about you than I know about myself." He lowered the flowers knee length. "You live alone with your cat. You love to read, know all the librarians by name and you don't cook."

"See. That's exactly the point. You hang around too much. I ..." *God.* Six months. Had he really been around that long? Suddenly his words sank in. "You've been spying on me? That's—" A claustrophobic sensation seemed to choke her. "That's an invasion of privacy."

His jaw clenched and he shifted his weight as though her words had

disturbed him. "Don't be offended. I'm a reporter. I make it my business
to know my assignments."

"And I do, too, like to cook." She jerked her hands to her hips.

"That remains to be seen." He grinned smugly.

The muscles rippling under his black, open-collared shirt quickened
her pulse, sent a flutter to her stomach—an emotion she found
disturbing. Why hadn't she ever noticed how muscular he was?

"You're Frank Prescott's son, aren't you?"

"Yeah, well, don't spread it around." He clasped then unclasped his
hand. "We all can't choose our parents now, can we?"

His tone was light, but there was no doubt in her mind that he meant
it.

"Didn't I see an article in the paper last week about him?"

"It's an ego thing. He just likes seeing his name in the paper." Roy's
mouth crimped.

"Don't you?"

"What?"

"Like seeing your name in the paper."

For a moment, he regarded her quizzically. "That's part of the job.
Comes with the territory. Anyway we were talking about you."

"Changing the subject, are you?" Her brows rose. "How does it feel
to have someone interrogate you?"

Awkwardly, he cleared his throat. "Point taken."

"Great. So stop following me around."

"I will if you're up front with me. Tell me what I want to know.
Spend time with me out in the open."

God. She'd love to get her hands on his face. She blushed. To
sculpt, she reassured herself. "I can't. After the last fiasco I could lose
my job if anyone from the university staff sees us talking." She glanced
away.

"Oh, that ridiculous line again. That's water under the bridge. Old
news. What are you working on this time?" He examined her face
searching for an explanation. His eyes were so chocolaty brown—and
she loved chocolate.

Her stance straightened defensively. "Yeah, well maybe it got you
front page news, but the university was left with egg on its face and a
year without funding for future projects. It was hell. Do you know what
it's like to have everything you do approved and scrutinized? It's like
living under a microscope."

Roy shrugged. "Lighten up. It wasn't your fault. How were you
supposed to know the information you gave me was falsified? Damn.

I've never met anyone so uptight about their job. Come on, relax a little. I didn't mean to get you so riled up." He placed a hand on her shoulder.

His warm palm sent a wave of tingling electricity through her. *No. Don't get involved. You'll only get hurt again.* Gabrielle stepped back, fighting the strong magnetic pull drawing her to him.

"You think I get to choose my own stories?" Roy stepped closer. The earthy scent of musk cologne wafted across her face.

"Hell, you gotta be on top for that."

On top? Gabrielle's heart pounded and she prayed her face wouldn't give away her erotic thoughts.

With a deliberately casual movement, he leaned in. His face only inches from hers, Gabrielle's breath caught. She stared at his perfectly formed lips.

"Besides, it wasn't like I wasn't offered that story. You guys offered it to me. Remember?" His breath blew warm against her cheeks. "I print what I see." He held his fingers up. "I quote: sixteenth dynasty statue found. One of a kind. Said to belong to Egyptian king. End of quote."

Those eyes. She could get lost in their dark depths. Her palms clammy, her breathing labored, she took an unsteady whiff of air.

"You had no way of knowing it was all a hoax planted by some overly desperate guy looking to keep his department open," he said, his voice seductively soft. His closeness made her thoughts spin.

He was right, of course. Still, reporters were banned from all future projects until the staff was certain their finds were legit.

His breath mingled with hers and her pulse raced.

And, like him or not, she sure as hell wasn't going to jeopardize her job talking to him.

"Look." She took a step back. "I don't have time to stand here and argue with you about past mistakes. I have to get back to work." She started to turn.

He grabbed her wrist.

She noticed how the muscles in his arm corded and his stance grew taut. Again her stomach quaked. His touch seemed oddly familiar, somehow comforting. It felt stronger than merely just two people who had met before and were somewhat attracted to each other. No, this underlying force of attraction seemed deeper, like she had known him well—loved him before.

She blinked, baffled. This was utterly insane. She twisted her hand from his grip.

"I've got to go." She spun on her heel in dazed exasperation and headed back to the tent.

"I know my stuff. There's a story here, all right." He skirted around her. "And by the way, I do know what it's like." He stepped in front of her blocking her way.

His gaze traveled seductively over her face and searched her eyes.

"Not too proud, are you?" she asked.

"Just honest." Again he stepped closer. Their eyes locked. An invisible force of electricity seemed to spark between them, drawing them closer and closer. Yearning radiated off his face like heat from a roaring fire. He was going to kiss her. The thought sent her heart in a panic. She blinked then abruptly stepped aside.

Both gazes froze on one another. She had the feeling Roy was as stunned by the deep attraction surging between them as she was.

An uncomfortable silence stretched between them.

He cleared his throat. "Now about that—"

"Please, don't ask," she silenced him before he had a chance to finish his sentence. "I can't tell you anything."

Grinning, he held out his hand. "At least keep the flowers."

Damn. He had such straight white teeth. She hesitated. *God, they're only flowers, not a proposal.* She took his peace offering. "Thanks." Then backed away. "What's with the earring? Going for a new look?"

"Now, don't you go and start too." He rolled his gaze to the sky and shook his head. "I'm still smarting from the jokes my coworkers ground into my hide." He brought his hand to his ear, fingering the dangling turquoise and silver feather.

"I don't have the foggiest notion why I did it." His brow crunched and his eyes held a look of puzzlement. "I was passing this store, went inside, and before I knew it I was letting some woman puncture my ear. I bought this to." He reached into his pocket and pulled out a beaded neck band. "Not exactly me, is it?"

"Well, do you have a dog? You could use it as a collar."

The huskiness of his laugh lingered in the air between them. "What are you, some kind of *heyoka*?" he asked.

"A what?"

A disturbed expression crept across his face as he stared at her in silence. "Clown. It's the Sioux word for clown. Only ..." He shook his head. "I don't know how I knew that."

Roy stared at Gabrielle, studying her face for a reaction. She reminded him of the Ivory Soap commercials, the ones where the women always had that clean, fresh outdoorsy-looking aura. Even in those baggy shorts and T-shirt she couldn't hide that shapely figure or that drop-dead pair of legs. "I must have picked the word up somewhere. I probably read the translation somewhere for an article." Boy, he was way overdue for a physical.

Gabrielle shrugged. "I guess."

There was something in those baby blues of hers; something he had never seen before, an intense lure, an abysmal connection that hit him squarely in the gut.

"Look. I've got to get back to work." She turned.

"No. Wait." God, her eyes were so clear he could swear he was looking into glass. A few strands of ebony hair fell to her cheek. She brushed the locks away leaving a smudge of dirt on her face. What he wouldn't give to be able to wet his finger and wipe that mark away.

He cleared his throat, bringing his mind back to the conversation. "Let me take you dancing sometime." He'd trade a dozen of those phony plastic women he had met at his father's club for just one of her.

Her gaze darted. A familiar emptiness nibbled at his soul. She wasn't going to say yes. "Or how about a cup of coffee?" It seemed his playboy reputation preceded him. Past mistakes weren't easily erased. "A quick cup, nothing more."

"I'm sorry," she said softly.

Rejection punched his chest like a solid fist, mid-center. Hell, last thing he needed in his life was a complication. He straightened his shoulders. And she was an emotional minefield.

"I'm in the middle of a project. I can't leave."

"Thought you'd say that, so I took the liberty ..."

Before she had a chance to argue he grabbed her hand.

"What?"

"Just come with me for a second."

"Roy, I—"

"Don't make me haul you over my shoulder," he teased.

Her eyes widened. "You wouldn't!"

"Just walk over there." He pointed to a tent a few yards from the one she'd been working in. "I'd like to show you something."

She slipped her hand from his, hesitated, then moved in the indicated direction. Her steps slow, she seemed to ponder her decision.

Roy quickly stepped beside her and reached the tent before she did. He opened the flap, gestured her in and followed behind.

A soft gasp escaped her. "What in the world?" She stared at the set table and chairs in the middle of the tent. "China? Silver? I ... I don't know what to say." Intense astonishment lit her luminous eyes. "I ...

How did you—"

"I bribed the guard at the gate and swore I was on an unofficial call. In fact, I had to give him my camera, which I might add, is like giving up my right arm. So ... what'll you say?"

She bit her lip, debating. "You swear on your precious camera, no shop talk?"

"Cross my heart. No questions."

"Well ..." An uncertainty crept into her expression. She glanced to the table then back at him. "You went through so much trouble ... But only for a few minutes. I can't—"

"I know, be seen with me. I understand."

They walked over. He pulled out her chair and she sat.

He settled into the opposite seat. "So. Tell me about yourself."

"What? You don't know everything?" She smiled.

"Not the important things." Roy picked up the coffee pot and poured. She teased him. That was a good sign. "Sugar?"

"Just milk. I can't believe you went through all this trouble."

"It was my pleasure."

Her spoon clinked the inside of her cup as she stirred.

Roy took a sip of coffee. He studied her face over the rim of his cup. No makeup, not a stitch. A natural beauty. This was the first time he'd ever been with a woman who hadn't plastered herself with makeup. He liked it. Liked it a lot.

"Well mister reporter man, what do you want to know? Time's ticking." She tapped her watch. Though her tone was light, he sensed her unease.

Damn. She was beautiful. A hot wave of desire swept across his body. "Your family. What are they like?"

"I really don't want to talk about them." A shadow of annoyance puckered her lips. She picked up her cup, her gaze fixed on the coffee inside.

"I can understand that." Seems they shared the same feelings. Last thing he'd want to do was spill his guts over a cup of coffee.

She glanced up. A flicker of relief crossed her face.

"Traveling. You've done a lot of traveling with your job."

Her cup hit the saucer with a clink. "You promised no—"

"I was just going to ask what your favorite place was."

"Oh."

Was that a blush beneath that dark tan?

"Strawberry?" He held out the plate.

She took a berry ...

"Egypt. India. Africa. It's too hard to choose I guess."

... took an erotic bite.

"Your childhood must have been amazing." He placed the plate to the table.

Her gaze dropped, as did her facial expression.

"What, did I say something wrong?"

Their gaze met and he swore he saw a sadness cloud those lovely blues.

"The same as any other girl." She shrugged. "My life." She fidgeted in her seat.

"No way. Camping out under the stars, campfires, living in the open—a kid's dream."

"Maybe some. Not mine," she said in a voice that seemed to come from a long way off.

"What was it like?"

"Lonely."

He placed his hand on hers. His heart hammered foolishly. A surge of blood shot to his groin.

Her breath quickened. She slipped her fingers away. "You must have had a great childhood, private jet, yacht, all those big fancy parties and galas one reads about in the gossip column. Like I said, I just read that your father donated a large sum of money to a relief fund for some flood victims. Paper portrayed him as quite a hero."

The speed of her voice, the nervous flutter of her hand—he was getting to her. "One shouldn't believe what one reads in the paper," he said, keeping his tone light, though the very mention of his father was pushing the pleasure of this moment away.

She grinned. "And this from a reporter?"

Her smile more intoxicating than a bottle of Dom Perignon, he felt a tug, a tightening sensation of arousal. He shifted his weight, making himself more comfortable.

"I would have given anything to live in a big fancy house ..."

Staring at her luscious lips, it was getting difficult to concentrate on her words.

"... live under any roof for a long period." She took a sip of coffee.

"And I would have given anything to get out from under it." The words slipped from his mouth before he had a chance to stop them.

An awkward silence hung between them.

"Boring. My childhood was boring." Damn. Had he just said that? His mouth, felt dry, like old brittle paper. He reached for his cup and took a drink.

"Oh."

Again, the silence.

She glanced away then back at him. "Make believe."

Said so softly, her words were barely audible. "What?"

"After my parents would dig up some ancient relic, I used to fantasize about living in that time period. I'd image whose hands crafted the vase or statue; imagine what it would be like to travel back in time. Silly huh?"

"No." Even her blush was an erotic turn on. "We all have our own way of escaping. Seems we have more in common than you thought. What are you working on now?"

She frowned. "You promised."

"For fun. What kind of piece are you sculpting—working on in your leisure."

"How did you know I—"

He grinned. "I haven't been peeping through your window, if that's what you're thinking. I happened to be doing some research in the library last week and over heard you talking with the librarian."

"A little boy. I'm working on a little boy and his dog."

Lightly he touched her fingers. "Maybe sometime you could show me."

The air grew thicker with palpable tension.

"Maybe." She pushed back her chair. "Look, this has been nice, but I've got to get—"

"Back. I know." He stood and they walked in silence toward the opening.

"You're not hiding the Abominable Snowman or some frozen caveman back in your tent are you?" Hell, he had to say something to lighten the mood.

"Don't be ridiculous. Whatever gave you that idea?"

Bingo! Her eyes darted from his for just a second. Maybe he'd hit on something.

"This was lovely."

Yes, you are. He took her hand. Squeezed her fingers lightly. "Promise me I won't have to wait another six months to get a little of your time. OK?"

"Thanks for the coffee … the talk. I've really—"

"Go." He let go of her hand and flipped up the tent flap. "I gotta get my camera anyway. I'm starting to feel a little lost without it."

Gabrielle stepped outside. She turned back, glanced at him and the sunlight hit her face, reminding him of the dream he'd had last night.

Indians. He'd dreamt of Indians. Long hair flowing past their shoulders, chests and faces painted in blacks and grays, they were engaged in some kind of battle. And there, standing in the middle of all the commotion, stood Gabrielle. Dressed in a white, beaded leather dress and moccasins, she looked angelic, a contrast to the devastation and ugliness around her. Then it was snowing; yet he got the feeling that it was summer.

When Gabrielle whipped open the tent flap, she came within inches of whipping George in the face. Obviously, he had been spying on her. Again she realized how much she hated having no privacy.

"I see you dumped the newspaper man."

"I didn't dump him," she said sharply. She chewed the inside of her lip. Sitting there sipping coffee, eating strawberries, feeling the intense attraction pulling at her, she had to restrain herself from bolting from the table. Why did he have to be so nice? Irritable, restless, she turned away not waiting for a response.

George followed behind her as she stepped around her workbench, dropped the flowers to the table then plopped into the chair, facing him.

Men were emotional disasters. No matter how cute. A gamut of perplexing emotions pummeling her mind, she stared absentmindedly at the tent's opening. *Why in the world did I agree to have coffee with him?* She rubbed her forehead. Tension throbbed beneath her fingertips. It had always been a professional relationship between them uncluttered with emotional garbage. Clean. Cut. She kept her distance. He did his job. Why now was her heart acting so foolishly? She didn't have the time— or the need—or the want, for that matter, for this foolishness.

She breathed in sharply. *Now he wants more—more than I can give.* Her chest felt as though it would burst and the need to run. To get away from her mother, Roy, her own remembered past, seemed to be stretching her nerves to a frazzled, thinning cord.

"Hey," George pointed at something behind her. "Why'd ya make that face to look like you?"

"What?" Gabrielle spun around and stared at the skull. He had to be imagining things. Or was he? She took a closer look. The blood drained from her face. *My God!* It did resemble her!

A claustrophobic panic rioted within her. She dug her fingers in the table's edge, blinked, and stared harder. Except for the nose, which was straight and fuller than her own, the damn thing looked too much like her. Why hadn't she seen that before?

The first thing that flashed through her head was a picture of her boss pacing. She could hear it now. He'd be rambling nonstop. *How could you have done such a stupid thing? Your own image? What am I supposed to think?* In fact, he'd be yelling: *What is the board going to think? How is this going to look for the university?*

Her breathing shallow, quick, she raked her fingers through her hair. She could take off the clay, change it, but deep in her heart, she knew it would be wrong. She bolted from her chair. Fired. That was going to be her boss's next line.

The room began to spin. George was mouthing something, but all she could see was that face—her face staring back at her. "I've got to get some air," she mumbled, pushing past him.

"Miss Gabby, are you all right?"

She halted in mid-stride and turned. "Nobody's gonna believe I didn't do that on purpose."

"So?"

"George." She paused. He wouldn't understand she felt like she had lost her objectivity. "It's kind of hard to explain." That for some unknown reason that skull had a strange affect on her, made her blood rush, her heart pound. What could she say?

"Your Unc—my ..." Anxiety, a volcanic erupting sensation pulsated her throat. "My boss isn't going to be happy with me."

George looked a little confused.

"He's going to worry about the press, the—" She waved her hand in the air. "Roy ... the newspaper! There'll be a field day!" She was gonna lose her job. God, she needed her job.

"Field day?" Nervous, George wrung his hands together. His face twisted in distress.

Gabrielle pressed her fingers against her throbbing temple. "George, listen to me." She took a deep calm breath, then exhaled slowly. "Don't show anybody the skull. OK?" She tried to keep her voice light so as not to upset him further. Skirting past her table, she hurried to the back of the tent, picked up a small wooden crate and wound her way back to the table. With great care she placed NAF inside.

"I'm going to lock her up in this box. If anyone asks you where the skull is, tell them I have it. Tell them I took it over to the Reservation to do some research." She had to get out, leave—now before Roy—before her boss—someone saw her.

"I'll be gone for a few days." Where, she didn't know. Anyway, far away where she could think. Where no one could find her. Where she could be alone.

"Then why—" He looked perplexed.

"I'm not really taking NAF with me." She hammered a small nail in each corner of the lid and quickly slid the box in the back of the tent between two other boxes. Finished, she spun back around to George. "I'm afraid to move her. She's not finished and well, I don't want to ... break her." How could she explain? She was in enough hot water. She couldn't take the thing with her. First of all, it was too delicate. Second, it wasn't her property. God forbid something happened to it. No. NAF would be safe in here. No one would even be looking for her ... she hoped.

Why she went back to the site by the river was beyond her. But here she stood, staring at the slow flowing water. She lifted her gaze and glanced beyond the river's narrow bank, across the barren prairie grassland where olive green and brown blades of grass swayed gently in the warm breeze and toward the steep bluff where Custer and the Seventh Calvary had fought. Where so many had died.

The hair on her arm rose.

She felt it—the eeriness of the place. Even stronger then before, it caressed her, ran its prickly fingers up and down her body. She shivered and hugged her middle.

"It's just my imagination." *Concentrate. There's got to be an explanation.* That skull did look like her. *God.* She dropped her head back and closed her eyes. She couldn't lose her job. It was in her blood. It was all she had—all she ever knew. What could she tell her boss?

She bit her lip, controlling the sob welling in her throat, straightened, and glanced around the grounds hoping to find an answer.

Everything around her was peaceful. Birds chirped. Yellow wild flowers basked under the sunny summer rays, and the river gurgled along its path. Nothing indicated the battle of all battles, the one that had sealed the fate of all Native Americans, had taken place there. White stone markers and a tall monument stood like silent soldiers commemorating the men who had died in the Battle of Little Big Horn. Somehow it wasn't enough. There should have been some big black hole in the ground. Something that said good men died here. Good men on both sides, those fighting to save a way of life, those trying to build a new one. Instead, only a vague anonymous void stood between the past and present; a present that seemed to reach out and strangle her.

She chewed her lip, wrung her hands. How could she hope to find the answer to her dilemma, when historians couldn't find the answers to what had happened that day?

A sudden flash, a reflection off the sun caught her attention. She stared down into the deep grave, trying to make out what it was. What had the crew overlooked? Her curiosity getting the best of her, she dropped to the ground, threw her legs over NAF's burial site and jumped into the hole. The glint came from a camera lens.

"Damn. Prescott has been snooping around. Great." She frowned. He hadn't just dropped by for a friendly chat. Having seen the large hole, he had to know more than he'd let on. Men! Bending over she picked up the lens. She'd been right all along. Deceiving thuds. They break your heart then leave you alone to pick up the pieces. She never should have agreed to talk to him. The glass cut into her palm.

A shadow suddenly veiled her vision. She glanced up. A giant black cloud billowed overhead. Electricity crackled through the air, sounding like live wires hissing in a bucket of water. Quickly she scanned the dirt for anything she'd overlooked. The wind lifted, making a tremendous swishing sound. Standing, she shielded her eyes from the whirling sand and torrid, rising winds. God, she hated storms. Ever since that time in the cave ...

Thunder rumbled, growing in severity, its deafening explosion booming. She shivered.

"It's definitely time to leave." She reached for the grass overhead and began to hoist herself to ground level when suddenly, the earth beneath her shifted. Her heart leapt. Sinking fast she hurled her arms up, in an effort to steady herself, but clasped nothing but air. Her first thought: quicksand. But that was impossible. There was no quicksand in Montana. Angry winds swirled around her. The pressure so strong, like a giant vacuum, she felt sucked up in its intensity.

Dirt slammed in her face making it difficult to see. Furiously she gulped in the air. Her arms flailed in an attempt to grab onto anything solid. A sound like pebbles pelting against a tile roof encompassed her. Thick oozing mud glued her feet to the shifting ground. Her body shook. Then suddenly the earth beneath her opened like a trapdoor....

Gabrielle fell, sliding into an endless pit, spiraling around and around, tossed about like in the center of a tornado. Hands clenched in a ball by her side, her hair flying above her head, she fell still deeper.

What was happening? A storm, even one like she'd just witnessed, couldn't bury a person alive. Could it? Her mind, a tangled web of confusion, felt unhinged. The sensation of falling, of whirling in circles, seemed even stronger then before.

In the darkness, a multitude of colors blurred before her. Reds, oranges, yellows and greens, it felt as though she were looking through a prism.

Stark vivid fear seized her body like a cold fist closing over her heart.

Then, in this perpetual hole of nothingness, a cacophony of sounds assaulted her senses. She heard a blast of gunfire, voices, music without any particular tune. Revolving like on a merry-go-round, with hundreds of voices all talking at the same time. Nausea rose in her throat. She closed her eyes.

And continued to fall.

Her anguished cry echoed. With trembling hands she covered her face. She was dying. Tears pooled in her eyes. Her throat swelled with misery. She didn't want to die, not yet. There were so many things she wanted to do. Maybe, she reasoned, when she opened her eyes she'd wake up.

She didn't.

Further and further she fell. The darkness reached around her and squeezed. The air, no longer a stifling wave of heavy molasses, cooled to a pleasant breeze, only to dissipate as rapidly as a shooting star, leaving in its wake a slap of cold air that sent waves of goose bumps up and down her entire body.

She wondered if she'd ever hit bottom. You never hit bottom when you were dreaming. She did, just as the jaws of darkness opened up and swallowed.

TWO

Wyoming Territory - June 1, 1876

*T*he Lakota warrior scratched on the side of his elder's lodge then entered. "Black Hawk, I have gone on the *hanbleceya*, vision quest to the top of the hill and have done what has been told of me. For four days I stood before our god, *Tunkashila*. I wore my robe. I ate no food. Drank no water. I held the sacred *chanunpa* pipe in my hands. Now I come to speak with you."

The holy one nodded without raising his glance, as the warrior moved beside him and sat before the fire. Black Hawk closed his heavy eyelids in meditation. He puffed on his *chanunpa* and a curl of smoke rose high into the air. "Tell me of your vision."

"There is a wolf with eyes the color of the sky and a woman surrounded by a white light. I cannot see her face. She has traveled far and is lost. I see two moons in the clouds of darkness and a golden circle with four sides." The warrior shook his head. "I do not understand this that I have seen."

Black Hawk listened quietly. He took another puff on his pipe then opened his eyes. "So when the spirit of *Tunkashila* comes, we do not ask questions. If you do not understand just hold onto what you have seen, the answer will come." He stood. "So, from now on you shall be known as Two Moons as spoken by your vision."

Black Hawk ran a roll of smoldering sage along Two Moons' head, then up and down his body. "I, too, have been on many a *hanbleceya*. So, at those times I have had to have courage, patience and endurance. I have had to have alertness." He patted the smoke into Two Moons' body with an eagle feather. "All these you must have to be an Earth Man."

After the purification ritual was completed, Black Hawk took his place once again beside the fire. "So, I had learned and you must learn. We go into the *Tunkan* lodge on all fours to be humble," Black Hawk's voice was calm and steady. "So, one must be humble, to see past his own blindness. It is of these I speak."

Two Moons hung his head. Black Hawk spoke the truth. His quickness of tongue had caused many a fight with another. The hardness in his heart over the white blood that ran through his sister's son, he knew, caused the boy much sadness. As for being humble ... He raised his chin up a notch. He left that for the women. "But—"

"When the Spirits deem it so, you will understand their message. Now go." Black Hawk gestured toward the *tipi's* opening. "Gather those spiritual items that are to be kept in your sacred bundle."

With a final puff on his pipe, Two Moons knew Black Hawk would say no more.

Two Moons looked ahead to the sacred mountains known by his people as *Papa Sapa*, the Black Hills. It was there he would begin his search for the medicine charms that were to be placed in his sacred bundle. Only then, with the protection from his own medicine would he have the power to fight off danger. Only then, would he be invincible to his enemy's arrows and have the strength he needed to be an even greater warrior.

He nudged his big gray forward and began the long climb up the narrow canyon and steep cliffs lined with ferns. Creeks heavy with water rushed along his trail. Giant cedars and larches, their needle-like leaves clustered and heavy, towered over his path, allowing very little light to penetrate. The air grew cool.

Tugging the corners of his vest up against his neck for warmth, Two Moons rode into a clearing, where the mountain ledge met a gunmetal sky. A storm approached. He could see it in the heavy dark clouds, could feel it in the winds that had suddenly become angry and whipped at the treetops.

Already the flakes were beginning to fall. One after another, faster and faster, they tumbled down from the clouds, building in their intensity, just as hurried and frantic as his growing impatience.

"*Wakan Tanka*, Great Holy Spirit." Two Moons raised his arms to the sky in prayer. "This warrior does not understand what you have shown me. Why a wolf of white with eyes like the sky? A sacred animal not of this world? How am I to fulfill my medicine if I know not where to search for such a beast?"

Sitting astride his horse, monstrous cold, wet flakes plummeted madly against his eyelids; they beat against his chest. "And where am I to find a coin with four sides? How can I find that of which, I do not understand? Even now, though it be the moon when the ponies are fat, when the warmth of the sun should shine upon me, you throw snow upon Mother Earth, making my journey a hard one. Am I to kill the sacred beast told only to me in the tales of the old ones?" His face to the sky, he listened for a reply.

Instead, there was only a silence—a hush, a breath, that whispered no answers in his ears.

His heart heavy, Two Moons opened his eyes and glanced to the horizon where a large black hawk flew low through the heavy snow. The bird's ragged shape soared through the white, battling the lashing winds.

"Anpo Wie, my old friend," Two Moons reached over and patted his horse's mane. "We must look for shelter." With a gentle heel in Anpo Wie's flank, Two Moons turned his mount around and sought sanctuary in the darkness of the woods.

Roy Prescott shivered from a sudden draft, though the sun beat down upon the tent like a hothouse. God, he hoped he wasn't getting sick. There was a story here; he could smell it. The last thing he needed to drag around with him was a cold. He pulled his collar up around his neck and peeked outside. Good. No one had seen him. He wasn't in the mood to explain to Gabby why he was poking around in her things—spying.

His stride quick, he moved away from the tent flap. He jerked the camera strap over his head and strode, camera in hand, over to her workbench. He had a job to do. A job he couldn't afford to lose.

So what the hell could she have found at the site earlier in the week that had caused such a commotion? By the significance of that hole, they had dug up something big. He hadn't been able to zoom in close enough with the crowd standing around her.

Gently he pushed aside an array of small brushes, picked up some clay and squashed it in his palm. The soft substance oozed between his fingers. So she was working on another skull. He grinned with satisfaction then dropped the clay to the table.

But why all the hush-hush? Either it was some poor old fellow from another century, or some poor dead guy missing from last month. Either way it was news.

The lens cover popped off beneath his fingers. He hurried over to a table scattered with papers and books, and started snapping pictures. A list of names caught his eye. He zoomed in for a closer look and shot. Never overlook anything. That was the sign of a good reporter. And God knew he had to prove to Dad he was up there with the big boys. He shot a few more pictures, then glanced around for other clues.

It has to be here somewhere. Rummaging around in a stack of wooden cartons that were piled in a corner of the tent, he found one that looked promising. With wild anticipation his heart pounded. Once again he glanced toward the tent's opening.

She'd be mad. He fingered the lid. Strawberries and coffee weren't gonna cut it.

"Ah, hell." He opened the box. It would be worth getting caught if for nothing more than to see the fire in those lovely blue eyes.

Wrapped in individual bags, rusty broken pieces of metal that looked like junk, were labeled and numbered. Disappointed, he carefully placed the bags back where they belonged. Quickly he opened another box.

Wrapped in a white cloth he found a large bone that looked like part of an arm. He shot a picture, wrapped it back up and unwrapped the package that lay beside it. Another bone.

He wiped his sweating palm on his shirt. What a rush. Gabrielle had hit it on the head earlier. He loved the hunt, the excitement of searching out a story then seeing it in print with his name at the top of the page. Adrenaline surged through his body. That was good; it kept him alert. Kept him on his toes. Again, he glanced around. No one had discovered him yet. He still had time.

He took a few more pictures from different angles then dropped the lid back on the box.

The skull had to be here somewhere; he could feel it. He moved to the next carton. It was sealed tight. Bingo! He hit pay dirt.

His gaze darted around for something to open the box with. He found a metal crow bar. Inch by inch, he pried open the lid. Being a reporter he'd seen a lot of things that should have surprised him, but damn. What was Gabby doing? He stared at the face, which at the moment, stared up at him. This certainly couldn't be what he was looking for.

He snapped a picture. His instincts were usually right. Why was Gabby wasting time making a model of her own face? It wasn't like her.

Before he got a chance to dwell on his find, the tent flap thumped open. He dropped the lid and turned around.

"What are you doing here?" George asked, his face ashen. His gait jerky, he hurried around the table toward him. "Miss Gabrielle, she ain't gonna like you in here. You're not supposed to be here."

As casually as he could, Roy took a step in his direction. "See, that's the thing. I've been looking for Gabby. Have you seen her?"

"She's not here." George's gaze fell. He stepped away. "You're not supposed to be here. I could get in a lot of trouble." He glanced over to the stack of boxes, wrung his hands together then glanced back. "Miss Gabby's gonna be mad at me."

Roy knew what it was like to be a little slow, to be an adult with the mind of a child. His own mother, when having bouts of schizophrenia, often regressed to her childhood. The last thing he wanted was to upset George.

"No, she won't be mad at you," Roy reassured him, with a gentle tap on the shoulder. "Don't worry. She's going to be mad at me."

George shook his head like a child who knew he had done something wrong. His eyes widened. His brows arched. "I don't want to get you in trouble Mr. Prescott. I like you."

"I like you too, George. I'll be fine, don't you worry. Now, you wouldn't happen to know where Gabby is, would you?"

George backed over to the table as though he were trying to shield the papers that lay about. "I don't know if I should tell you."

If his instincts were right, something was very wrong. And it wasn't about the story anymore. He took a step closer to George. "You know I like Miss Gabby, don't you?"

"Yeah."

"I won't hurt her or get her in trouble now, would I?" He placed his hand on George's forearm in a reassuring gesture.

George shook his head.

"That's right. All I want to do is talk to her."

"She's …" George hesitated. He jangled some loose change in his pocket. "At the reservation," he added in a huff. "Said she was gonna spend a few days there."

"Which one?" Frustration strained Roy's voice.

George shrugged.

"Well don't worry. I'm going to leave now and go find her. Okay?" Roy forced a smile.

"Ask her if I did good," George shouted as Roy flipped open the tent flap and stepped outside.

It was growing dark when Two Moons left the cave once again in search of his medicine charms. His failure thus far stung like a thorn in his side. And with each futile attempt made, each hour he searched in vain, that thorn cut deeper and deeper, making him want to scream from the mountaintops. Only once he had found what he needed, could he return to his village with pride.

He could hear the trees creaking as they struggled against the howling wind. Then in the distance, a different kind of howling pierced the air. Two Moons' heart pounded. His body taut-erect, he stood rooted to his spot and listened. His eyes sharp, his senses' alert, he moved quickly through the deep snowdrifts. Aware of everything around him, of every branch he passed laden with snow, he took each step in silence. He inched closer and closer until he could see the wolf.

With a quickness born from experience he drew an arrow from his quiver, placed it in his bow and aimed. The arrow whizzed through the air, straight and sure. Two Moons' spirits lifted. At last part of his vision would come to be. This was a good sign. At last *Tunkashila* had heard his prayer.

The joy in his heart fell, as his arrow missed its mark. The wolf with the speed of the wind took to the shadows of the trees.

Two Moons ran, ran as though his life depended on it. All the pride, all the hope he had felt earlier tumbled around him. He would not let it. He would not let his spirit lose faith. He would not let the wolf win.

Through the high snows he struggled, up the steep incline, sliding down the other side. Sure of foot. Sure of his purpose. Again the lone white wolf stood before him. His bow ready, Two Moons aimed.

A nighthawk screeched from up above. The bird's large wings flapped like thunder. The wolf raised his head to the sky; then in a flash, he disappeared through the trees.

Perhaps if his quickness of thought hadn't gotten the best of him, he wouldn't have screamed his anger like a wild cat caught in a hunter's trap. He wouldn't have stomped at the ground in frustration only to lose his footing and find himself now sliding out of control down the hill. His breath slammed from his chest in a rush. Dizzy, he landed belly down at the foot of the hill.

A tangled web of long wet hair clung to his face. He growled, wiped his eyes clear, and then shook his head in disbelief at the sight that lay only a few steps before him.

A woman lay deep in the snow.

Her long black hair appeared stiff, clumped with ice. She wore the cloth of the white man, Two Moons thought with disgust, noticing the long red skirt that clinched her ankles and the long sleeved shirt gathered at her wrists.

He got up, trudged over to her. Her chest rose and fell in a faint but steady rhythm. She was still alive, but for how long?

The wolf howled in the distance, his deep wail echoing off the mountains.

Two Moons began to pace, making deep grooves in the snow. The desire to run to the beast surged through every inch of his body, yet he knew he could not. To leave the woman here would mean her death.

He raised his gaze to the distant woods. "Another time, my old friend. Another time," he promised sadly as he bent down and scooped his find up into his arms.

He spied the markings on her moccasins. She was his enemy—a Crow, enemy to his people. Yet, it was growing increasingly difficult to remember that, as Two Moons, knowing she would die from the cold, sat in the dimly lit cave, peeling layer upon layer of wet, frozen cloth from her damp, limp, body. Dark lashes fluttered for a moment then lay still against her closed lids. He brushed her cheek lightly with the back of his fingers. Her skin felt like a softly tanned hide, smooth, dark earth brown and hot with fever. Her full, lush lips quivered as he drew his hand away.

His heart raced. His breathing heavy and swift, he yanked down her skirt, trying to focus his attention on the bright colored cloth clenched between his fingers. He threw the skirt aside, wiped his dry mouth with his hand, then rubbed his taut neck with his palm. In the distance the wolf howled, tormenting him. Challenging him to battle. Calling him a fool.

Two Moons' rage began to build as hot as the need burning between his legs. Always before had he been a man in control of his body's desires. He, Two Moons, warrior of his people could have any woman he wanted; yet, he chose a higher path in which to follow.

He glared at the woman before him. He should have left her to die. It was his right as her enemy. Yet, even as he thought those words, he was drawn to her. Kneeling by her side he stripped the last layer of cloth from her body, for not to do so would mean her death.

Her skin in the fire's light seemed to glow like the golden embers. He dragged his gaze away from her breasts, to her flat stomach. He smiled. Knotted around her waist she wore a small protective rope that continued down between her legs, barring any man's entry to that part of a woman, which all men sought. Pleased she had not yet been touched, he fingered the cord that lay against her thigh.

With a jerk he drew his hand away and lie down beside her. He gathered her tightly in his arms and pressed his hot body against the cold threat of death hovering over her. Then he reached beside him to his robe of fur and with a heavy sigh, drew the blanket up around them.

THREE

S urely she was dreaming. A comforting ebb of warmth enveloped her body. Gabrielle, with half-closed lids, snuggled closer to the object of her comfort. In her dream, a man lay beside her. His face inches from hers, she could see the fine straight line of his nose and the deep-set ridge of his brow. Long straight hair, an almost iridescent blue black, cradled his neck. She could almost feel the strength of his arm lying protectively across her shoulders—could almost feel his warmth. His smooth muscular chest, bare and hairless, glistened like it had been rubbed down with oil. Around his neck he wore a bone and beaded choker—Roy's choker.

Lying next to him, Gabrielle felt safe and protected in a blanket of comfort that only in her dreams could she find. Only in her dreams would she allow a man, any man into her world. A world where they would always be together, where no one would leave the other behind. That was the luxury of dreaming.

Something soft tickled her jaw. She brushed the imaginary object away. God, she didn't want to wake up, not yet. She wanted to hold on to him, to touch him and be touched. She rolled onto her back, rubbed the sleep from her eyes and stretched. Jet black eyes stared back at her. Shock jolted through her. Instantly awake she watched as her Indian, with the swiftness of a cat, leaped to his feet and disappeared.

She sat with a start. Her breath caught in her throat. Her gaze dropped. Dear God, she was naked! Bewildered, she grabbed the fur blanket that lay in her lap, drew it up to her chin and frantically glanced around.

A cave. What was she doing in a cave? She hated caves. She clutched the blanket close to her breast. Her hands shook. She squeezed her eyes shut. *Make this horrid nightmare go away.* She had to be dreaming, she had to be.

The musty dank smell of mildew, mixing with the acrid smell of smoke filled her lungs. The crackling hisses and pops of dry twigs burning in a fire, accosted her ears. Her eyes opened with a flash. Blinking with bafflement, she stared into the space before her. Giant pillars of stone seemed to reach out, crowding her.

"OK. There has to be some logical explanation." She took a deep calming breath. "It's just another dream. Only this time I'm not dying. That's it. I'll wake up now at any minute and be back at the site." She shifted around to her left. "Everything is fi—"

He stood by a small fire. His dark eyes glared at her. Confusion mixed with fear. Something was very wrong; reality had crossed into fantasy. She was no longer dreaming.

"Who … Who are you?" She glanced around. "Where am I?"

His body taut, his hands clenched into fists, he stood in rigid silence like an animal ready to pounce.

"What do you want? And what have you done with m …" Her voice cracked. "My clothes?" Trembling, she drew her knees to her chin and held the blanket up to her neck. Why wouldn't he answer her? Didn't he understand?

His shadow looming on the wall behind him, larger than life, made her pulse race. He glanced to the fire where unfamiliar clothing dried over forked poles.

He did understand. Studying her intently, his eyes narrowed. "*Nituwe he?*" he asked softly.

She shook her head. "I—I don't understand."

Wearing nothing but an Indian breechclout, barely covering his groin and a pair of fringed leggings, he looked like a throwback from another century.

"Why are you dressed like that?" It was a stupid thing, asking about his clothes, but it was all she could come up with at the moment. She had to say something to stall for time.

He glanced down, confused. Leggings hugged his lean powerful legs. Legs, Gabrielle realized, that with one quick stride could bring her closer to her death.

Suddenly anger lit his eyes.

Terror compressed her belly like a vise.

Frantically, she inched away from him. He was crazy. Small rocks scrapped against her bottom as she dragged the heavy blanket with her. Something pinched her waist as she moved. Her inner thighs rubbed against coarse fibers. Glancing down she caught a glimpse of a rope tied around her waist, extending down between her legs. Horrified she glanced up at him. Was he some kind of psychopath? What else had he done to her body while she lay sleeping?

Her back hit the cold damp wall of the cave. Her breath caught. She was trapped. Trapped in a cave with a half-naked madman. Gabrielle choked back a frightened cry. If he meant to kill her why hadn't he? Had he only been waiting for her to wake up so he could—

He took a step closer.

"No! Wait!" Her hand shot up in front of her, a small useless barrier between them. He meant to rape her first.

Swallowing with difficulty, she found her voice. "Please," she begged. "Please don't kill me."

He seemed surprised by her words and a spark of hope boosted her confidence. "You look like a reasonable person." Her gaze darted, searching for a way out. "Maybe ... maybe we can just talk about this."

A few yards away an archway of rocks formed an opening leading to a tunnel of darkness. Quickly she glanced back at him. "You don't really want to hurt me."

His silence sent a chill to her spine.

Sharp jagged rocks pressed into her back as she burrowed even deeper against the wall. A wave of cool air wafted across her bare shoulders. She shivered. Without clothes she wouldn't get far.

She needed a weapon. She needed time.

He took a step closer.

"Please wait! Think about what you're doing."

He stopped, regarding her with somber curiosity.

Her attention fixed past him, she could see a rifle leaning against the wall. If only ...

The corners of her jailer's mouth turned up in a knowing grin.

Gabrielle's heart fell.

He parted his legs in a solid stance and crossed his arms in front of his chest. Eyes of steel challenged her to make a move.

The scream died in her throat. No one would hear her and he knew it.

"*Kuwa yo?*" With a slight gesture of his hand, he indicated she move away from the wall.

"N... nooo. I think I'm fine here." Did he think she was a fool?

Out of the corner of her eye she could see a stone, the size of a baseball. She dropped her hand to the ground and groped around. Her fingers touched the rock's rough surface. With deliberateness she dragged it toward her.

Forcing a smile, her hand trembling, she inched the rock up her side to rest in her lap beneath the folds of the blanket.

Again he gestured she move.

Her fingers closed tightly around her weapon. A tense silence hung heavy in the cave like a guillotine's blade waiting to fall.

Taking a step closer, he reached out to her.

Panic, an electrifying shudder surged through her. "Stay where you are," she screamed. She jerked her hand up and held the rock above her head.

Dark brows rose in astonishment. He whipped out a knife. His mouth took on an angry twist.

The rock felt like lead in her palm. "Get away from me. I ... I swear, I'll use this. Don't make me use this."

Eyeing her with suspicion, he hesitated then held out his hand to calm her. Watching her intensely, he knelt down. His eyes riveted, he placed the knife by his knees and slowly brought his hand away. With a slight nod he gestured she do the same.

"OK. Don't move. I'm going to put this rock down, " she assured him. "See? I'm putting it down."

The hint of a smile tipped his mouth as she brought the rock down a notch. *He's crazier than I thought.* Gabrielle flung with all her might. With a thud, her weapon hit his temple.

His eyes widened with shock. His brows arched. As he brought his fingers up to touch the trickle of oozing blood, Gabrielle jumped up. He started to rise.

With a strength she didn't think she had left, she wailed out and kicked him in the one place she knew would hurt. He doubled over in pain. She heard him groan as she ran past him.

Her surroundings blurred. The only vision before her was the rifle— her chance to escape. Her heart raced. *Almost there. Only a few more steps.* She reached out her hand. *Just a little closer.* She stretched, her shaking fingers touching the cool metal of the gun's barrel.

A guttural barbaric roar, close at her heels, startled her. She jerked her head around. The gun slipped from her grasp as hard fingers gripped hold of her ankles and pulled her off her feet.

Air rushed from her lungs. Her chest hit the ground with a thud. The gun was so close, inches away from her fingertips. She thrust out her arm, stretching as best as she could to reach the weapon.

He threw his body atop of her, crushing her breasts into the dirt and her chin to the ground. She cried out in pain. His hand slammed down over the weapon and her fingers. With a forceful shove, the gun slid from her grasp.

Abruptly flipped onto her back, she stared into his dark hard eyes. Gabrielle jerked her arms before her, shielding her breasts from his gaze. For a moment she thought she saw a look of concern in his eyes. She was wrong. His expression was one of pained tolerance. The veins in his neck bulged tautly.

Furious at her vulnerability, seized by a blinding fury, Gabrielle reached up and with all her might gave him a shove. The force of her blow did little to move him. "Get away from me you lunatic!"

He sat back on his haunches, studying her. The weight of his buttocks atop her thighs pinned her legs to the ground.

Without thinking of the consequences, her reasoning out of control, she jerked her body forward and pounded on his chest like a wild woman.

He grabbed her wrists and held them tightly. She struggled against the unrelenting force of his hold. Her hair whipped her eyes and clung to her mouth. She couldn't see ... she didn't care. She screamed, frightened, furious.

His strength overwhelming, he shoved her backward. Together they hit the ground.

Her high-pitched scream bounced off the cavern's walls. An angry snarl crossed his tight lips. Before she could break free, he gathered both her wrists in his one hand, thrust them above her head and pressed them firmly against the ground. He pushed himself up onto his forearm and raised his torso off her. His hips and pelvis pressed heavily against her. She could feel his hard erection against her thighs.

"Stop. You don't want to do this," she pleaded.

Struggling against him, she twisted and turned her head from side to side. "Nothing's happened. They'll let you go free. Nothing's happened. Please stop."

He studied her a moment, a puzzled look that made her wonder if he really didn't understand her.

"You're never going to get away with this. I'm sure my friends ... the police are out there right now looking for me. And ... and ..." Her voice sounded thin, high—hysterical.

His silence.

"I'll see that you rot in jail. I swear," she promised between ragged breaths. Again she tried to break free of his deadly grip, twisting and turning her wrists, but she stopped, realizing the more she struggled, the more her body ground seductively against his.

An expression of amusement crossed his eyes, then quickly disappeared, replaced with an intense gaze of desire that made her want to vomit.

As a heavy darkness seeped into her taut chest, Gabrielle closed her eyes against the onslaught she knew to follow.

* * *

Two Moons stared down at the woman whose ice blue eyes only a moment ago had shown such courage. She was a strong one in mind. That pleased him. With her eyes now closed, his spirit fell. All the desire he felt, the pure physical fire burning in his soul, fell flat. To be weak in spirit was to be dead.

Guilt stabbed his brain. He did not mean to harm her. Was she, or was she not the woman of his vision? The one with the eyes of the *wasicun*, white man's eyes? The wolf had been a sign. He had only to follow that wolf to find her. But what of the gold rope the woman of his vision wore? This woman beneath him wore no such rope. Perhaps he had been wrong. Perhaps after all, she was just a woman.

The warmth of her stomach pressing into him made him feel strangely uncomfortable. He sat, hooking his knees around her hips.

Releasing one wrist, he caressed the side of her cheek. Her skin reminded him of golden honey and felt soft against his finger.

Dark lashes flew open once again. Her blue eyes pierced the distance between them. With the quickness of a rattler she twisted her head to his wrist and bit down hard. With a jerk, Two Moons reached over with his free hand and yanked her arms back over her head. He stared down at the imprint her teeth had left on his skin. He would expect no less from a Crow woman. Her spirit pleased him.

But, she should not have betrayed his good sign of faith earlier. The bump on his head pounded from the rock she had flung and his groin still throbbed. Wasn't that just like the whites, to say one thing and do another? Although they both shared the same color skin, her heart was white.

She struggled against him. Her hips ground into his groin. His heart thundered. His body grew hot and tightened painfully. He dropped his gaze from her face to her breasts. The loud breath she took as she tensed thrust the dark tipped points out toward him. A knot of desire welled in his belly. He had not tasted a woman's sweetness in a long time. His blanket he had not shared with anyone.

"Let me go. Let me go." Her legs lashed against him.

He stiffened. Twisting so desperately to get away, her hip pushed aside his loincloth. Two Moons could feel his hard erection dangerously close to the junction of her inner thighs. All he had to do was cut the ropes, jam his knees between her legs, thrust and she would be his. His possession. His slave. He could use her to satisfy the need that was growing like a wild fire out of control.

But he would not. Not now, not unless she came to him. It was a promise he had made to himself long ago, when he had seen what a man's unwanted advances could do to a woman.

Blue eyes stared up at him, a glaring reminder. Her soul was that of the white man, his most hated foe. "*Inila.*" *Be still!* His jaw clenched. He tore himself off her body and stomped toward the fire to retrieve her clothing. Disgusted more with himself than with her, Two Moons flung the garments at her, turned and stormed out, needing to place some distance between them.

In her prison of stone and earth, Gabrielle had no knowledge of time or place. The hours seemed to drag as she sat against the wall of the cave, struggling with her emotions. She wrestled with her mind and its relentless questions; struggled to keep her eyes from closing when sleep wanted to take hold. Each time her lids fell, panic surfaced, forcing her to stare bleary eyed at her surroundings.

After she'd dressed, her captor immediately returned as if he'd been waiting outside the entrance of the cave in case she decided to try to escape. Little chance of that. Her futile attempt to free herself from his overpowering strength had left her mentally and physically exhausted. Why had he changed his mind and not raped her? She had seen it in his eyes. He knew he had complete control over her, that she was powerless against his strength.

Gabrielle shivered more from the thought than the cold lingering in the air. Through heavy lids she noticed the fire had died down, leaving in its wake, simmering charred embers and a thin wisp of gray smoke that rose to the roof of the cave, then disappeared into the darkness.

She strained to see through the dark shaft and listened for the sound of her captor's footsteps. Hope and the silence surrounding her, gave her the strength to stand. From lack of sleep, her body felt heavy, her legs weak. She caught her toe on the hem of her long skirt and stumbled forward. Where were her own clothes, her shorts and her boots? And why in God's name was she wearing what looked to be a chastity belt around her waist? Earlier in the day, she tried pulling the crude looking rope off, but the knots were tied too tightly.

Her skin grew clammy. What kind of game was he playing? What did he want with her? Was she to be the sacrifice in some kind of sick ritual? Gabrielle's head pounded. He *was* crazy. She had to find a way out; now was her chance.

Cautiously, her attention focused on every silent footstep, every swish of her skirt, she moved toward a tunnel she prayed would lead quickly to the outside world and safety.

"Damn it." Sharp rocks cut into the soles of her bare feet. Hobbling over to a pair of moccasins that lay neatly side-by-side near the fire, she bent down.

Before she had a chance to stand, *he* appeared from the shadows. She gasped, startled. All hopes of escaping for the moment disappeared.

Carrying the carcass of an elk over his shoulder, he glanced at her before he dropped the dead animal to the ground. Then, ignoring her, he knelt beside his kill. His arms raised toward the cavern's ceiling, he bowed his head and began to chant.

Fascinated, intrigued, Gabrielle stood motionless, afraid to move. She had gone to many a powwow, but never had she seen anything so personal and private as the prayer service going on before her. Her brief feeling of exhilaration crashed however, when she realized she could be the next victim.

His back toward her, quietly, yet as quickly as she could, she hurried toward a passageway she hoped lead to a shorter tunnel, then outside.

Before she could get far, he yanked her head back by the ends of her hair. Spun around, Gabrielle felt her back hit the wall. His hands gripped her shoulders tightly.

"Ow." Thinking he was not paying attention to her had been a mistake.

"Let go." Gabrielle squirmed, trying to break free of his hold. If he meant to kill her, she'd fight him tooth and nail. He pressed her shoulders into the wall. His chest heaved slightly. His nostrils flared like an angry bull.

"Let me go." She tried to kick him.

He backed an arms length away.

Frustrated when her kicks came up short, she shook her head and screamed. His wide brow creased in an annoyed frown. Deep-set eyes peered fearlessly into hers, demanding she stop.

"You don't scare me," she spat, trying to muster up the courage that seemed to be slipping with each squeeze of his hands.

When he abruptly released his hold, Gabrielle's only thought was to get away, yet the closeness of his body, like a solid wall of lean muscle, barred any further movements. Her knees began to shake.

"*Hacib wínyan.*"

She didn't understand a word he spat, but his anger came across loud and clear. Before she knew what was happening he drew out his knife.

The terror on her face made him cringe; yet Two Moons could not bring himself to tell her he understood her fear. He brought his knife up. Her mouth dropped. Her brilliant blue eyes widened. Dismissing the guilt tightening his chest, he met her gaze. The discomfort he caused her would soon pass. Her small loss would be his good fortune.

He sheared off a small piece of her raven hair. She cringed against him. For a brief moment as he stared into her eyes, he wondered if his actions were foolish. A lock of hair from his Spirit Woman would be good medicine, a good charm to wear in the battles to come. But if she was not …

He made a fist, enclosing the cut strands in the center of his palm. With his free hand he fingered a strand of her long silky mane between his fingertips. For now he would keep this charm close.

"*Éna un.*" He brought his closed fist up a little below his shoulder; then with a quick short motion brought it downward a few inches. Surely, she would understand the word "stay," in sign talk? "*Éna un.*"

Satisfied when she didn't move, Two Moons walked over to his kill and knelt down. He placed his knife on the ground within grasping range beside him, then slipped his finger inside the small medicine bag around his neck and pulled out a short piece of leather. Quickly he tied the strip around the cut strands of black hair, dropped the small bundle inside his bag, then slid his knife back into the rawhide sheath that hung at his side.

His thoughts on the woman behind him, he flung the heavy carcass over his shoulder and stood. Enough time had been spent here with her. His mother would be waiting on his return. Black Hawk would be waiting on his words. Two Moons kicked the dying embers with his foot until the fire no longer burned, then he turned on his heels to face her.

"Come, we leave," he said in Lakota, knowing his words were foreign to her.

Before she had a chance to answer, he yanked her forward.

"If you are well enough to think of escaping, you are well enough to leave," he said again this time in Crow. "We go."

She showed no knowledge of his command to go. Annoyed at her lack of response, he grabbed her arm, pulling her behind him.

This one was indeed a stubborn one, either brave, or crazy in the head. Two Moons tugged on her arm urging her forward. He could hear her cry out in annoyance, could hear her mumbling under her breath. He understood every angry word she threw at him between clenched teeth.

Glancing behind, he gave her a disgusted look. She showed no knowledge of her own language, or that of his signing. Even the Crow understood signing. *Wasicun winyan*, white woman. White man's blood ran deep in her soul. Perhaps that is why she did not understand. She chose to speak in the tongue of his enemy.

By the time they reached the outer entrance of the cave, bitterness burned in Two Moons' gut. The thought that she had forsaken her people's tongue for that of their white enemies' chilled his heart.

Releasing his hold on her, he removed the elk's body from his shoulders and placed the carcass over his mount's back. With a swift yank, he pulled down the rope that hung from the horn pommel of his saddle. He clenched the rope then pivoted around to face his captive.

She stared down at her hands. Her brows slanted, creased with question, she studied them as if she saw them for the first time. He grabbed her wrists and pressed them together. Anticipating her next move, he backed away. She thrust out her foot to kick his shins. He shot her a glance of triumph. If he were not careful, he would feel his own knife in his back. It would be wise not to trust her.

She struggled to get away from his hold. With quick fingers he tied the rope around her wrists. She screamed and shook with impudent rage. He yanked the cord, slamming her close to his body and stared into her eyes. He'd had enough of her tricks. She would follow his commands. That was *his* way.

Placing his hands around her small waist, he hoisted her upon Anpo Wie's back then swiftly jumped up behind her.

She was in trouble. His sixth sense had never failed him before. He never questioned it. It was one of those unexplainable things that was just a part of him. His reporter's instinct, he always called it.

Roy drove up the steep mountain road, his thought's heavily centered on Gabrielle. Something wasn't quite right. George's words nagged at the corner of his mind. *Ask her if I did well.* Just what did that mean? Was George covering up for her?

Roy's gaze fixed on the narrowing road before him. Maybe he was on a wild goose chase. He'd been to the Crow Reservation, where he had checked with every official and gift shop counter person he could find. No one had seen her. He drove over to the village of Lame Deer where he'd been told to check in at the Northern Cheyenne Community Center. Perhaps she was there.

She wasn't.

Just what had she been up to? Why sculpt a piece in her own likeness then hide it? And George, he definitely was hiding something.

No. Something wasn't quite right. She couldn't just disappear into thin air.

He checked his watch: 6:50 p.m. He turned on the radio and fiddled with the button until he found the news. "Today's high ..."

He drummed his fingers on the steering wheel, tuning out the weather report. Where was she? Gabrielle Camden, with the face of an angel. She was a stubborn one indeed. But he'd break that shell of hers. He could tell she liked him. Well, maybe a little. She tried to deny it, but he saw the interest in those lovely blue eyes of hers. There was some kind of strange electric charge whenever they were together. He felt it, just as sure as that streak of lightning slashing through the sky.

The radio announcer's words drew his thoughts back to the present. "Hey, did you know that on this very same day, June first, back in eighteen seventy-six there was a blizzard. Thought with all those hail stones earlier we'd been in for a repeat. No snow in the forecast, however, temperatures ..."

"Damn near feels like a blizzard in here." Roy shivered. He turned off the air and rolled down the window, allowing the warm evening's air to flow in. The sky, a slate gray, was heavy with the gathering clouds of a storm. A black hawk winged silently above the treetops. Gracefully the bird rode the air currents down until it disappeared into the thick forest of trees.

A blast of hot air wafted across the side of his face. As heavy and as thick as honey, it sent prickly goose bumps up the nape of his neck. Strange, this weather— hot and sunny one minute, stormy the next. As strange as the strong feeling tugging at his gut, that something bad was about to happen.

FOUR

M y *God!* What was wrong with her hands? *They're so dark.* It was as if she'd spent an entire month in the Caribbean without any sunscreen. Gabrielle stared down at her bound wrists. What could have stained her hands such a deep clay color, surely not the soil from the cave?

The horse stumbled over a rock, jerking her forward. She grabbed the mane to keep from sliding, just as her captor's hands reached around her waist and pulled her closer. Hands, she noticed, that were the same color as hers, which didn't make any sense. Had he done this to her? Why? Did he wish her to be someone else? Is that why he had painted her skin the same color as his?

But ... She stared. It didn't look like paint?

She brought her fingers to her face, touching her cheeks as if there would be some difference in its texture. Was it also so dark?

She glanced around. And the snow. Where had it come from? Heat and a storm, those she remembered, but certainly nothing that indicated this amount of snow. In June? What was going on? Where was she? Twisting her head from side to side, she tried to make sense of her surroundings.

The forest, thick, lush, dark, was so different from the dried, vast open prairies of Eastern Montana and the excavation site.

How long had she been unconscious? Surely someone besides this mad man had seen her. Did her captor have a car hidden somewhere? Could they be to the southwest of Little Big Horn, somewhere in Yellowstone Park? Or had he taken her down south to the Black Hills? Someone must have seen them.

Something wasn't right, yet she couldn't quite put her finger on it.

A hawk cawed overhead. She raised her gaze to the sky.

A startling realization hit her.

There were no overhead wires above the treetops, no telephone poles. Gabrielle blinked and hastily glanced around. There were no roads or road signs. She hadn't heard a single car whiz by. And where were the scenic overlooks with their hordes of tourists? A wave of dizziness blurred her vision. She gripped the horse's mane tightly.

Suddenly exhausted, she let her head sag. She was so tired, it hurt to think. Any thoughts of escaping for the moment, evaporated under the darkness of her closed lids. From the moment she had awakened in that cave she'd felt as confused as Alice down in the rabbit hole, with no rhyme or reason to anything. In fact this whole mess had started when she had climbed down into that grave.

Minutes passed. Hours. Neither one spoke.

Gabrielle tried to keep up her spirits by searching every new area for signs of her chance to escape, hoping, praying for any signs of civilization; telling herself that although they were well off the beaten path, soon they'd have to come across someone.

But as the day grew longer, any hopes she harbored slipped like the setting sun. She felt as isolated and as alone as the large yellow sunflower they passed; as frightened as the flock of birds scattering from the tree tops as horse and riders rode by.

Dense blue spruces surrounded them at every turn. They made their way past a wall of granite where a gully of water, formed by the melting snow above, trickled down its face. Riding close by the mountain's side, the icy cold spray cut through the thin fabric of Gabrielle's sleeve. She shivered.

Strong arms reached out and drew her closer against his hard chest. She jerked away, his touch poisonous. "Don't."

The last thing she wanted was to be close to him. She'd rather freeze than feel the heat of his body against her back, no matter that the cold seeped through her thin blouse, chilling her.

When the horse stopped, Gabrielle fell forward. Strong arms again caught her. She twisted away, shifted her position and glanced back at him. "Don't touch me."

His black eyes sharpened dangerously.

She stared back at him. "I'm not afraid of you. You know that? So you just keep your hands off me." She prayed silently her voice wouldn't crack, that he couldn't read her fear, the fear that had grown with every passing hour—the fear she was trying so desperately to hide.

She raised her hands. "Untie these."

He gave no indication he understood.

"I said, untie my hands."

Not a muscle moved.

"Don't you understand anything?" she screamed. "I'm going to fall of this beast if you don't untie me."

Gently he grabbed her shoulders and tried to indicate that she lean against him for support.

"Not on your life."

A strong gust of wind blew over her. She shivered.

Keeping his gaze on her, he reached behind with one hand and began fumbling with something resting on his horse's hindquarters. With a flick of his wrist, he shook out a brightly colored blanket and dropped it over her shoulders. Then, without a word, he kneed his mount.

Lurching forward, she had no choice but to face front and lean back against him to keep from falling. She'd been on a horse twice in her life. That hardly made her an experienced rider. The ground looked so far away. She leaned back a little more, hating him, hating the feel of his face so close to hers, of his steady breathing in her ear. She hated being cradled by his thighs and the way her body seemed to mold naturally against him. She rounded her shoulders to keep away, to stay erect. But the effort was so hard.

She hated not knowing his next move, or what her fate would be. She was an independent woman, always knew exactly where she was going, what she wanted out of life. This feeling of despair, of fear, of not knowing what lay around the corner, frightened her more than the man himself.

Two Moons tried to ignore the feel of her soft body against his. He tried to focus on the words he would tell Black Hawk on his arrival at the village. He tried to think about the smile his return would bring to his mother's face. But all he could think about was how *she*, the woman who sat before him, would look with a smile on her face. Even when she'd screamed at him a moment ago, he had wondered.

When he thought about the warmth of his lodge and envisioned himself sitting by his fire, the only fire he could feel was the one burning in his loins every time his mount rocked her against him.

"Anpo Wie, steady." He spoke the horse's name softly in Lakota, glanced down and patted the gray's side. Against his will his gaze traveled to another's side, where slender ankles and shapely legs dangled close to his. Every muscle in his body clenched at her nearness.

Annoyed at the desire tightening his loins, he jerked his gaze up. The wind blew strands of her long hair in his face. He cursed under his breath. He wished he understood what the spirits had shown him. Wished he knew the path he was to follow, or how this woman, whom he now held against his chest, was to be a part of his journey.

Her head fell back against his shoulder. Her long lashes lay against her face. Her eyes were closed. An overwhelming sense of protection surged through him.

His face raised to the sky, his voice but a whisper, he prayed. "*Tunkashila*, why do I need to question you so? *Taku wakan*, this sacred mystery you have shown me, I do not understand."

They came upon the village nestled in the valley as the last rays of sunshine fell upon the earth. Two Moons stopped on the distant hill. He reached around his captive to grab the long rope bound at her wrist. His chest pressed deeply into her back. She stiffened. She feared him greatly, he thought as he slid off his mount's back. Her blue eyes stared down at him with confusion. She could not know he would never let her ride into his village by his side. She was his prisoner. That was how his people would see her. She would walk behind him, no matter how painfully the guilt sliced his belly. Two Moons reached up to her. She snapped her head away, refusing his help.

"Down," he ordered in the Crow tongue.

No response.

Annoyed, he tugged on the rope.

Still, she refused to look at him.

This time she will understand. Tight-fisted, he yanked the rope.

Her hands jerked toward him, as did her attention. She stared at him in silence, then swung her leg over and sat facing him. She glanced to the ground. Her eyes widened. Her face grew pensive.

Two Moons placed his hands around her waist. He waited for her to struggle. She didn't.

Quickly he lifted her down. For a moment, he held her close, wrapped in his arms, a silent moment that quickened his heartbeat and blurred all vision beyond her face. She wrenched her body away, breaking his hold … breaking the moment.

Two Moons flung himself on Anpo Wie's back. With a flick on the reins, he started down the hill. He glanced over his shoulder. His captive stumbled blindly behind him. Her dress from dragging in the snow had become wet and appeared heavy against her legs.

A chorus of dogs announced their arrival. A rush of women and children immediately surrounded his captive. Before she could say a word, they jerked and yanked at her clothing. They lashed out with angry words as well as their hands. "*Toka!*, Enemy! *Letan kigla yo!* Get out of here!"

His captive's arms shot up as she shielded her face from their onslaught.

"*Henala!*" he shouted above the enraged crowd. *Enough.*

The beatings stopped as curious eyes looked up at him.

He slid off his mount. The women separated to let him pass. His sister's son, Curly, stood before him, waiting for an acknowledgment he could not find in his heart to give. Without a word, Two Moons brushed past him, strolled over to his captive and stood beside her.

"The one with the blue eyes is my captive, yes," he said in Lakota. What could he say to make them understand he wished her no harm? If she truly were his Spirit Woman, they would not harm her; yet he himself did not know for sure if she was.

"My brothers, I understand your anger. She is a Crow, enemy of our people. But she was not among those who killed your husbands and sons. She is as you are, only a woman. Do not take your sorrows out on one who has not gone to battle."

"Has Two Moons turned soft like a woman?" a voice challenged. Little Wolf, his rival, marched over to them. "Or perhaps you have gone crazy like your sister."

Furious at the insult thrown at him, Two Moons stomped over to Little Wolf before he had a chance to get any closer. "Your words, my brother, have the bite of a serpent's tongue. Be careful where you spit your poison."

Two Moons towered in height over Little Wolf. He could take him down in an instant, and after that torturous ride with the Crow woman's soft body rising against his own, he was itching for a good fight. Let them see once and for all who the better of the two was.

Little Wolf backed away at Two Moons' threat. "Our women have a right to grieve out their anger on our enemies," he hissed between crooked teeth. "What right do you have to stop them?"

Two Moons thought a moment. He had no right. He knew the women's actions were more to frighten Blue Eyes, than to really hurt her, to bring her down to her new level of acceptance. But, he could not tell them that their blows had hurt him far more than they had hurt her. Perhaps he had gone soft.

"I ask you again," Little Wolf challenged. "What right do you have?"

Two Moons turned and glanced over the heads of the crowd to his captive. Her gaze caught his. He could read the fear in those eyes and something else. He saw a pleading need for his help.

"I do not have the right. Nor do I take it. But she has been sick. Her body is weak. I have brought her back as a gift to my mother who could use a younger one's hands to help her."

By now others had joined the crowd and stood near watching. Two

Moons continued, choosing his words with care. "If I had brought back a small bird as a token of my love, would you smash it to the ground and destroy it?"

A soft murmur sifted through the crowd as the women turned to one another in discussion. Buffalo Calf Woman took a step forward. "There is much work to be done and to have another among us to help lessen one's burden would be a good thing."

Her round face scolding, she glanced over to his captive, then back to him. "We have heard your words and we understand."

Her plump arm raised toward his captive, Two Moons could see scars in Buffalo Calf Woman's flesh, self-inflicted cuts made in grief when she had lost her only son at the hands of a Crow brave.

"But, she will come to understand her presence here is lower than that of a dog until she proves herself otherwise," she said, her voice heavy with loathing,

Two Moons nodded. His captive was safe for the moment.

He glanced back to Little Wolf who stood glaring at him with hatred in his eyes. Always there was strife between them. Ever since they had been boys, when he had gown taller than Little Wolf, when he had shot faster, rode better, the hate in Little Wolf grew no matter how he had tried to stop it. Now, it was too late. They acknowledged one another but kept their distance.

Looking at him, Two Moons knew Little Wolf once again had lost the fight. Little Wolf knew it too. His mouth twisted with loathing, he turned and stalked away in defeat, yet Two Moons knew the battle was not over.

Gabrielle stood in silent fear ... watching ... waiting with held breath. A Sioux encampment with conical tepees of various sizes and colors dotted the clearing before her. Yet, despite her curiosity, she was too afraid to tear her gaze off her captor.

She wished she understood what he said. His deep guttural words seemed composed, oddly gentle, considering the anger of the crowd. Was he trying to woo the crowd to his opinion? Were they discussing her fate? A sickening wave of terror welled up from her belly. Were they all crazy? Would they beat her again as they had started to? Her face stung from the slaps the women had given her. Her arms felt black and blue from their pinches.

It was only when the shorter man with the crooked teeth clenched his hand at his side, spun on his heels and stalked away, that the tension in the air broke and the mood of the crowd shifted. Relief washed through her. Her legs quivered as she watched the women shuffle away.

Gabrielle sighed. *Thank God.* Whatever her fate, for the moment she would live. Or ... perhaps not, if the burning look of disdain in her captor's eyes meant anything. He marched over and grabbed her arm. His hand strong, firm, he nudged her forward past rows of brightly painted tepees and strung hides. A group of old men sat smoking long pipes and glanced up, barely giving her notice. Continuing in silence he nudged her past little ones, whose wide dark eyes beheld hers with curiosity as they played in the melting snow. When they passed a group of men with grins of lustful interest, Gabrielle wished she had been left with the women.

Tepees, horses, costumes—a movie? She drew her gaze away, scanning the village for something, or someone who looked familiar. Nothing did. Shoved through the flap of a tepee, she stumbled. She jerked her gaze around. "Hey, watch it."

Her captor's lips curled with disgust. He nodded she move forward.

An old woman sat quilling a dress. Gabrielle stared into black eyes that looked familiar. This woman was her captor's mother. They shared the same strong chin and high cheekbones; had the same proud demeanor about them. Her long, dark braided hair was streaked with gray. Her weathered features lined with creases and age, were softer, less threatening.

Gabrielle felt a moment's hope. "This is a game, right? Candid Camera?"

The woman scowled and put down her work. She adjusted what appeared to be elk teeth sewn on a shawl then stood stiff and dignified.

She might as well be on an auctioneer's block, Gabrielle thought as she watched the woman scan her up and down. She returned the other woman's gaze, regarding her critically.

Gathering her courage, she took a step forward. "In case you didn't hear me the first time, what kind of crazy game are you all playing? I demand to know where I am."

Mother and son spoke, ignoring her. Their words were guttural, sometimes angry and argumentative. Gabrielle didn't need to understand a word to know they were discussing her. Her stomach churned with a mixture of hunger and anxiety. Her hands shook. She clenched them to keep them still. Her gaze transfixed, she studied the old woman's face, trying to read her thoughts.

A stern, tight-lipped expression confronted her.

The woman reached out to feel her arm. Gabrielle stepped back.

With a grunt and a shake of her head, her captor's mother turned, leaving Gabrielle alone with her son.

He marched toward her. Gabrielle's pulse pounded. He grabbed her wrists. She jerked them back. His endless black eyes flashed with anger, holding her mesmerized. His hands tightened around hers. His dark brows wrinkled with contemplating thoughts, then he glanced down and untied her hands.

Rubbing her sore wrist with her fingers, she watched, relieved when he turned without a word and followed his mother.

Her knees weak, Gabrielle sank onto a pile of buffalo skins. This village, these people, nothing appeared to be as it should. This was not some erected town built on a reservation for a movie. This was too real.

Her eyelids felt glued to the tops of her brow. She glanced around, barely blinking.

Halfway up the inside walls of the tepee cream-colored cloths embroidered in horizontal stripes, beaded in yellows, blues and reds, decorated the walls. Bold symbols, figures of wolves, birds and two moons, had also been painstakingly painted on the skins. Animal skin covers were arranged neatly on the trampled dirt floor. A shield painted with two crescent moons hung from a forked pole over in the corner. Everywhere she looked, everything she saw shouted what couldn't be. This wasn't the year two thousand anymore.

On shaky legs she stood and stumbled over to a broken mirror hanging off a hammock-like mat. Hesitant, her fingers shaking, she brought the mirror to her face ... afraid to look ... afraid of what she'd fine, yet curious.

A soft gasp escaped her lips. Her body stiffened. Her face was as bronzed as her hands.

She jerked the mirror away. Why? What absurd reason could he have to do this to her? It didn't make sense. Nothing made any sense. Vigorously, with her sleeve, she tried to wipe the brown from her cheeks and forehead. Frustrated when the color remained, she rubbed and wet her face and hands until they hurt.

Blue eyes stared back at her when she slowly raised the mirror and took another peek at her reflection. The dazed expression staring back couldn't be ... No. It just couldn't be!

A faint thread of hysteria began working its way across her brain, squeezing like a tightening screw. She rubbed her eyes. She looked the same, yet she didn't. Besides its color, the face staring back at her couldn't be more than nineteen!

Again she brought her hands to her face, running them along her features, feeling her bone structure for shape and texture like she was sculpting a piece for the first time. The oval face with the slightly pointed chin and full lips, felt like hers. And the nose ... Gabrielle looked at her profile. Her nose turned up at the end. It wasn't as broad or as straight as the nose she saw out of the corner of her eye.

Her hands began to shake. That reflection—the remembered touch of sculpting those same contouring lines—it was the skull; the woman's skull she had found and had so carefully reconstructed in clay.

She put the mirror down, nearly dropping it. She wore a dead woman's face!

Pacing back and forth, her fingers pressing against her temples, Gabrielle pinched her eyes closed. In the darkness fanning before her, vibrant colors of yellows and oranges flickered. A murmur of distant voices rang in her ears.

Startled, her eyes shot open. She'd experienced all those sensations before. Only this time, her feet were on solid ground. She wasn't dreaming or sliding down the center of the earth. Gabrielle ran to the tepee's opening, held her breath and peeked outside. As impossible as it seemed, there could be no other explanation for the countless number of people out there living their lives in a manner unfamiliar to her.

The authentic moccasins on her feet, the color of her skin, her captor and the untamed wildness about him ... Why hadn't she seen it before? And the skull that resembled her. It all made sense, in a confused kind of way. There could be no other explanation.

Wasn't it Jules Verne who believed time travel was possible? But why her? Why now?

Staring into the space around her without focusing on anything, her mind spun. Could it be? Was it really possible? Could she really have traveled back in time? Finally, her mind like an imaginary top, slowly wound down to a drop dead stop. Her legs gave way. She sank to the ground, wide-eyed, staring blankly at nothing in particular. Her head throbbed with the realization that her world as she knew it no longer existed.

Two Moons knew what they were all thinking as he walked over to his friends. The grins on their faces said everything: They wanted her.

"*Hau kola*, hello my friends." He clasped a hand on his best friend's shoulder.

Shadow Elk acknowledged his greeting with a nod, but it was Walking Hunter who spoke. "The one you bring into our village has a face and body to tempt even the strongest of the Great Spirits. We will all look to your lodge."

"Blue Eyes will share no man's blanket but my own," Two Moons began. He tried to keep his voice light, masking the annoyance that built with each word of lust spoken by his friends. "I have claimed her as my property and I will not share her, even with you my friends." He laughed. "It would not do to have you fight amongst yourselves like a pack of angry dogs over a bone. That would be my doing. So I will sacrifice myself to save you."

"Such a sacrifice. I think you are too good to your brothers," Shadow Elk joked. "Such a sacrifice I think Kills Pretty Enemy would not be happy with."

Shadow Elk was right, Two Moons thought. Kills Pretty Enemy would be angry he had brought Blue Eyes back with him. At one time he had thought to share his blanket with Kills Pretty, but his heart was not hot for hers. She did not understand why he chose to walk alone. His mother did not understand. Still, she held tight the hope that the two of them would get together. It could never be.

"The day grows late. I will leave you to your own amusements as I will be too busy to accompany you." Two Moons turned.

It was clear by the good-natured remarks and the slaps of approval on his back that they all understood his message.

Two Moons re-entered his lodge. His mother stood inside. Her chin lifted toward his captive. "What do you call her?"

Two Moons studied his captive. She raised round clear blue eyes to find him watching her. "She is called Blue Eyes."

"She will cause you trouble." Rattling Blanket frowned. Without another word she left his lodge.

Two Moons squared his shoulders. Blue Eyes and he were to follow the same path, if only for the moment. Until the day came that their roads forked, she would be his to protect. If she truly were his Spirit Woman then he would not anger the Spirits. If she was not, *hecetu*, so be it.

He took off his vest and hung it neatly over his backrest. He slid the leggings down his thighs, over his calves and ankles, then folded the clothing and laid it beside him on his bed of fur. He knew what was expected if he was to call her his own.

His heart heavy, he glanced down at her, seeing the intense terror etched across her face. She started to rise to her knees. He threw himself over her. Together they fell back against the blanket. She struggled against him. Her hips ground into his as she thrashed about wildly. Her soft breasts heaved against his chest. He clasped his hands against her cheeks to stop the frenzied motion of her head. With gentle fingers he brushed the hair from her face.

The fear clouding her beautiful blue eyes pained him now as it had before when the women of his village had showed their anger at her presence. Had it not been so recent—the memory of loved ones killed by his enemy's hand—then perhaps they would have acted differently. One day she would come to see the kinder more generous side of his people.

He slipped his hand off her face, to the cloth at his hip, untied the knot, then with a flick of his wrist, yanked off his breechclout and dropped it to the ground.

Gabrielle couldn't believe he had brought her here to his home to rape her, but his nakedness said exactly what he had in mind. His chest weighed heavily, crushing into her rib cage, making it difficult to breathe. His groin pressed against her thigh. She could feel the rapid rhythm of his heart against her breast. The cool air on her legs, the touch of his hot hand against her thigh, sent a jolting stab of panic to her chest. She struggled to sit, tried to force her skirt back down.

"Get your hands off me! You disgusting pig! Let me go!" Kicking and thrashing did little to prevent him from sliding his hand up her leg as he shoved her back down to the blanket.

"I won't let you do this. I won't!" The bravado in her voice diminished as the pressure of his thumb in the hollow of her collarbone increased. She understood only too well she was no match for him. He wanted her to know he was stronger, showing her that with just his thumb he was in control.

She stared at him, trying to read what was in those cruel dark eyes of his. Hoping if he saw her fear, he'd change his mind. Was this his pleasure to rape her now amongst his people? Did he wish to let them hear her screams? Gabrielle clamped her lips tight. She would give him no satisfaction.

He lifted her skirt. Cool air assaulted her bare torso. She clamped her thighs together, struggling against him. In the blink of an eye, he reached across her and grabbed a thin piece of rawhide. With the agility and swiftness of one trained in battle, he bound her wrists to a supporting lodge pole. Her heart pounded erratically. She watched in horror as he brought his knife up from the ground beside him. She jerked her knees up, tried to turn away from him; but he rolled her flat on her back, straddling her legs. As he thrust her thighs apart with his hands and cut the chastity rope, Gabrielle's last thread of hope unraveled. A cry escaped her lips. A cry she had promised only she would hear.

She stared up into his eyes, trying in one last effort to get him to change his mind. In their depths she saw not lust, nor hostility, only a sadness she didn't understand.

As quick as he had straddled her, he was off, kneeing beside her. As he yanked the rope from her waist, it scratched against her flesh, burning her. A swift shadow of anger swept across his carved face as he lowered her skirt. He grunted with annoyance then turned his body away from her gaze.

When he lay down beside her, she nearly jumped out of her skin, relieved he had not raped her—confused. When he threw the blanket on top of them and rolled over, she shrank as far away from him as she could. Finally when she no longer felt him moving beside her, Gabrielle breathed more easily and closed her eyes.

FIVE

The patches of fog grew thicker as Roy drove his pickup higher up the mountain's winding road. The dense gray mist, thick as pea soup one minute, clear the next, made his eyes feel dry from strain. The road seemed almost invisible. He never knew what lay around the corner until he came upon it. He bit his lower lip in concentration. Every fiber in his body grew taut. A tense silence enveloped his truck, as thick as the air outside.

Like a slow descending curtain, dusk snuffed out the last of daylight. He took one hand off the wheel and flipped on his lights.

"Shit!" The word left his mouth a few minutes before the road curved. Nothing but air and open space loomed before him. With a jerk on the wheel, he swerved his truck to the right and avoided driving over the edge of what appeared to be a thousand-foot drop.

When at last the road widened and the mountains were behind him, he pulled over to the shoulder and stopped. Leaning back against his seat, he closed his eyes and exhaled. Damned if his sense of doom earlier hadn't been right on the mark.

Beads of sweat pooled on his forehead. He wiped his face with his wrist and opened his eyes. He reached under his seat for his first aid kit. Inside the box, gauze, bandages, antiseptic pads and various medical necessities were arranged neatly and organized in their respective places.

He could still hear his father's words: *Everything in its place, a place for everything.* He popped an aspirin in his mouth and swallowed then reached for the radio and turned it on. Surprised when nothing happened, he fiddled with the volume and pushed the various buttons.

Stone dead. That was odd.

A loud bark sounded in his ear. Staring out the side window, Roy strained to see past the rolling mist.

A large white dog broke through the fog. The beast came pretty close to resembling a wolf, and Roy hesitated before he leaned out the window. "Hey boy. Where'd you come from? You lost?"

Blue eyes stared back at him as the dog in silence wagged its long bushy white tail.

Thinking to check for a collar, he opened the door and stepped out.

Before he had a chance to bend down, the dog skirted around him and jumped onto the front seat.

"Hey fella, nice try, but I don't think so. Come on out." He patted his thigh. "Come on, get out."

He reached across the seat and pulled on the animal's fur, keeping his distance from the beast's mouth in the event that the dog might turn on him. "Come on now," he urged again. "And don't give me that look."

He straightened and then crossed his arms in front of his chest. "This is my truck and I don't have— "

Suddenly a flash of lightning and an exploding crash of thunder interrupted his words. Huge raindrops fell, shattering against the ground, hitting his back.

"Damn it!"

With a quick shove, Roy pushed the dog over and jumped to his seat. The door closed with a thud. As he rolled up the window, a strong gust of wind breathed heavily against the glass, causing it to rattle. The rain grew in intensity. It pelted the windshield like pebbles thrown from above.

Struggling out of his damp leather vest, he folded it neatly over the back of his seat then turned on the ignition.

"I'll take you as far as the next town and then you're out." He put the truck in gear, stepped on the gas then glanced at the animal beside him. Blue eyes. The damn dog had blue eyes. Seemed unnatural, if you asked him. Clear blue, piercing eyes. That reminded him.... He picked up the phone and dialed.

"George, it's Roy Prescott. You remember me?"

"I ... I think so." George sounded uneasy.

"Good. Ms. Camden, did she come back yet?"

"Ms. Camden ain't here. I told you. She ain't here."

"George. I know. Calm down. I'm just worried about her. Where'd you say she went?"

There was a pause of silence. "I don't know."

Flexing, unflexing his hand, Roy took a deep calm breath. "What do you mean you don't know? I thought you said she had gone up to one of the reservations."

"Oh. Right." George paused, hesitant. "She'll be gone a few days."

"What reservation, George?"

"I don't know. She'll be back. Told me so."

The hair on Roy's arm rose.

"George, listen to me. I have a terrible feeling something's not right. Now, I don't want to scare you, but think, where'd she say she was going?"

"I don't know," he wailed. "Said she'd be back. Couple of days or so." George sounded agitated.

"OK. Don't worry about it. When she gets back, tell her—George? George?"

Silence answered him.

Roy stared at the phone in confusion. What the hell was going on? First the radio, now this? He placed the receiver in the holder and stared into the darkness.

The beams of his fog lights cast an eerie glow to the dark winding road, and the swirling mist engulfed his windshield.

His neck muscles tightened. His lids grew heavy from straining. He blinked then focused his attention on the dark road. Settling back against his seat, he arched his shoulders forward, then back. The joints in his shoulder blades crunched.

Again, a weird premonition of impending disaster overcame him. He shook his head and wiped his sweaty palm on his pant leg.

The wind pushed his truck with a heavy hand. Leaves whirled up from the ground, hit his windshield then were swept away by the rapid swish of his windshield wipers.

Rounding the bend, he was starting down the mountain, when a crackling bolt of light hit the pavement blinding him. His shoulders jerked.

Out of nowhere a black hawk, the size of an eagle, swooped down and landed in the road before him. Grasping the steering wheel tightfisted, Roy swerved to the right to avoid hitting the bird. The pickup's speed increased as it skidded down the road's incline. He slammed on the brakes. The steering column shimmed in his hands. The car swerved to the left. Now off the road and onto the shoulder the pickup rocked, throwing him forward.

A tree loomed up ahead. Sensing the impending danger, the dog dropped his head in Roy's lap. "Hang tight fella. It's gonna be a bumpy ride."

Roy's eyes widened. He thrust his arms out tautly and braced himself against the wheel. He heard a yelp, felt the weight of the dog being jostled beside him. Roy sank down in his seat.

Thoughts came to him like a movie reel on slo-mo, dragging across his brain. He was go... ing to hit th ... at tree.

Tree branches creaked in the wind. A hawk cawed. But inside the sweat lodge, Two Moons, his legs crossed, sat in silence focusing his thoughts to the pit of hot stones before him. Flames of golden amber crackled in the burning fire. The door flap of the *tunka tipi*, sweat lodge, shut out the evening's light. In the darkness the stones glowed a deep red and gold.

From his leather pouch, Black Hawk sprinkled a fine dust over the rocks, filling the room with the woodsy smell of cedar. Two Moons thrust his cupped hands into the sacred smoke and drew it toward him.

"*Tunkashila*, Grandfather, creator of all, look on us. We offer you all we have. All else belongs to you. So hear us, your children." Black Hawk sprinkled more cedar onto the stones and waved his eagle wing fan over the flames. "May this sacred cedar carry our words to your ears, so that you may hear and guide us."

Steam hissed. Wood popped. Smoke rose fiercely, filling the lodge with a gray mist, as he sprinkled handfuls of water onto the fire.

Hot vapors washed over Two Moons. The fierce heat burned his nostrils as he breathed in deeply. His shoulders rose and fell in shallow rhythm with his chest. Smoke stung his eyes and his lids fell shut. Sweat poured down his forehead, tracing a path down his cheeks. He tasted its salty wetness on his lips, as he began to pray for guidance.

Blurred visions wafted in and out of his consciousness. The steady beat of a drum, the ceaseless vibration of a rattle, kept with the rhythm of his heart, as it beat faster and faster. Black Hawk's guttural low chanting carried him higher and higher.

Darkness embraced his mind and he welcomed it—prayed for a vision, prayed for guidance—until Two Moons entered the world beyond, floating on a smooth, transparent mist, surrounded by a glowing yellow light. Cold droplets of rain hit his face as he burst through the clouds and found himself running beside the wolf. Suddenly he and the beast became one. Images, fast and furious, sped past him. He sensed danger, fear, as the earth beneath him shook. He clenched his hands. A sharp pain cut across his chest. He winced. Then the darkness swallowed him.

From the distance he heard a song. Soft and whispered, carried over the breeze, it flowed like a gentle gurgling river, filling his soul with peaceful contentment. As quickly as it came, it disappeared. He was back in the lodge, confused, lost and lonely.

A breath of cool air swirled in, fanning his steaming body, striking him back to reality.

Black Hawk signaled to the doorman to keep the flap open. "The spirits have spoken."

"I do not understand what they have shown me."

"You are beginning a new circle of life."

Two Moons nodded. "I saw a hawk flying over me. As its legs touched the ground it grew larger and larger. Its giant wings gathered me up and carried me above the clouds. Then I was on the ground, but the earth beneath my feet was black. As I ran, the white wolf with the eyes of the sky, was beside me."

"He is one of your animal spirits. So, he guides you in and out of the spirit world."

Two Moons nodded. "I held in my hand a small box that talked in my ear—"

"I have heard of such. So, it is said that in this year, in a village called Philadelphia, a man with the name Bell has made such a box."

Two Moons continued to talk about his vision, while Black Hawk smoked his pipe in silence.

"Lost, I walked through a heavy gray mist. Then I came upon a man riding in a wagon with no horses."

"A horseless carriage," Black Hawk replied. "Yes. On my visit to talk with the Great White Father, I, too, have seen these wagons."

"Black Hawk, this wagon ..." Two Moons leaned closer. "... from its jaws of wrinkled metal, it spit smoke."

Dark and confusing, images blurred: a black hawk, a white dog, clouds of gray and a loud crash. Slowly Roy regained consciousness and became aware of being slumped over the steering wheel. His movements sluggish, he straightened and leaned back. An excruciating pain attacked his chest. He hunched forward to relieve it then closed his eyes. Motionless for a moment, he took a long deep breath and tried to regulate his breathing—tried to recall what had happened. He had hit the tree. Thank God. He was all right. But, what about—

He glanced sideways. The dog was gone. How? The window was still closed. The windshield wasn't broken. Clutching his chest, he raised himself on his other hand and stared out into the darkness. He couldn't see much; everything beyond a few yards was pitch black.

With great care, he reached for the doorknob and pushed the lever up. When his feet hit the ground, they buckled slightly beneath him. Dizzy, he leaned against the door for a moment then slowly walked around to assess the damage. The front left of his truck crumpled into the tree. The hood had popped open. He fanned away the smoke pouring out from the radiator and leaned closer to the hood to take a better look. He could hear steam hissing, could feel its heat upon his face.

"Your jeep will not carry you any further."

Startled, Roy hit his head on the hood of his truck. He cradled his head with his hand and whirled around. An old man with braids and a dark floppy hat, stood behind him.

"Where …?" Roy's gaze darted about him.

The old man seemed to read his mind. "Not far." He waved the beam of his flashlight over his shoulder. "Just a short walk up the road. So, you and I will go there."

"But my truck. I …" Momentarily distracted by a severe pain in his ribs, Roy paused for a moment. "Right. I'll need to call for a tow truck."

"Come then. We will see to all your needs later." The old man turned away, not waiting for an answer.

Reluctantly, Roy reached to the back seat for his camera, turned and followed him, his movement's stiff and awkward. "Did you happen to see a white dog? He looked kinda like a wolf. He was in my truck before …"

"I let him out."

Roy stopped dead in his tracks. "You let the dog out, but left me unconscious in the truck?" What was wrong with this picture?

"He asked to go out. You did not." The old man paused and glanced at him from beneath bushy, gray brows.

Roy couldn't believe he had heard correctly. He frowned in exasperation.

"So, besides," the old man continued, "I knew you would come to."

For a man with so many years under his belt, he sure moved fast. Roy took a few quick steps to catch up with him. "I hope the mutt is all right. Must live around here, huh?"

"He runs with the wind. Mother Earth is his home."

"I guess you can't collar the wild part in him. Trying would probably kill him. I can relate to that." A heavy weariness began to seep into his body, as he tried to concentrate on just keeping in rhythm with his companion. His chest ached. His head pounded. Sweat poured down his forehead. And if things weren't bad enough, he could swear he knew the old man from somewhere.

SIX

A breath, hot and heavy, fanned Gabrielle's cheeks—a warning sounded in her ears. Gabrielle awoke with a start. Yellow eyes stared down at her. She choked back a cry, frightened, afraid to breathe. He was so close, nose to nose. She could smell his animal odor. She clenched her hands. The ropes that held her immobile tightened against her wrists. Paralyzed, her body numb with fear, she kept her attention focused on the beast hovering over her and silently prayed the wolf would leave. Bending his head to her chest, he sniffed her. She cringed. Where was her captor? She knew without turning that he no longer slept by her side. Had he left her to die? Was this to be her end, like this? Torn apart limb by limb by this beast? *Please, dear God.* She prayed it wouldn't be so.

The wolf raised his head. His cold wet nose touched her ear. She shivered, clenched her eyes tightly then ... screamed. Her bloodcurdling cries shattered the silence. The wolf backed away.

A thud, a bright flash of morning's sunlight startled her. She twisted her head, glanced over her shoulder. The front of the tepee open, a crowd of nameless faces peered in at her ... laughing.

She heard her captor's cool, authoritative voice above all the chatter. She watched as he pushed his way through the crowd, the only face she had come to know. Walking over, he knelt between her and the wolf and cut the ropes that held her prisoner. His dark eyes filled with sympathy, he said not a word as he held out his hand. Gabrielle scrambled to her feet ignoring him and ran to the door of the tepee.

"Get out of my way." In vain she tried to elbow her way through the opening. Like a solid wall, the crowd wouldn't budge, not one inch, not one person.

She didn't want to run to her captor like a frightened child, didn't want his protection, but she ran to him anyway, without knowing why he'd protect her. And when his strong arms wrapped around her and she lay her cheek against his chest, she felt safe; not just from the wolf, but from all of those who found humor in her fears.

"*Kopegla sni yo.*" Although the words he spoke were foreign, the degree of warmth and concern in his tone, settled in around her like a well worn blanket. Her heart slowed to a steady thump. Surprised this man whom she hardly knew could have such an affect on her, she raised her eyes to his. The look of pleasure glistening in his dark pupils was the last thing she had expected to see. Or want.

Embarrassment turned to rage. She jerked her body from his and took a step back. "Damn you!" How could she be so stupid? How could she even at a time like this be attracted to him, this stranger, this person from another world whom she knew nothing about?

"I fail to see the humor in all of this." Her voice rose an octave, mingling with the raucous sounds of laughter. She spun around on her heels and faced the crowd. "Stop it ... all of you!"

A small boy, no more than four of five, stepped through the opening. His face round, his cheeks chubby, he looked like the little Indian dolls she'd seen in the reservation shops back home. A head of glorious dark brown wavy hair, which didn't quite fit the picture, cascaded down his shoulders in wild disarray.

"Do you speak English?" Silently she prayed, that being half white, he might understand her.

In the depths of his hazel eyes she saw his lack of comprehension. She bit her lip until it throbbed. Anguish and desolation extinguished any spark of hope. His smile, a genuine honest smile, said without words what everyone else around her already knew. The wolf belonged to the boy. And when the child wrapped his arms around his pet and nudged the beast to follow him, she felt like a fool.

"Get out of here. Leave me alone," she screamed. "I—I don't belong here." Emotionally drained, her voice weakened. She sighed and drew her body away. Her shoulders sagged in hopelessness and defeat.

Her captor studied her silently before he glanced over his shoulder at the crowd. He issued what sounded like a command. Then with a wave of his hand he shooed his tribespeople away, all but the small boy and his pet.

Their gaze met. Her heart jolted. He reached for her wrist and held her firmly. His guttural words were soft as he urged her closer to the wolf. "*Kola.*"

Was he crazy? "No. Please. I don't want to." She pushed his hand, tying to break his hold. He brought her fingers still closer to the wolf's head.

She pulled back.

He stopped her.

"*Kola.*" Once more, he encouraged her to touch the animal's head. Friend or foe, she didn't care. She yanked her hand from his.

"I said no. Now why don't you just leave and take that beast with you?"

He opened his mouth to speak, changed his mind and clamped his lips closed. Anger lit his eyes. Taking the boy and his pet with him, his strides quick and furious, he left her to stand alone.

Surrendering to her exhaustion, Gabrielle collapsed to her knees. What was she doing here? These people hated her, and it wasn't really her they hated, but the woman whose body she'd been switched into—a woman whom she knew nothing about.

Lonely, overwhelmed, frightened by the unknown, by the mystery of quantum physics that had catapulted her back through time, she cradled her face in the palm of her hands. Had she lived this life before? Was the skull the key, her look-a-like? Was she here to change someone's destiny, or merely to die?

Her mind whirled making her dizzy, as multitude after multitude of questions accosted her from all directions. Did anybody realize she was missing? Did anybody even care?

Roy! He'd be looking for her. His bloodhound instincts wouldn't give up, that much she knew.

Her head pounded and she pressed her thumb knuckles into her temples. She was grasping for straws. Her current situation was scientifically unrealistic, there was no explanation, but she was sitting here, wasn't she?

A stab of guilt lay heavily on her chest. She'd pushed him from her thoughts so many times, like she did anyone who wanted to get close to her. Would she ever see him again? Would she ever get the chance to tell him about the attraction she had buried deep inside, or would she be stuck in this time warp forever? *Please Roy, find me.*

A warm hand on her knee jostled her from her thoughts. Hastily she withdrew her hands. An astonishingly beautiful young woman, with finely sculptured high cheeks, a delicate small chin and huge almond-shaped eyes stared back at her. She looked like she could be a model for *Vogue* magazine.

With gentle fingers she brushed a strand of hair from Gabrielle's eye. The warm and compassionate smile that touched her lips, shattered the last of Gabrielle's self control, and she broke down and cried. The woman gathered her in her arms like a doting mother, shouldering her pain.

When the tears subsided, Gabrielle drew away slightly, embarrassed. "I ... I didn't know the wolf was a—" She hiccupped. "A pet. And—whatever his name ..."

"Two Moons."

Gabrielle brushed a tear from her cheek. "Well he ... he ..." A tear fell on her lip and she wiped it way. "The scars on his back—all night I thought ... I thought I was going to die."

"Shh. Dry your eyes and have no fear. Those scars you saw are the marks made by the pale faces. It is not our way. No harm will come to you."

"You ..." Gabrielle stared, dumbfounded. "You speak English?"

"Yes. Many of my people have learned the way of the white man from the men who trap the beaver. My mother taught me, as I will teach my *wakanyeja* ..." She paused, searching for the English word. "Children. My children." She smiled. "My name is Chahanpi."

With the back of her hand Gabrielle wiped away her remaining tears. "Mine's Gabrielle."

"Gab-ree-l." Chahanpi struggled with the word. "Pretty. I am named after the juices that flow from the tree. *Cha,* meaning tree; *hanpi,* sap. Why are you called by your name?"

Gabrielle sat back on her haunches and took a deep calm, reflective thought. Native Americans did not necessarily keep the name they were born with. Each name had a special meaning associated with a brave deed, or a personality, or a sign, something that said something about the person. What did her name mean? She shrugged. That was a good question. "My mother named me after the angel Gabriel."

"Angels. Once I saw a picture book with a beautiful woman with wings. They are like our man beings, is that not so?" Chahanpi asked, in a soft, gentle tone.

Looking at her, Gabrielle was reminded of spring rain, light, warm and refreshing.

"Do they not come from the land above?" Chahanpi asked before she could answer.

"Yes. I guess if you believed in spirits, they'd be up there."

Chahanpi's luminous black eyes widened with awe. "You are truly blessed with such a special name."

Blessed wasn't the word that came to mind when she thought about her life. Losing her brother and her father wasn't being blessed and what about Jeffery, her childhood friend and Robert, her fiancé? She had thought they would be around forever. *Fool.*

Wasn't it fitting though, she thought with a touch of cynicism, that given her luck with men, her mother had named her after some guy.

* * *

"It is true then." Kills Pretty Enemy grabbed Two Moons' arm. "You have brought a woman with blue eyes to your lodge."

Two Moons gently pried her fingers off him and placed her arm by her side. "It is of no surprise. I heard your laughter above all the others," he answered in a low composed voice.

Kills Pretty's mouth took on an unpleasant pout. "You will give her away."

"No."

"You cannot mean to take her as your first wife. What about me?"

Two Moons studied Kills Pretty for a moment. She was indeed a beautiful, strong-looking woman, with a proud tilt to her square jaw and generously full curved lips. Her long braided hair was as dark as a starless night. She would make any warrior proud, would bear him many fine sons. Even her name was one of bravery. Having no brother of fighting age, she had gone into battle and had killed a young man, avenging her younger brother's death. Any man would be lucky to call her his own.

He picked up a long dark braid and fingered its softness between his fingertips. "Do not concern yourself with what I chose to do." His voice calm, his gaze steady, he continued. "It is not your place to question me." He dropped her braid and turned.

"I have waited many moons for your presence at my lodge. Have listened through the night's air to hear your song."

Two Moons stopped in mid-stride. He had never even considered having a flute made for her. To share a blanket for talk was one thing, but the flute's magic was so powerful it might lead to marriage. No. He was not ready for that.

"Do not wait for me at your door." He turned. "Listen for another's song."

"I will wait for your song," she answered stubbornly.

"Then you will wait many moons."

A soft rattling from behind made him turn. His mother walked toward him. Pausing for a moment, she wrapped her elks-tooth blanket more snugly around her shoulders. A picture of his father came to mind. He had given her the very first elk's tooth to sew on that robe. Now that he was dead, Two Moons made sure her blanket was covered with the teeth of the elks he had killed. She wore it constantly, even when the sun was high in the sky. He guessed it made her feel as if a part of Walking Proud was always with her.

She glanced up. Her gaze found his. The pride that never wavered in her eyes whenever she looked at him, shamed him. He did not deserve to be placed high in her heart. If it hadn't been for him, his father would still be alive.

"Where is that no-good girl?" She stepped up to his side. "I could have fetched the water faster myself. Some help you have brought me. I cannot even speak my mind to her. Do not the Crow speak in sign as we do?"

His gaze shifted from her, to Blue Eyes, who was trying to balance heavy water bags over her shoulders without spilling them. Weariness settled under her eyes. Her steps were slow and unsteady.

She had gotten no sleep last night. He knew because he'd been awake most of the night himself. Every move she had made, he had felt. Every sigh, every breath had set his body on fire. Her closeness had been unbearable. It had taken every ounce of strength to fight the need to wrap his arms around her, to taste her lips, to feel her body once more beneath his, this time surrendering to his desires. The desire he had seen in her eyes as she had openly examined his body had set his blood aflame.

Blue Eye's tripped on the edge of her skirt.

Two Moons' heart lurched. His breath held. She caught herself, straightened, and only then did he breathe.

Aware of Kills Pretty's laughter and his mother's voice, aware of the snickers of the other women, he kept his attention on Blue Eyes. His mother's words rang in his ear. "Watch her." He would watch her like a hawk, if for nothing else than to make sure no knife found its way into her back.

SEVEN

*U*p at the crack of dawn, the caravan moved forward. Trudging behind the dog-driven drag, Gabrielle shielded her eyes from the gritty dust being kicked up from the long poles dragging before her. The blistering sun beat down, cracking her lips, parching her throat. She swallowed with difficulty. Her steps slowed, putting distance between herself and the travois.

She'd always thought of herself as a trooper. Had never complained when her digs had brought her to remote places without water or electricity. Working long hours was part of her nature. But nothing had prepared her for the endless days of walking, of hauling countless bags of water, of sleeping under the sky with nothing but a bunched-up blanket for her pillow and the hard ground for her bed.

Mothers with babies strapped to their backs, walked effortlessly and chatted with those around them. Children scampered about with the dogs, and Gabrielle wondered where they all got the energy.

She could feel Two Moons' gaze on her back. An imaginary rope tugged at her shoulders beckoning her to turn around, pulling her toward him. He was always in the background watching her. Did he think she was going to run away? To where? She dug her fingers into her palm. What did he want? He never stopped the women from pushing or ordering her around. Other than at night when he lie next to her, he barely spoke to her.

Yet at times when those around her treated her poorly, she thought she caught glimpses of anger in his eyes. Was his anger directed at her, or toward the others?

Tilting her head to one side she stole him a glance. He sat tall and proud in his saddle. The wind brushed long strands of his black hair away from his face. The notched and beaded eagle feather wrapped in his hair reminded Gabrielle of Roy's earring.

Dark eyes studied her keenly. Gabrielle's cheeks flushed. Damn sun was too hot! She wiped her arm across her brow. Then, with hurried steps, she caught up with the rest of the column and focused her attention on the long line of men, women and children parading before her.

* * *

From his spot beneath the tree, Two Moons watched Blue Eyes drag the lodge poles from the travois, watched as she struggled to carry them, dropping them to the ground at her feet. No one offered their hand. No one would, until she proved herself worthy. He knew this. But it did not stop the tightening of his gut, as woman after woman walked by ignoring her. Buffalo Calf Woman yelled and gave her a shove. He thought for moment Blue Eyes might protest, but it seemed she did not have the strength. For the last three days, she had not had a moment's rest.

They called her *witkowin*, crazy woman, she who is afraid of pet wolf. The words burned in his heart. She had surprised him by running into his arms. The strong sense of wanting to comfort her, of happily sheltering her in his arms had caught him off guard. She had thought he had found her fear funny. Maybe it was better that way. The blade in his hand pressed heavily against his palm. The whites were his enemy and she chose to be white. It would be best if he remembered that.

"*Hau Kola.*" Shadow Elk stepped into the shade of the tree.

"*Hau Kola,*" Two Moons replied.

"That is a fine-looking arrow you are working on."

Two Moons placed his knife down on the rock beside him and brought his arrow to his eye, looking it over for any curves or flaws. "Yes. It will fly straight and true to its mark."

"That it will, my brother. You have done fine work."

Extending his arm before him, Two Moons placed the arrow down against his arm to measure its length. Satisfied when it reached from his elbow to the tip of his little finger, he picked up the two pieces of sandstone that rested beside him. Pressing the stones together with the fingers of his free hand, he slowly twisted and pulled the shaft of his arrow through the center hole he had formed with the two grooved stones. Fine shavings of wood fell into his palm.

"I find it takes many suns to smooth down that rough bark till it is the way I like it. Is that not so?" Shadow Elk asked.

Two Moons blew the shavings away, turned his head and glanced at Shadow Elk. Although his friend's words were directed to him, Shadow Elk's attention was on the four women standing in a circle in the clearing a short distance before them. Two Moons watched as the women turned. Chattering among themselves, they glanced over at Blue Eyes, who was having difficulty balancing the lodge pole upright and placing it into position.

"Do not let the words of others trouble you, my brother," Shadow

Elk said softly. "With time, the one with the blue eyes will learn and will find her place among us."

Two Moons glanced back at his friend. "For three nights now I have had to listen to my mother's talks that Blue Eyes knows nothing of the women's work. She is a Crow. Their work is the same. Is that not so?"

"Yes." Shadow Elk frowned. "So I think maybe it is because of her white family she has chosen the white man's ways."

Two Moons shook his head. "I want to believe that is not so, but I fear you are right. I do not understand this. Look." He nodded in her direction. "She does not eat. Already she grows thin."

"I have heard that the pale women sit around making music and have their men feed them." Shadow Elk grinned, then nudged Two Moons' side. "Perhaps she likes nothing more than to play games. Has she sung for you?"

Two Moons rapped his friend's shoulder with his arrow. Ducking, Shadow Elk feigned a look of grievance then winked. "I wager she sings a sweet tune, if you but know where to touch."

"You, my good friend, best keep your thoughts to your own woman and not concern yourself with mine," Two Moons answered in jest. He slid down off the rock. Blue Eye's cry caught his attention. He glanced over to see her staring down at her hand.

His mother ordered her to pick up the wood that lay scattered at her feet and to place it by the fire. Blue Eyes just stared in silence.

Two Moons dropped his unfinished arrow into the quiver at his side and casually began to stroll in the women's direction.

Shadow Elk followed. "I have angered you?"

Two Moons glanced to the man beside him. "Nothing you could ever say would anger me. You are my brother. If not for you I would still be rotting in some white man's cage. Your face was a welcome sight that day at the soliders' walled village." Two Moons stopped abruptly and placed his hand on his friend's arm.

"I owe you my life."

"I would gladly give up my life for yours." Shadow Elk replied. "When the spirits tell us, you and I will go back to Long Hair Custer and his blue coats who hide at the fort. We will get our revenge."

Two Moons could see the anger in his friend's eyes, could hear the cutting edge of hatred in his voice.

Shadow Elk's face clouded with uncertainties. "The scars, have they healed?" he asked, concerned. "I can have Chahanpi rub some salve on them, unless you had thoughts of another's hands on your back?"

Two Moons glanced at Blue Eyes. "You, my friend, have thoughts for only one thing. I think you'd best marry Chahanpi with great haste."

Her arms now laden with wood, Blue Eyes failed to notice the rock in front of her. His stride quick, Two Moons moved closer. He caught her before she hit the ground. The wood spilled over his arms with a rolling thud. The women turned, watching as he gathered her up into his arms. He glared at them. Let them all talk. He turned on his heels and carried her away.

She gave him no resistance and wrapped her arms around his neck in fear of falling. He would never let her fall. Carrying her to his lodge, he nudged open the flap with his shoulder and walked inside. Kneeling, he sat her down on his bed of buffalo skins. A streak of dirt smudged the side of her nose and cheek. The urge to wet his finger and wipe that mark away, made his hand itch.

He reached over and picked a small twig from her knotted hair. His gaze traveled over her face and searched her eyes. Her silence and lifeless stare made his heart heavy. He would rather feel her claws upon his chest than see the defeat in her pale blue eyes.

He straightened and glanced to his backrest for his carry bag. Seeing the parfleche hanging there, he walked over, opened the leather flap, and reached inside. The clean white cloth in hand, he bent down, picked up the water bag by his feet and returned to her side. Kneeling once more, he unlaced the bag and dipped the cloth into the tepid water. She tensed as the cloth touched her cheek.

Through half-opened lids she watched him. His eyes riveted on hers, he gently wiped the grime from her neck and shoulder. Already, his body anticipated what his eyes did not see and he became aroused. Slowly, he pushed aside the cloth from her other shoulder exposing her skin. His heart began thumping like a played drum, increasing its rhythm with each inch he moved the cloth downward.

Hesitating, he stared into the space beyond her. He had traveled this dangerous path before. Would it be wise to do so again? He knew her body too well. Knew every curve. Knew how soft she would feel beneath his hands and how that softness would make him hard and ache to hold her close. His body begged him to take her. Every day watching her had been torturous. Every day the battle between his body and his mind exhausted him. His silent vow haunted him. She was his slave to do with as he pleased; yet he would not take her against her will.

When she worked along side the other women his eyes were on her and her alone. He'd notice the way her hips swayed when she walked and the movement of her breasts under that thin cloth she wore. Every time she bent down and he saw her shapely legs, he longed to kiss the hollow spot in the back of her knees. Never had a woman had such an effect on him.

With great care he slowly slid the cloth over her collarbone, then down to linger at the swell of her breasts. His fingers quivered. A heat spread to his groin, an intense surge of desire that would grow until he ached with a hardness he knew would be impossible to stop. He had but to leave, just leave—

Her eyes flew open. She grabbed his wrist, stopping his movements. "Ouch." Her cry, a bare whisper, was like an arrow piercing his heart. Hastily she withdrew her hand. He caught it. For an instant her eyes widened with alarm and his only desire for the moment, was for her not to fear him.

A moments panic sliced through Gabrielle. Not from the man who held her hand tightly in his, but from the awakening of feelings she had long ago buried away. Feelings that had died at the altar when her fiancé, Robert, had left her standing there. She had vowed to never trust men, to never let herself fall victim to their desires, to shield herself from hurt and betrayal.

"*Takomni wacinmayaye yo.*"

Her pulse beat erratically at the sound of his voice. She wished she could understand what he was saying.

She trusted him. Somehow she knew deep down in her heart she would be safe with him. A feeling of deja vu, as if they had shared this moment once before, overwhelmed her.

He bent his head, brought her hand closer and examined her finger. He glanced to his hip, drew out his knife, then glanced up at her. Her heart pounded but not from fear. Drawn into the deep, endless darkness of his eyes, she was vaguely aware of the slight scraping sensation on her skin as the tip of his knife gently picked at the splinter.

He had the most sensual eyes, compelling, magnetic; and his face— "I'd love to sculpt that handsome face of yours."

The words came out in a rush, slicing the tension in the air-shattering silence. It didn't matter. What did he understand? Not much. "And those perfectly formed lips—God, you have great eyes."

She studied his face imagining the feel of his high cheekbones beneath her fingers. She knew just how she'd mold that proud square jaw line, how she'd create those thin lines of age around his eyes and—

The warmth of his lips against her finger fanned her growing need. She drew in a sizzling breath as he opened his mouth, placed her finger inside and sucked.

"Please ..." The heat of his mouth, like the flick of a match on its cover brought an instantaneous fire to her limbs. "Don't," she begged, slightly light-headed.

She couldn't think straight. Didn't want to. Knew she should.

"No, I ..." She swallowed dryly. *Shouldn't.* The silent word echoed in her head.

He released her finger and leaned closer. She could almost feel his lips upon hers. A shiver of anticipated excitement rippled through her. She closed her eyes.

Outside the drums beat wildly ... as did her heart.

A second passed—an eternity. She remained absolutely motionless and held her breath. Waiting. Hoping ...

Nothing happened.

Gabrielle's eyes flew open. An unwelcome blush crept into her cheeks when she realized he had changed his mind. She watched as Two Moons jerked his body away, stood up in a frenzied wave of motion and with long purposeful strides, headed outside.

"Bring me a bottle of the white man's whiskey," Two Moons demanded to Chahanpi who stood by the fire stirring the steaming broth. Too surprised to do anything more than nod, she turned, not waiting for an explanation. He knew what she was thinking. Firewater was the white man's bad magic. His father had told him that as a boy. He himself had said the same many times when others had downed the fiery liquid during their celebrations.

He watched as she disappeared inside a lodge, then came out hiding the bottle in the folds of her skirt.

"She does not sleep well at night," he explained when she reached his side. Neither did he. Two Moons frowned and glared at Chahanpi. Why should he care if Blue Eyes was exhausted, or try to help? She was the same as every pale face he had met who said one thing and meant another. No, she had said. But her telling stare had spoken differently, confusing him.

Chahanpi cast her eyes downward, but not before he saw the amusement in her gaze. They all thought Blue Eyes' lack of sleep was his fault, he thought with cynicism. Little did they know.

She handed him the bottle.

Two Moons crossed his arms before him. "You see that she drinks it."

"I will bring her some fresh clothes?" Chahanpi asked, searching his eyes for an answer.

"Bring her what you want. It matters not to me."

He glanced to his lodge where he knew Blue Eyes sat wondering why he had left like the twisted winds. He had come too close to giving in to the hunger that still burned in his loins. But her words had said "stop," and he had vowed never to force himself on an unwilling woman.

He glanced toward his sister's lodge. Gentle Fawn, the reason he could not quench his thirst for Blue Eyes. His thoughts strayed to that horrible night when his sister, wracked by gut wrenching cries, had fallen asleep on his lap. That night he had seen the scars a man's unwanted advances could leave. He could not forget what *Hay O Wai*, Yellow Hair, had done to his sister. Now a half-bred child lived among them. Now his sister lived in shame.

Abruptly Two Moons turned his gaze back to Chahanpi who stood silently observing him. A faint smile touched her lips. Was his attraction to Blue Eyes so apparent? Did the entire village think him a fool?

"Well, what are you waiting for?" he questioned harshly. "See that she gets cleaned up."

A stab of guilt attacked as he watched Chahanpi scurry toward his lodge. He shouldn't have taken his anger out on her. It wasn't her he was angry with.

The scars still raw upon his back, how could he forget what the Long Knives had done to him and his family. He closed his eyes, recalling the father who no longer walked this earth. Many moons had passed and still the memory so fresh and vivid, filled his mind as thick and heavy as the clouds of dust had filled his eyes that day. In every battle he now fought, with every blast of the white man's stick of fire, he was instantly back to that day, hearing the lead whistling overhead as bullets tore through the poles of the lodges. The screams of the women as they frantically gathered their children in their arms still drummed in his ears.

He had stood in the midst of his burning village watching his friends and those he loved dying around him. In the confusion that followed, he saw his father mounted on his big, gray war pony, riding toward him, calling his name, telling him to run with the other children and hide. It had only been when the bullets pierced his father's back that he'd had the courage to move. It had been only then, standing over his father's body, that he had realized his father was dead. It was then that he, a child of ten summers, had sworn a vengeance on all those that were not of his people.

Two Moons stopped pacing and opened his eyes. The sun sat low behind his lodge. Blue Eyes was not of his people. It would be best he remembered that. Still ...

He could not let any harm come to her. Screams of frustration stuck in the back of his throat. If she were not his Spirit Woman, he should send her back to her people. He did not need her here to tempt him with her womanly curves. Yet, if she was the woman in his vision, she should be treated not as a slave, but with honor. How was he to know the truth?

He clenched his jaw in silent determination. He would not let the people of his village think Blue Eyes crazy as they did his sister. If he had to put aside his hatred for the white man's tongue and speak to Blue Eyes, he would do so; he would give in to the white man's ways this once, if for nothing more than to tell Blue Eyes what was expected of her. This he would have to do.

It was time she knew his secret.

EIGHT

*I*t was barely morning when Gabrielle felt Rattling Blanket nudging her side. Gabrielle rolled over, ignoring her. Why didn't that woman leave her alone? *God.* She had never missed her own home's peace and solitude more than she did at this very moment. Every day, everywhere she turned, eyes watched. Every time she did something wrong, there were gossiping old biddies to spread the news. And it wasn't much better trying to sleep next to Two Moons, whose physical closeness throughout the night was a constant turn on, or listening to his mother who kept her up half the night snoring.

Jostled roughly a second time, she sat up. "All right already." She yawned and stretched, easing away the night's kinks, then stood. The clean dress Chahanpi had given her clung heavily against her body and despite its smooth appearance, felt slept in. She glanced down at the knee-length, elk-skin garment. A few more days without a bath, and she was going to need a gallon of perfume! She wrinkled her nose and turned her head away.

He always smelled so clean, as though he had just showered, she thought, annoyed, studying Two Moons' sleeping form. Even his clothing, whether it be the fringed leather buckskin leggings, or the quilled skin vest he wore, hung with perfection on that lithe body of his. Damn his rotten soul! None of the other men had that same clean look. Maybe if he smelled of bear grease and sweat she'd be less attracted to him. And why didn't he sleep in more than that breechclout—

She hurried toward the opening, paused by the door, and stole him a quick glance.

Why had he chosen last night to release her? For the first time in days, he had left her hands unbound. Did he sense she no longer feared him? Maybe he thought the whiskey Chahanpi had brought her would have knocked her out for the night. It had, for the most part. Thank God. She would never have fallen asleep thinking about the way he had left her practically kissing the air. Why had he fled from her as if he couldn't run away fast enough? The bum. She'd felt like a fool. He just got up and left, abandoned her like all the other men in her life.

The camp bustled with activity. A large number of unfamiliar tepees had been erected during the night. Painted with colorful pictures of horses, stars, birds and various geometric shapes, all were arranged in big circles, with each opening facing the rising sun. Women from other tribes stood around laughing and chatting with women she had come to recognize. Fires burned and meat boiled in pots. It was going to be another hot day. Already she felt sticky. Summer's heaviness hung the air.

Rattling Blanket stood in the clearing, waiting. "*Opeya*," she ordered.

Gabrielle had heard that word enough times to know she was to come and follow. Quickly she started after the older woman, only too happy to get away from Two Moons. Led to the riverbank where women of all shapes and sizes frolicked in the water, Gabrielle stopped.

Could it be she was finally going to be allowed to bathe? She glanced over to Rattling Blanket, who dropped her dress without giving any indication that she was to do the same and joined the others.

Chahanpi hurried over. Gabrielle smiled, relieved to see a friendly face.

"Come, you must join me." Chahanpi stepped in front of her.

Gabrielle glanced over Chahanpi's shoulder to see a group of young girls splashing and bobbing about in the sparkling water. "I don't know...."

Chahanpi stripped off her dress and stood before her, uninhibited by her nakedness. "You must. It is Two Moons' wish that you bathe with us. Besides," she laughed, "you stink."

Gabrielle watched as she ran to the water's edge, turning once to call her. She couldn't help but notice Chahanpi still wore the crude chastity rope around her middle. The first time she had read that Native Americans had worn a "chastity rope" she'd been surprised. She'd always been under the impression that only medieval women wore such a device. It was amazing how two very different cultures were, in many ways, so similar. Still, she frowned. How could any woman stand to wear the barbaric thing? Was she ever glad to be rid of hers.

"Come. The water is fine. Come join me," Chahanpi shouted, before she plunged into the river's depths.

Gabrielle hesitated. Maybe she was being a prude, but stripping down to her birthday suit and joining in wasn't something she was comfortable with, no matter how inviting the water looked. What about the men? Didn't these women wonder if the men from the camp could see them?

She glanced down to her bare feet and her dirty ankles. She could feel the sweat pouring down between her breasts. The hot sun beat down on her shoulders. She chewed her lip, debating. This might be her only chance. She glanced to the river shaded by bending pines and larches whose branches drank the river's coolness. Swift waters ran over small rocks, foaming white and inviting ...

Chahanpi was right. She did stink. Glancing quickly behind her, Gabrielle pulled off her dress and ran. If her mother could see her now, she'd never hear the end of it.

She hit the water with a splash. Ducking beneath the cool surface, her tension subsided. Heaven. Truly heaven, she thought as she kicked her feet and moved her arms before her. At the sound of children's laughter, Gabrielle glanced to the shore to see the little boy who had been her savior. At his side ran that wild beast of his. She was reminded of an article Roy had written about how man should try to be one with nature and learn from it. Too bad he wasn't here to see this, she thought, longing to see a familiar face, one of her own century.

"Curly is of Two Moons' family," Chahanpi remarked casually, as she floated over. "Though it is sad, Two Moons does not acknowledge him."

Speechless, Gabrielle stared back at her. A son? He had a son? What did Two Moons' wife think about her presence in her husband's lodge all these days? Could it have been her cynical laughter she had heard the morning the wolf had been in the tepee?

God, what an absolute jerk she was to have been attracted to him.

"The boy is part white. That is why Two Moons refuses him, isn't it?"

A momentary look of discomfort crossed Chahanpi's face as she nodded in agreement.

"How cruel of him." Gabrielle frowned. "Where's the boy's mother?"

Chahanpi held out a lump of lye soap. "Gentle Fawn is at the camp. You will meet her."

"Thanks." She took the soap, leaned forward, flopped her hair into the water and lathered. It had never entered her thoughts that Two Moons could be married. Would his wife hate her? Would she take her anger out on her? Where had she been hiding all these days?

Gabrielle scrubbed hard. The gritty bar of ash, salt and grease hardly made for a sudsy head and she wasn't sure if the greasy smell made her hair clean or made it smell like fried hamburgers, but at least it was better than using sand.

"I understand you do not get much sleep." Chahanpi chuckled.

Gabrielle scooped a handful of water over her head and rinsed out the lather.

"Well, it's just that I'm used to sleeping in a bed."

"Is that the only reason?"

Gabrielle nodded. Her long hair whipped her shoulders as she flung her head backward. "Yeah. What other reason would there be?"

"Oh, I don't know." Chahanpi grinned. "If I had a strong handsome warrior like Two Moons lying next to me all night, I doubt the dreammaker would find me sleeping."

"Oh, don't be ridiculous. I hardly even notice him let alone dream of him."

"You wear no protective rope. So you are not a stranger to the ways of men. I think you tell me small lies when you say you hardly notice him." Chahanpi giggled and splashed water in Gabrielle's face before she disappeared under the surface.

Gabrielle wiped her face as Chahanpi resurfaced. Then it dawned on her. Her eyes widened. "No." She gasped. "I mean he took it off. I had one." She groaned, embarrassed.

"Then you and Two Moons—"

"No. We never—Good God, no!" Gabrielle stood and hurried out of the water to find her clothing.

Chahanpi followed her. "Then it must have been to tell the others."

With a yank, Gabrielle pulled the dress down over her head, struggling and wiggling as the leather stuck to her wet body.

"Tell them what?" She popped her head through the neckline.

"That you are his woman." Chahanpi's luminous eyes shone full of question.

"His what? I'm nobody's woman." Indignation and annoyance flushed Gabrielle's cheeks. "We've done nothing. That son of a—" She turned with a start, smothering a groan. "That's why he took it off. I just thought ... that no good son of a bitch," she mumbled under her breath. It was bad enough they all thought she and Two Moons slept together; but what really pissed her off was that for a damned moment, when his dark eyes had softened and his voice had dropped to a breath of a whisper, she had wanted him to.

"I'm sorry that I have caused your anger. I did not mean—"

Gabrielle shook her head. "I'm not angry at you. It's Two Moons, that's gonna get a piece of my mind. I swear when I get a hold of him I'll break his thick neck!"

A look of horror crossed Chahanpi's face. "Please—" Her voice cracked softly. "Do not do such a foolish thing." Chahanpi touched her arm. "I fear if harm comes to Two Moons, you will be in grave danger. It is not a wise thing you wish to do."

Gabrielle halted her steps and laughed. "I'm not going to hurt him. Like I could. Breaking his neck, it's just something you say when you're angry. I'm going to tell him how I feel. Really, that's all. Don't take it so literally."

Chahanpi shook her head slowly. "Then it would be wiser if you were angry at me."

Gabrielle lifted her chin. "I'm not afraid of him."

All morning Gabrielle stewed over her embarrassing discussion with Chahanpi. Everywhere she went, it seemed as if the women were talking about her. There was no escaping their stares and whispers.

A tepee more colorful than the others caught her attention. Walking over she stopped beside it and ran her finger over the various muted green, brown and blue paint that outlined the grass, depicted the rivers and the sky. Black, gray and brown wolves of all sizes were drawn around the middle.

Intrigued by the ostentatious nature of this home compared to the rest of the village, she couldn't resist taking a peek through the unlaced opening. The interior was very similar to Two Moons' home, except unlike his tepee where everything was neatly arranged, someone cluttered this place to the hilt.

"Come."

The voice from inside startled her. She flinched.

"Come in."

She took a hesitant step through the opening, then regretted her foolishness.

The man who stood before her had the face of an unfinished sculpture—sharp, angular, with cheekbones that were too pronounced and a wide nose that looked as though it had been broken once too often. His appearance, though small in stature, was compensated by his muscular body. She recognized him as the same man who had argued with Two Moons her first day in camp.

"This was a mistake. I'm sorry." What a jerk she was. No one here could be trusted. She should never have let her guard down.

Seductively he scanned her body.

"Forgive me. I'm intruding." She turned to leave.

Roughly, he spun her around. "No. You will stay."

Gabrielle wrenched her body away. "No. I think not."

He pulled her tighter.

She shoved her hands between them and pushed. "You disgusting pig. Let me go."

His solid hold wouldn't budge. He pulled her tighter. "You dare to speak to me with such disrespect?" He reached behind and yanked on her hair.

She winced.

"I, Little Wolf, will teach you to respect me. Perhaps you will not be so high and mighty when you feel me between your legs." His grip pinched her arm.

She tried to break free.

"It will be such a good ride." He ground the word between crooked teeth, then grinned. "I will ride you harder and faster than he ever could. You will go back and Two Moons' arms will no longer be enough. From now on, I will be in your dreams."

He rubbed his body up and down the length of her. She could feel his hard erection. He jerked her dress up.

"Let her go or you will answer to me." Two Moons stepped through the opening.

All fear for the moment forgotten, Gabrielle stared, dumbfounded. He spoke English! The shock of discovery slammed into her.

His stare fixed on her, he continued with brutal detachment. "She belongs to me and I wish no man's hands but my own upon her."

He spoke English. *That son of a bitch!*

Little Wolf spun around to face Two Moons, dragging her with him, his unrelenting grip tighter than before. "Your woman was in my lodge," he jeered with triumph. "She came of her own free spirit. Perhaps you do not please her and she seeks another's pallet to warm."

A vein throbbed in Two Moons' neck. "What she wants, or whom she desires, is not up to her," he said, his voice controlled, chilly. "She is mine and I shall do with her as I wish. I choose to keep her for my own amusements."

Releasing her abruptly, Little Wolf went for the knife at his side. Two Moons, anticipating his move, did the same.

Gabrielle held her breath, not sure if the knife were meant for her or Two Moons. She edged away from Little Wolf and watched with numbed horror.

The air thick with tension, both men sized each other up. Sweat dotted Little Wolf's brow as he studied his opponent. A muscle twitched in Two Moons' cheek as he watched Little Wolf hesitantly slide his foot forward. Two knives, held at shoulder height, were poised to plunge at a given moment.

Gabrielle's mind raced as fast as her heart. They were fighting over her and it was all her fault. What if Two Moons got hurt or worse, killed? What would happen to her? Where would she go? Who would be her protector against those like Little Wolf, who wished her harm? And more important than that, how could she live with herself knowing once again she was to blame for somebody's death.

Little Wolf, his face taut, his stance tense, dropped his knife at his side. "Now is not the time for this battle between us. But one day …" He raised his knife before him. "When the sun is high in the sky and the Great Spirit deems it so, we will see which of the two is the better man. *Heceto*, so be it. Go."

He turned and rapped her mid-back shoving her forward. She tripped into Two Moons' arms. Without a word he caught her, grabbed her wrist and pulled her after him.

Although relieved the battle between the two men had come to a halt, Gabrielle, furious Two Moons dragged her away like some Neanderthal cave man who had just won his woman, screamed at the top of her lungs.

"Let go of me, damn it!" She stumbled after him. "I'm quite capable of walking on my own."

Two Moons shoved her through the opening of his tepee.

She whirled around to face him seconds before he stepped through the opening.

"And what are you so mad at? I'm the one who should be mad. You speak English. You never told me you spoke English." Breathless, her chest heaved. "All those times, you never answered me, you pretended not to understand." God. The things she had said. He had understood every word.

"I understand you fine. I chose not to speak to you. There was nothing I wanted to say." His calm voice and steady gaze annoyed the hell out of her.

"Damn you!" She whirled out to slap him.

His iron grip locked on her wrist and stopped her before her fingers reached his face. A forbidding shadow crossed his eyes.

"Why?" She bit down on her lower lip and yanked her hand from his. "Why now?"

"It is my wish, now." His tone, laced with anger, was surprisingly composed.

"That's it? That's your explanation? Period? End of discussion?" she asked curtly. "Well since you understand me, I think it's cruel and inhuman to hate a child because of something he had no control over. So what if he's half white. He didn't choose to be. Here's a new word for you, prejudice."

Two Moons scowled, clasped then unclasped his hand.

Before he had a chance to speak, she continued, "And what about your subtle message to the others? Polygamy may be your belief, but it's certainly not mine. I refuse to be part of your—your harem!" Her voice sounded shrill, even to her ears. "And what about your wife? Certainly she—"

"Wife? You talk nonsense." He stared at her, his black eyes as unreadable as a flat slab of stone.

"It's too late for that I-don't-understand-you look. Of all the no good—What could I have been thinking? I wouldn't sleep with you for all the tea in China!" She clenched her hands at her sides afraid she might be tempted to fly at him again. "How dare you let the others think I'm your woman? How dare you?"

He cast his hands up in the air. His dark eyes reflected his anger. "I know not of which you speak. I have no wife. It was better when you thought me ignorant of your tongue. Now I must forever listen to your ceaseless prattle. I do not have the desire." He spun around ready to leave; then hesitating, his hand on the partially opened flap, he turned. "They think you are touched, witkotkoke." He ran his index finger in small circles by his temple. "Crazy. Why do you make them think you are?"

She watched as he approached her.

His somber eyes examined her enigmatically. "I speak to you in the tongue of the white man only to prove to my people that you are not."

"I'm not crazy and I resent the fact that you think I am." He wasn't married? For some unknown reason, that pleased her.

He placed his hands on her shoulders. "Then tell me why you act as if you know nothing about our ways? Perhaps you prefer the white man's way." His grip tightened as he brought her closer to his broad chest. His biceps bulged. His firm lips were taut. He expected an answer. And what was she going to say? Gee, sorry, but they didn't offer Tanning 101, or a course on gutting rabbits in college. Or would he rather hear: Could it be because I'm not of your century?

"I'm trying, aren't I?" she answered, aware of his musky scent, so male so sexually stimulating.

"You were a many days ride from the fort when I found you." Two

Moons noticed the confusion cross her face. What was she hiding? He was well aware of her mouth, as she chewed her lips nervously. They called to him like a bear to honey. His gaze dropped from her face, to her shoulders, to her breasts. The dress she wore was too small and seductively clung to her body, accenting every curve. Annoyed at his body's weakness, his gaze flew back up to her face. He had come to talk, nothing more, he reminded himself. "Tell me. Had you thought to meet your lover in the woods only to find yourself lost?"

"No."

Two Moons' brows rose. "Then tell me why it was that I found you?"

Perhaps the Blue Coats had sent her to find his village so they could send their army to kill his people. A Crow scout would never get past the *akicitas*, guards, but a woman—yes. Perhaps she had been on her way to his village when her horse had thrown her. Once she gathered the knowledge she needed, she could return to the fort and the Blue Coats would know how many braves there were in the village. They would know where his people were.

Their eyes met. She glanced away then back at him.

He brought his finger to her face and ran it slowly across her smooth warm cheek. "I see no disfigurements on your body, so I am right when I say you did not run from an angry mate."

"Where I come from, they don't cut up a woman's face for being promiscuous." She took a deep breath, struggling with her thoughts. "Look. I'm no adulteress and they didn't kick me out of the fort."

"Then what sin banned you from the fort you call your home?"

They stared at each other through the silence that followed. He wondered if she would be truthful in her word as all red brothers were; or would her tongue be forked like a serpent's and ring false like the white man's word? If she were truly the woman of his vision, then let her prove it by the truth of her words.

"I don't have a husband."

She chose to avoid his question. *Hecetu*, so be it.

Gabrielle couldn't answer him; didn't know what to think. She certainly couldn't tell him why he had found her; didn't know for herself how she came to be here. But she was sure of one thing: He couldn't just change the conversation and think he was going to walk away from her until she got some answers.

"Don't you dare turn away from me. I want to know why you cut that damned rope off!" Gabrielle grabbed Two Moons' arm before he had a chance to leave. "If you think that just because you're stronger than me ... that—that you can force me ... well, you're wrong. I refuse to—"

"You refuse?" Two Moons' face tightened with strain. He yanked free from her grasp and puffed out his chest, reminding her of an angry bull. His eyes narrowed. All he needed was horns.

"You refuse me nothing. I am the warrior. I own you." His angry words so close to her face and the flash of fury in his piercing eyes, made her cringe. "You do as I say," he demanded.

"*Witkotkoke*." He shook his head, took an abrupt step backward and dismissed her words with a wave of his hand. He turned to leave.

"Oh, so we're back to I'm crazy, are we? I'll show you how crazy I am," she shrieked. She grabbed a leather bag by her feet and flung the satchel at him with all her might. With a thud, the bag hit him between his shoulder blades. The look of surprise on his face when he turned to face her would have made her laugh, if she hadn't been so mad.

Mumbling beneath his breath in Lakota, in words that sounded a lot like swearing, he glared at her. His chest heaved. Before he had a chance to straighten, she hurled another parfleche at him.

"Foolish woman—" He ducked and brought his arms up as a shield. His head bobbed to one side as she flung a moccasin at him. "Stop, or you will feel my hand upon you," he ordered.

"Over my dead body!"

"When I am through with you, you will wish that you were." He dodged the other moccasin.

Empty-handed, she glanced around. Out of the corner of her eye she saw him approaching. Quickly she sidestepped him, turned and reached for the pipe bag that hung from a peg beside her.

"Wait!" He threw his hands out before him. His steps halted. The intensity in his voice made her flinch. "I promise. I will not come any closer. Just do not touch that bag. It is sacred to me." He dropped his hands to his sides. Outwardly he seemed calmer, but his eyes flashed in a familiar display of warning.

"If you move, I swear, I'll rub my hands all over this thing."

"When you swear, to whose god do you swear? Mine or the white man's God?"

"What difference does it make?"

"If it is to the white man's God, then I will be forced to break my promise."

She hesitated. He took a step forward.

"Fine. Yours." She took an arm's length step back widening the distance between them. "Stay there and don't move," she warned. "I want an answer and it better be the truth."

"My words are never twisted. I will tell you what you wish to hear."

Suddenly, oddly uncomfortable, she bit her lower lip, glanced away, then back. He watched her with keenly observant eyes. She was acutely conscious of the way he held himself, straight and tall. Widening his legs, he crossed his arms. His stance emphasized the force of his thighs and the narrowness of his hips. Drawing her gaze to his face, she blushed miserably when she saw the approval in his eyes. Was her attraction to him so evident? Her heart thumped erratically. God. She wanted to die.

"Why did you ... ah ..." She clenched her clammy palm and squared her shoulders. Her embarrassment quickly turned to annoyance. "Why did you remove that rope? Did you think to shame me in front of all the others?" She marched up to him. "I will not be degraded. Not by you or anyone else."

"It was not my intention to shame you."

Momentarily distracted by the way his eyes blazed down into hers, all she could hear was the rapid thumping of her heart.

"I thought to spare you." His throaty voice was low and soft.

His intense gaze made her nervous and hot. "What? Spare me from what? Whom? I don't need your help." She turned her back on him. He cupped her elbow and abruptly spun her around.

"Then perhaps I was wrong." Angry, his brows knotted. "Perhaps you would like for me to give you to the others." He jerked her to his chest. "But first, you will spread your legs for me." The cold tone of his voice chilled her more than his words.

He took her mouth with a savage intensity that was both punishing and demanding. Her knees buckled as he crushed her closer. When he drew away, he left her lips throbbing. She leaned back, struggling to break away, only to find her movements barred by his strong grip locked around her waist.

"Let me go." Lightheaded, her voice barely a whisper, she continued. "You certainly have the wrong idea."

"Tell me. Surely you cannot be so blind as to not know that a man, any man has the right to lay claim to a captive and can share her with whom he pleases? Had I not let the others think I had bedded you that I alone lay claim to you, right now you might have found yourself wrapped around Little Wolf's shaft. Perhaps you would prefer him to me?"

"No, he repulses me."

A smug look on his face, he pressed her closer and ran his hand slowly up and down her back. "Then I am right when I say that I please you."

She glanced away. He hadn't raped her. Hadn't forced himself on her at all. He could have had his way with her anytime over the past few days and even at the cave. All along his intention had been to save her virginity? Hell, Robert had already stolen that as well as her heart.

With gentle fingers he turned her face back. "Answer me," he demanded, his voice low.

His warm fingers against her cheek fueled her racing heart. Her throat pulsed rapidly. "How do I know you didn't have an alternative notion in mind when you cut that rope?" She never should have brought the subject up.

"You don't." A slow, sly grin touched his lips. "You haven't answered me. Do I please you?"

Gabrielle hesitated, feeling trapped. "Thank you for coming to my rescue before with Little Wolf...." Feeling like they had reached a crossroads—a truce, maybe. "I don't find you repulsive," she mumbled under her breath.

It was the first time she heard him laugh.

Two Moons reached out and ran his finger against her cheek. She inhaled sharply at the contact. So she desired him. "It brings me much happiness that you find me good to look upon. You ..." He took her face in his hand and held it gently. "Are also very pleasing to the eye."

The desire to feel her lips pressed against his made his throat dry. *Do not go down this path*, a voice called out in his mind.

Ignoring the words whispering in his head, he slowly slid his hand to her neck. His fingers caught a lock of her hair and he twirled it against her cheek. He touched her lips. The tresses fell from his grip as he ran his finger gently back and forth against her warm mouth. His lips throbbed with wanting. *Stop. The spirits will be angered. A vow, a promise will be broken.*

She leaned closer. Blood rushed through him like an awakened river. *She is willing. I break no vow.*

The desire he saw shining in her eyes broke his resolve. Claiming her lips, he crushed them to his. Their tongues blended, twirled and darted, back and forth, around and around. He drank in her sweetness, savoring every movement. Every erotic plunge, darting in and out of her mouth sent a fire of desire to his throbbing limbs. Any thoughts of guilt faded into the back of his mind.

Breaking his hold, his arms encircled her. With one hand in the small of her back, he lifted her in the cradle of his arms. His gait, hurried, anxious, he carried her to his pallet and laid her gently on the fur. Before his heart could take a second beat, he lay beside her. *Think on this what you are about to do,* the voice whispered again.

He searched her eyes and saw the tenderness, the passion brimming forth. She wanted him and he her. He unlaced her dress and pushed aside the leather revealing her breasts. Fondling one sphere, he watched the golden nipple grow taut. Quickly his hand slid to the other breast and he swirled his finger around her dark orb. Again, her body responded to his touch. He leaned forward and let his tongue follow the same path left by his finger. Skillfully caressing her swollen nipple, he heard her moan; then he swallowed her taut nub in his mouth and sucked.

Pressed against her, she squirmed beneath him. Slowly he reached to the bottom of her dress and drew up the cloth. His hand touched her bare thigh. A sense of urgency drove him to straddle her. *No gold rope. She wears no four-sided piece of gold. She is not of your vision.* A sense of uncontrollable wanting made him push all thoughts of denial from his mind. He stared down into the depths of her blue eyes. *Look at her. Take a good look. She is not of your people. The gods will curse you.* The silent words beat against his brain, shouting, echoing. *A wrong will be done. Be strong. Fight.*

Angered by the guilt quickly speeding through his mind, he rolled off her and stood.

She stared at him, surprised. And he knew as he threw open the flap of his lodge that she would be hurt. He knew he should tell her it was not her fault.

Without glancing back, he hesitated. Pride knotted the words in his throat. He stepped outside. The flap fell shut.

This was not a path that he should walk.

NINE

G abrielle stared at the closed flap of the tepee where moments ago Two Moons had left in a rush. One minute they were fighting and then the next ...

She sat up and yanked down her dress. Damn him! He had done it again. He'd knocked down her defenses until she couldn't think of anything but feeling him inside her, and then he just walked off in the middle. Without an explanation yet!

She jerked to her feet and paced back and forth, her footsteps grooving a path in the tepee's dirt floor. She was the bigger moron. God, did she ever learn? You'd think that being dumped once in a lifetime would have taught her that men were fickle, afraid of commitment, afraid to stick around. What did he think would have happened if they'd made love? Marriage? Fat chance. She'd almost made that mistake once. She certainly didn't love Two Moons. Desire ... perhaps.

"Damn you!"

She strode to the opening and threw open the flap. What could she have possibly been thinking? She stared outside—

She hadn't been thinking; that was the problem. She had let herself fall victim to a man's whims. Let herself fall for a pair of strong arms, and eyes so chocolaty dark that she felt as though she could lose herself in their deep depths.

She sighed. Fool that she was, she missed making love. It had been such a long time since anyone had touched her like he had. Not since Robert had, she felt so wonderfully out of control. *And I paid for that dearly enough.*

A sharp pain attacked her abdomen. She dropped her hand to her belly as another cramp attacked. Great. Could things get any worse? Blood trickled down her leg.

Gabrielle ran to her pallet of fur and pulled from beneath, the white blouse she had worn her first day in the village. Quickly, she ripped the fabric into strips and tied a few pieces around her body. God, what she wouldn't give for a bathroom and a box of tampons. She straightened her dress and stepped outside.

The aroma of stew wafted toward her. Food! McDonalds would be heaven-sent at this moment. God knew what she was eating—birds, squirrels, even prairie dogs. Eating an animal, after she'd been forced to clean it, was enough to make her want to become a vegetarian. Irritation thinned her lips.

Ah, hell. She'd have to confront Two Moons eventually.

She sat next to a woman who was busy pulverizing some boiled meat. Staring at the crude rawhide bowl where the meat, mixed with bits of fat and dried berries were being ground with a granite meat pounder, Gabrielle couldn't help but be amazed. Hundreds of years from now, some archeologist was going to find those artifacts and wonder who had used them and for what purpose. And here she sat, seeing it first-hand.

Gabrielle glanced to Two Moons who sat beside a tepee painted with black and blue geometric shapes. Curly, her little hero, sat on his lap. The boy looked so small against the wide expanse of Two Moons' bare chest. His arms looked so strong wrapped around Curly, and his bronzed skin slicked with grease, shone smooth beneath the sunlight. She couldn't help but remember how it felt to be pressed up against that broad chest, or how his musky male scent had sent her senses reeling. They were studying an arrow, Two Moons running his fingers along its shaft and Curly nodding with understanding at something he was saying.

Two Moons turned slightly. The sun illuminated the scars on his back and she wondered, as she had so often lying next to him at night, how he'd come to get those crisscrossed marks. Even from this distance, they were noticeable. Somehow, she couldn't imagine him doing anything wrong enough to warrant that kind of punishment.

Curly dropped the arrow. As Two Moons bent over to retrieve it, the medicine pouch he wore around his neck swung forward. She wondered what was inside that little bag. What magic items did he wear to ward off evil spirits and protect him from his enemies? Those were the things that made the man; things that were dear to his heart. Would there be a precious stone or the claw of a grizzly inside?

He glanced at her. The raw sexual magnetism that seemed to emanate from his body, made her heart jolt. His bold stare, so intense, so purely provocative, sent her mind spinning.

"You keep your thoughts from my man," a hard voice from above her ordered.

Gabrielle looked up. Standing overhead was a statuesque woman, with a wide girth to her shoulders and with arms that could probably lift a fifty-pound weight without flinching.

"You can have him," Gabrielle lifted her chin, meeting the woman's icy gaze.

She could feel the scrutinizing stares of all those around her, waiting and watching.

"You speak with the same forked-tongue as your true people. I see the way your eyes search his."

"I don't know what you're talking about. Why don't you go kill a rabbit or something? I've got work to do." Gabrielle grabbed a stone gavel and began mashing berries in a bowl on her lap. Maybe if she ignored her, Miss Jack Lalaine would leave.

"He is mine, you blue-eyed dog."

"That's it!" Gabrielle jumped up. The dish fell to the ground with a thud. "I'm sick and tired of everyone pushing me around." Her fingers poking imaginary holes through the woman's collarbone, she continued. "You'd better watch who you're calling a dog."

The woman drew in a heavy breath. With a sudden thrust, her hand came up, reaching for Gabrielle's hair.

"Kills Pretty!" Chahanpi's voice rang out before Kills Pretty touched Gabrielle's head. Gabrielle ducked, then spun sideways facing Chahanpi who was walking toward them.

"It is my wish that no harm come to her. If you want me as an enemy, then disregard my words." Chahanpi's words, though softly spoken, had a steel edge to them.

Kills Pretty dropped her hand. Her mouth thinning with frustration, she hesitated a moment. Icy contempt flashed in her eyes; then without a word, she knocked Gabrielle in the shoulder as she pushed between them.

"Don't mind Kills Pretty Enemy. She is jealous."

Kills Pretty Enemy. That was an appropriate name for a bully Gabrielle thought as she watched her walk away. "Of what?" What did Chahanpi hold over her head, to make the woman shake in her shoes?

"She wishes to become Two Moons', *mitawicu*, his wife." Chahanpi stepped before her. "But, it is you who shares his tepee."

Now Gabrielle understood the depth behind the woman's hate.

She noticed a young woman with doe eyes staring at her with a mixture of anxiety and concern on her round face.

"Who's that young woman over there?"

"Where?" Chahanpi turned. Her gaze followed Gabrielle's pointed finger. "Her name is Gentle Fawn. She is Two Moons' sister and the mother of Curly."

"Curly?" Her little hero? Chahanpi's words came back to her. *He is of Two Moons' family.* Now it all made sense. "Then I must go tell her what a fine boy she has."

"Not now. Sit. Let us talk about Gentle Fawn." Chahanpi gestured to the ground.

Gabrielle sat.

Chahanpi settled beside her. "Gentle Fawn does not live in the same world as you or I. During the long snows many soldiers walked our lands. They came to us, smoked the *chanunpa*, told us they wanted peace. When they returned to their camps, they forced many of my sisters to go with them." Chahanpi paused. Her gaze on Two Moons' sister, she watched as Gentle Fawn entered her tepee, then she continued. "Gentle Fawn was one of the women. They told her she had the greatest honor. She was to bed down with the soldier-chief."

A flash of grief ripped through Gabrielle. Rape. It had happened so frequently between both the Indians and the whites, neither side caring if their lusting needs destroyed those "chosen" multitudes.

"Gentle Fawn stayed with the soldier-chief for many nights. Then the soldier-chief's wife came to his camp. Now Gentle Fawn could not stay. She was an embarrassment to the soldier-chief. He sent her away, used and broken."

A heaviness settled in Gabrielle's chest. In a small way she could sympathize with her. She, too, had known the fear, the threatening terror of rape. With a shiver of recollection she recalled being in the cave with Two Moons and then in Little Wolf's tepee. Two Moons would never have raped her, she knew that now, but what about Little Wolf?

"Gentle Fawn is a proud woman," Chahanpi continued. "For many moons she kept her silence as the soldier-chief's child grew within her. Then on the day of Curly's birth, through her screams, her mind left us to find peace in her own world. Two Moons, he always worries about his younger sister. He is a good man."

Gabrielle shot Two Moons a glance. He studied her intently with what appeared to be concern. She wondered for a moment, what he would have done if there had been a fight. She had no doubt that he would have eventually stopped them, but whose side would he have taken? Did he have feelings for Kills Pretty? Were they lovers?

She glanced away, annoyed. A swift stab of jealousy twisted her heart. He had asked her if she was crazy. Maybe she was. She was sitting here wondering if he was attracted to her.

"Thanks for coming to my rescue, again," Gabrielle said.

"You are my friend. I would do no less."

Friend. What a novel idea. When was the last time she had one of those? "What month is this?"

There was a faint glint of surprise in Chahanpi's eyes as she studied her thoughtfully.

Great. If she didn't think I was crazy before, that ought to do it. Gabrielle bit the inside of her lip. How could she explain how she had no knowledge of her whereabouts, or the day, the month, or for that matter why she couldn't tell a poisonous berry from a good one. Hell, no wonder they all thought she was crazy.

"It is the moon of the ripening berries," Chahanpi answered, her voice low, soft.

Gabrielle tried to recall what she had read about the Native American calendar. If she remembered correctly that would mean it was June.

The sound of Rattling Blanket's laughter rose above the women's voices.

Gabrielle frowned. "That woman works me like a slave."

"You belong to Rattling Blanket," replied Chahanpi.

"I belong to no one."

"You were a gift to Two Moons' mother. It is her right to do with you as she wishes. It is our way."

"Well, sometimes I don't agree with your ways," Gabrielle snapped in annoyance. "If anyone was treated the way I'm treated, the civil rights activists would slap a law suit on that woman so fast, her head would spin," she mumbled under her breath.

"What?"

"Oh, never mind. You forgot a bead." Gabrielle pointed to a blank spot on the garment Chahanpi held in her lap.

"No. That was my intention. Only *Tunkashila* is perfect. It reminds me to be humble. Only he can create something perfect, the rest of us make mistakes."

Chahanpi's words, like the entire attitude of the people in the village, whose every day's actions exuded spirituality and a respect for their creator, was one of the things that truly awed her. Living with these people was like living in a monastery without walls.

She believed in God, but never went to church. As a child, she'd been taught to say her prayers. But growing up in a household where love and respect were almost nonexistent, she had come to wonder if God perhaps had ceased to listen. And the death of her younger brother had put an end to her talks with the Almighty.

Not happy with the way her thoughts were going, Gabrielle abruptly changed the subject. "Anyway, now the entire village has other things to talk about, right?" She was sure the little scene between Kills Pretty and her was the hot topic of discussion.

"Talking about people reminds us of the right and proper way of life. How else, if not by other's mistakes, are we to learn? Is it not the same way where you come from? Two Moons, believes you lived at the fort."

Gabrielle shrugged. "We call it gossip." She couldn't explain where she had come from. Perhaps it would be better if Chahanpi and everyone else believed she had come from the fort. What could it hurt?

"Then it is true. You lived among the whites. Do not make that known. Others will not be as understanding as I, with good reason."

"Why?"

"It is one thing to be Crow, another to live among the ones with the pale faces. The Crow scouts at the fort send the soldiers to fight against my people. You cannot change the white blood that runs through you, but there are those who do not understand why the *Upsaroka*, Crow help the white soldiers. Even as we speak the Long Knives search for us, look to bring us back to live on their reservations."

"I'm sorry."

"It is not within your power to change the journey my people must follow."

Oh, but it was, Gabrielle thought. She was the only one who could do something. She knew how it all played out. There had to be something she could do.

Two Moons could not stop the way his heart raced or its irregular pounding against his ribs as his gaze beheld Blue Eyes' loveliness. The darkness of her hair like a raven's wing, shone under the sun. Her skin of golden honey was clear and flawless. If it were not for the color of her eyes, she would right now be sharing his blanket. He knew his thoughts were twisted. Hatred for the whites burned in his gut like a raging fire, yes. But at moments like this, when his loins ached and his heart raced, when that damned little voice from the corner of his mind spoke to him, he cursed the vow he made long ago. Only his spirit woman would share his life.

At the sound of Curly's voice, Two Moons focused back to the little boy who sat in his lap. "Have you listened to my words?" he asked.

Curly looked at him with eyes that showed intelligence and spirit. "Yes, and I will be a brave warrior like you."

A knot of guilt tightened Two Moons' chest. How could the child think such worthy thoughts of praise when in the past he had shown him little, if no, attention? Even this day, it had been an effort to take him upon his knee, to push aside his hatred for that part of the boy, which reminded him of his white enemy.

Black Hawk's words ran through his head. *One must learn to see past his blindness to become an earth man.* Curly was his blindness. He did this for his sister. She needed the boy—needed someone to bring her spirit back to the living.

"Rattling Blanket ..." Blue Eyes' voice brought his attention back to the women. "I belong to no one."

What trouble was Blue Eyes causing now?

He lifted Curly from his lap, placing the boy on his feet. "Go then and practice what I have taught you." He gave the boy a gentle pat on his backside and Curly ran off with the arrow in his hand. The child smiled with open gratefulness before he disappeared into the bushes; a smile that should have brought gladness to his heart but only served to further his guilt.

Out of the corner of his eye, Two Moons saw his mother walking toward Blue Eyes. With haste, he stood and started toward them. The tension between the two was strong enough without Blue Eyes' barbed words.

"Rattling Blanket wishes you to follow, there are many buffalo hides that need to be cleaned," he said when he reached her side.

She stared at him. What was going on in that pretty head of hers? Would she refuse his mother as she had refused him? He knew not what the word *harem* meant; nor did he like the tone of her voice when she said it earlier.

He grabbed her arm and spun her around. "Come. I will show you what needs to be done." Before she had a chance to argue, he dragged her after him.

He stopped when they reached the area where a buffalo hide had been laid out across the ground and stretched taut between wooden stakes.

"Here." He released her and thrust her forward toward the circle. "This one has been dried under the sun and is ready to be worked." He picked up a short, hoe-like tool and held it to her. "You will use this. It is called *wahintke*."

She looked at the tool then glanced down at the hide. An unsettling frown tipped her lips.

"I will show you."

Dragging the tool back and forth across the hide, he was well aware of the stares he received from his friends who stood a short distance away, observing him. He couldn't hear their whispers but knew when he heard laughter, he was the brunt of their jokes.

"You must scrape the skin to an even thickness, like this," he said trying to ignore them.

"But—"

He handed her the tool. "When you have finished, we will turn it over and remove the hair."

"We need to—"

"I do not wish to talk. You will work. I will stay and watch." He sat beside her and pulled his knife from its sheath. He picked up a branch and began whittling. Glancing over to his friends, he noticed they still watched him closely. Before the sun set he would be hearing their heckling remarks.

"It must have been a beautiful beast," Blue Eyes said softly.

Two Moons stopped carving and looked at her. She stood beside him, scraping the hide as he showed her. She learned quickly. This pleased him. "He was a worthy adversary."

"There are so few left; it's a shame."

"It is not my people who kill them all," he spat, jumping to his feet, "but the Long Knives and white hunters who kill for sheer pleasure. It is like a game to them. The white men come to our land like the rains without end. Like a mighty flood they will wash away all that is good and precious to us, including the buffalo."

"They'll come back. You may not believe me, but one day your children will see the buffalo again. The government will protect them." Her silky voice was low and filled with compassion.

"More white man's promises I will never see. How do you know this?"

"I just do. Eventually, we all learn by our mistakes. Even the white man."

Was it possible for the *wasicun* to change their ways? Were her words that of the spirit world? Could it be that the great *Wakan Tanka* had sent her to him so he could help his people understand?

He reached into an open parfleche hanging on a pole and handed her a mixture of brains, liver and fat. "Rub this into the skin to soften it."

At the sight of it, she paled and covered her mouth with her hand.

He frowned. If she were of the spirit world, would the mere sight of the buffalo's fat make her sick?

She reached for the parfleche.

"It is late." He pulled the drawstring tight and placed the pouch on the ground. "You have done enough for now." He glanced at her, hearing the words Shadow Elk had said: *It will take time. She will come to know our ways.* He hoped his friend was right and she learned quickly before the others sent him to live with the *winktes*, those men who dressed like women and did women's work.

Two Moons drew in a heavy breath. Perhaps he would teach her.

Gabrielle, in a much needed moment of solitude, stared across the hazy, violet dusk-lit plains where hundreds of horses grazed on blades of yellowing grass. Her languid mind drifted, like the wispy white clouds, as she gazed over the rise of the bluffs, where camp lookouts patrolled the perimeter of camp.

Even here, away from the center of the village, there was no escaping the constant pounding of the rhythmic drums, the stomping of moccasin-clad feet in ceremonies without end. Yet, even with the hoards of people, with all the commotion everywhere around her, she felt lonely, a disturbing feeling she hadn't had in a very long time.

A tug at her skirt brought her attention to her side. Curly looked up at her, smiling.

"Hello." She bent down. "Let's see …" She brought her finger to her chin in contemplation. What was the word for hello? "*Hau.*" She smiled, pleased she could recall it.

"*Hau. Nituwe he?*"

"Nit-tu-we he?" She had no idea what that meant. She touched the tip of his nose and returned his smile. "You're my little hero, did you know that? I never did thank you."

"He asks who you are. Your name." Rattling Blanket walked up beside her.

Startled by her knowledge of English, Gabrielle gave her a sidelong glance of utter disbelief. How many others in camp understood but chose to ignore her? "My name is Gabrielle," she said to Curly, before she straightened. "Would you tell him …"

Before she had a chance to finish, Rattling Blanket, in Lakota, issued what sounded like a command and pointed to a group of cottonwood trees. Curly seemed pleased by her words. A beaming smile lit his face before he scurried away.

"I was only going to thank him for taking his pet wolf away. Why do you dislike me so?" Seeing that Rattling Blanket was about to leave without a word, Gabrielle hastily continued. "It's more than just because I'm Crow, isn't it?"

Rattling Blanket's mouth pulled into a sour grin. "Your presence in my son's lodge is not good."

"I didn't ask to be brought there. In fact, I had no say in the matter at all," Gabrielle retorted.

"My son only sees what is your face, not the dangers that lie in your heart."

"I bring him no danger." She could help him. She knew what the future held.

"Kills Pretty Enemy can give him many fine sons of our own blood. She can see his lodge is strong; his wishes are fulfilled. What can you offer?"

"Well, I can ..." What was she thinking? She didn't want to give him anything. "I know that ..." Nothing. She knew nothing she could tell Rattling Blanket without sounding like a fool. Gabrielle shrugged. "It doesn't seem as if I have a choice in the matter. Your son, for whatever reason, wishes my company."

Rattling Blanket shot her a look of disgust. "You do not even know the difference between a poisonous root and one that is food. It is like I said: You will bring him trouble." She snorted, turned and in Lakota ordered her to follow.

They entered the tepee. The essence of cedar wafted through the air from a fire built in the center of the lodge. Gabrielle stepped to the left only to find Two Moons' hand on her arm stopping her. Displeasure hovered in his eyes as he waited for her to move. She knew what he was thinking, that she should know by now that when you enter a tepee, you should step to the right then walk counterclockwise toward the setting sun to find your place.

She clenched her hands at her side and watched him walk to his honored seat and settle onto a mat of loosely woven tulle.

This blatantly macho, male-dominated era was beginning to get on her nerves. He watched her walk over to the fire. She could feel his gaze upon her back as she picked up a ladle and dropped the boiled meat into his polished horn cup. If it weren't for the fact that his mother sat nearby, she had the good mind to feed herself first. She strolled over and handed him his meal.

After serving Rattling Blanket, Gabrielle sat along the perimeter of the tepee where all his belongings were kept. She tried to force down her dinner, but the buffalo stew and thick fry bread formed a lump in her throat.

"Here." Two Moons' words startled her; she hadn't noticed him rise. "This will help it go down easier." He handed her a cup of honey. "Some say it to be poisonous, but I can assure you I have eaten enough of it to tell you it is not."

She took the cup, poured the heavy golden liquid over her meat and nodded her thanks. Out of the corner of her eye she noticed Rattling Blanket's disapproving glare. "Your mother doesn't approve of your kindness."

"My mother knows it is not a man's place to serve a woman."

"Then why do you?"

"You will do me no good if you do not eat."

"Right, just stick the feed bag on the horse's face and regardless of whether he's hungry, he'll give you a good day's work. Is that it?"

"You talk in circles. Eat." Two Moons strode back to his spot and sat.

Maybe she was just tired. After all, he was only trying to be nice to her. She took a nibble of meat. It tasted somewhat better laced with honey. She swallowed.

A vision of the hide she'd scraped and the mush of brains he had wanted her to rub into the skin, entered her mind and the meat tasted sour in her mouth. It had hurt his male pride explaining and lifting the buffalo skin for her. The fact that his friends stood around with teasing stares and snickers made his act of kindness that much more considerate. She suspected he wasn't going to live it down.

Gabrielle glanced over to Two Moons. He watched her. She could see the concern in his eyes. He nodded, pleased she had tasted the stew. He brought his fingers to his lips indicating that she should continue to eat. She dropped her gaze, took another bite of dinner and wanted to gag.

Hearing his laughter, she looked up. The smile on his face was enough to knock her socks off—if she'd been wearing any. She wished he would do so more often. He was less intimidating when he smiled. A flicker of jealousy shot through her, when he touched his mother's hand with tenderness. She could see that he loved her—that she adored him. How lucky they were.

If only ...

Gabrielle set her dish down beside her. What was the use? Her mother was light-years away.

TEN

*T*hey came upon a small wood-shingled house nestled in the woods. Roy followed as the old man led him inside. In the darkness that embraced him, the only light, other than from the flashlight, came from a single log burning in a fireplace. The essence of cedar wafted through the air. A thin wisp of smoke rose from an incense burner on the mantle.

The old man moved about with ease, leaving him to stand alone near the doorway. Then, to Roy's surprise, instead of flipping on a switch, he struck a match. Within seconds the light from a kerosene lamp brightened the area.

"No electricity." He blew out the match.

Roy stared at him, astonished. "No? Well, I guess it beats paying the electric companies."

"No." The old man answered. "The power line's dead. So with your accident, you must have pulled down the wires."

"Oh. Right." How stupid. Just because the old man reminded him of a fictional character from some old time movie, didn't mean that he lived in a bygone era.

"Sit," his host suggested, pointing to a battered, old leather sofa. "I will get you some good medicine for that headache."

"No, really. Thanks. I already had an aspirin. Can I use your phone?" Roy glanced around the dimly lit room.

He doubted the old man heard him as he ambled out of the room in silence. Either that, or he chose not to reply. Odd fellow. Seemed to look at him as if he wasn't there. Gave him the creeps.

Roy glanced around. A freestanding fireplace was set in the middle of the room. Open and screened in on both sides, he could see straight through to the other side of the room where a lone chair sat facing him. Odd. Except for that chair, all the furniture was arranged along the walls.

Various Native American artifacts, a buffalo horned headdress, a tomahawk and a few odd-shaped instruments he had no knowledge of, lay scattered about.

Roy carefully made his way over to the sofa, sat down and placed his camera on the table before him. A sharp jab of pain stitched his side. He drew in a quick breath and stretched out his arm to relieve the cramp.

A cool smoothness accosted his fingertips. He glanced to his side. His heart jolted. Hidden in the shadows a huge black ceramic bird stared back at him. Yellow eyes blazed at him through the darkness. The bird's extended wings and opened beak instantaneously brought him back moments before his crash. The hair on his arm prickled. He snatched his hand away. Was it just his imagination, or was that bird haunting him? Damn thing made his skin crawl.

Sitting alone in the dark room with the light from a single lamp casting distorted shadows on the walls, definitely played havoc on his nerves. He sensed a presence beside him. He snapped his head to the left.

Only the darkness filled his vision.

"Good God," he muttered. What the hell was wrong with him? Perhaps his accident had left him a little more shaken than he thought. Suddenly agitated, Roy stood. His feet sank into the thickness of a bear rug. Picking up the lamp, he walked to the other side of the room. Abstract-styled paintings of varying sizes hung on the wall. He raised the lamp to take a better look.

"So. You like my work?"

Startled by the voice beside him, the lamp jostled in his hand. The old man's footsteps had been so silent.

Roy leaned closer, examining the brush strokes. "Interesting." He placed the lamp on the table.

"All that is life revolves like the earth. So it is with my paintings." Handing him a cup of what resembled tea, he continued. "This one here is particularly interesting." His host pointed to a long rectangular portrait. Assorted geometric symbols filled the canvas. "A battle scene," he explained. "Your father being a military man could relate to this one."

Roy's jaw clenched. Even up here, isolated in the middle of the mountains he couldn't escape his father.

"So. The white represents the color of snow. These two long green lines indicate the flight of arrows. The points at the end are the wounds made by the arrows."

If you asked him, they resembled double-sided pitchforks. A sharp jolt pierced his heart. A muscle spasm. Roy arched his shoulders back. "And this?" He pointed to a large, green, diamond-shaped figure then brought the cup to his lips. The strong, sweet smell of whiskey filled his nostrils. His hands shook as he pushed the cup away and placed it on the table beside him. "What did you put in there?"

His host studied him with curiosity. "The water from the walnut tree, honey for sweetness and bourbon. It is good medicine for your head."

"Thanks. I think I'll pass. You know what they say, firewater's bad medicine." Firewater? That was a first. He'd called his drink of choice many things over the years, but firewater?

"You like honey, correct?"

Roy stared. "Yes, how'd you know?"

"Good guess." Not explaining further, his host pointed to the painting. "That is the body of a man. So, the dark blue color means the man is dead. The small white rectangle enclosing that red spot near his heart, is the wound that brought him down. And this ..." He reached to the top of the painting, to another lighter blue diamond. "So, this means he will live again in the new world."

Abruptly, his host turned and started walking away. "So come. Let me show you this one."

"A phone. I didn't see a phone I could use," Roy quickly followed after him. "I've got to—"

He stopped short and grabbed a hold of the table beside him for support. It was probably just the dimness of the room and slight pounding in his head that caused the room to blur, but he suddenly felt a little too warm.

He glanced up. The old man stood facing the opposite wall, waiting. "This one here shows what you whites call the Sun Dance."

Slowly making his way past the battle picture, Roy stopped and stared at the various painted shapes that seemed to resemble bronzed men. Bent at different angles as if in the midst of dancing, they formed a circle around a center pole, painted in bright red. The sun sat low on the horizon. A sphere of yellow and burnt oranges, it cast a golden hue to the ground. In the distance the muted shape of a black hawk floated down among the hills. That damned bird again, Roy thought. "It's beautiful."

He needed to sit down. Once again, a light-headedness overcame him. His chest hurt. And where was the phone? His gaze darted around the room. He needed to call for a tow truck.

"So. Let me explain about this ritual. Here. Sit." His host pointed to a carved caned rocker.

Thankful just to get off his feet before he dropped, Roy tried to concentrate on his host's words.

"When a Sioux warrior finds himself in a life threatening situation, he might offer a prayer to his father, the Sun, to save him from death. Not that he feared death mind you, but for the sake of those who love him. So, it is that vow, that gift of life we celebrate."

His host took out a pipe and lit it. "We make lots of preparations. Everything must be prepared just so. Spiritual foods and waters brought, everything facing the west. The tree is cut and carried. It is erected and decorated with carved figures, representing the man who is fulfilling his vow and giving thanks publicly."

A puff of smoke rose to the ceiling. "So when all is ready—when the steady throbs of drums pounded in song, I looked to the sun. I blew my whistle." He paused and reached into his pocket.

As Roy stared down at the crude bone whistle handed to him and listened to the old man's staid calming voice, he felt oddly lured into the image of that celebration. He could almost hear the sharp, high-pitched cry of the whistle....

Shrill, high-pitched screeches pierced the air. Dancers pounded their feet to the ground, keeping rhythm with the rawhide drums.

Two Moons stood ready. Soon it would be his time to honor the spirits. To thank them for the visions they had sent him. To give back what they had given him; his life in times of battle, his family and all that was good and decent around him.

"You have waited many moons for this day to come, hey my brother?" Shadow Elk placed a hand on Two Moons' shoulder.

He nodded. "It is a good day to celebrate." He had participated in many dances to the sun, but never before with the knowledge that he finally had his own vision. Many a buffalo skull had been planted in the river as a sign that the great father had granted him no vision. Today would be different.

"Little Wolf will be jealous that our people will come to you for advice on matters of great importance."

"That is of his own doing. He chose to pay for someone else's vision. There is no shame to that."

Shadow Elk dropped his hand. "Honored one," he jested, "what words of wisdom do you offer?"

Two Moons grinned. "I will be the one to seek your advice. Black Hawk tells me I have much to learn."

In the distance a group of women sat observing the ceremony. Two Moons noticed Blue Eyes among them. His body craved her. Even now, when his only thoughts should be on his task ahead, she tormented him from afar. He knew *Tunkashila*, the great father, would be angered. Still, the sight of her made him grow rigid.

He clenched his hand at his side. He should just take her and get it over with. Perhaps then, when he had his fill of her, would he find the contentment he yearned for. That was how it should be.

"You are restless my friend. Perhaps you have been without a woman for too long." Shadow Elk's brow rose. "Any man would be tempted by her beauty. Your will is stronger than mine, my friend." Shadow Elk grinned. "I always wondered when that strength would give out."

Two Moons grunted. For days now, as was their custom before a ceremony such as this, he had been separated from Blue Eyes. He had slept, eaten and sweated with his brothers. And as much as he looked forward to the celebration and all the preparations that went on before it, his thoughts had been with her from the moment the sun was high in the sky till it had set at night. Throughout the days his anxiety about her well-being grew as much as his longing to see her again. He had wondered if she were safe or causing trouble. Did his mother keep an eye on her as he had asked? And what of Little Wolf? Would he find the two of them together again?

Shadow Elk's expression stilled and grew serious. "We have ridden together into many battles; have watched each other's backs; been to many an enemy's camp and have stolen many horses. Hey, my brother?"

"That we have."

"The one with the blue eyes steals what I cannot steal back."

Two Moons' brows drew together. "I do not understand your words."

"She steals your heart. Let her steal it."

"That is not so."

"It is true. Even now, though your words are spoken to me, your eyes seek hers. I see what you are too blind and too stubborn to see. Do not fight what is meant to be. She is a good woman. She will be the half that will make you whole. Besides ..." Shadow Elk rapped his arm. "She is better looking than me."

Two Moons grinned. "At last we agree."

Dragging his gaze from the woman whose body he desired above all else he watched his sister walking toward him.

"She is pretty. Her song fills your heart. I can hear it," Gentle Fawn said softly.

"I know not of whom you speak."

"I think that my big brother knows too well, if he would only listen to the music. Listen. Can you not hear it? Look. She is singing to you. Look—"

He turned to find Blue Eyes watching him.

Was there a song in her heart for him? *Look at me.* His silent words floated through the air. Their eyes met. Boldly his gaze clung to hers, searching for an answer. Eyes, as blue as the summer sky, widened. The heaviness in his heart lifted. So his sister was right. This warrior was desired. And so it should be. His mouth twisted wryly. He arched his shoulders back, jutting out his chest with confidence. She had said she found him good to look upon. Perhaps soon she would come to him and then …

"Do you see the man with the sun in his hair?" Gentle Fawn grabbed Two Moons' arm. "Do you see him? He is coming."

He glanced around. "Yellow Hair is far away. Do not worry little one," he assured her.

"It is not of Yellow Hair that I speak."

"If not of the white man's general, than of whom does she speak?" questioned Shadow Elk.

Two Moons frowned. Did his sister really see the man who had visited him in his visions, the man who wore a black box around his neck? Or despite her words, did she confuse him with Yellow Hair?

"Perhaps your sister sees more than she wishes us to know," Shadow Elk whispered.

"Enough. I have already had an earful." Two Moons grinned. He hid his fisted hand at his side. "Go find our mother and see what words of wisdom you can offer her," he joked. He gently placed his hand on her arm. "Go find your son—"

He felt her stance tightened. "Curly is a fine boy," he quickly added, before she had a chance to run from his words. "He is like his mother, independent and courageous for one so small."

Reflected in his sister's eyes he saw her horror, knew she thought of the day she had conceived him. A heavy feeling of sadness settled in his chest. He gave Gentle Fawn a soft nudge and watched her hurry to Rattling Blanket's side.

"I see the scars are not fully healed." Shadow Elk spoke to Two Moons' back. "Will you not let me take your place today? For you, my brother, I would gladly drag a hundred buffalo skulls across the furthest prairie."

"That I know you would, my friend. However, this is something I must do. I do not fear the pain."

"Of that I am sure. There is no one here who would think otherwise. But I say again, the scars left by the white man's whip still shine red upon your skin and I would gladly take your place."

"No."

Shadow Elk nodded and placed his hand on Two Moons' shoulder. "Come my friend. The drums are singing to a faster song. We must go."

Strutting past Blue Eyes and Chahanpi, Two Moons kept his eyes before him. If he looked at her now, his mind would not stay straight on its course ahead. There would be time enough after the ceremonies to think about her.

He stopped before his elders. Their fingers touched his face, striping him with the sacred red color. They painted his chest, his shoulders, his arms. They placed the cedar wreath atop his head, then handed him a whistle.

A strange sensation shot through his hand. It was almost as if another's hand, beside his own, held the bone whistle. Perhaps *Tunkashila* was guiding him through his task ahead. That was good a sign.

Two Moons turned and started toward the buffalo skulls. At his side, Shadow Elk held the leather thongs in his hands. At the base of the tall ceremonial pole, tethered with colorful strips of cloth, they stopped. Two Moons turned toward his friend. He was ready. He was not afraid of the pain. The tip of his friend's knife pressed into the swell of his shoulders; its sharp bite cut his skin. Blood began to trickle—

"No wait." Kills Pretty hurried over and stopped before him. "You must stop or the spirits will be angry."

Enraged by her interruption, Two Moons' eyes narrowed. Everyone stared at him. He could hear the whispers rising around him. He clenched his teeth to control his anger. The muscle in his jaw twitched.

Before he could address her, Kills Pretty reached inside her bag and pulled out a white cloth stained with blood. "Look, look at what your precious slave does to you. Did you know it was her moontime? She bled while in your lodge? She has defiled you and everything you own." With a smug look of victory on her face, she held the rag out to him. "See the proof of my words. Here is the white man's cloth she wore when you brought her to our village."

He stiffened. His gaze riveted on the fabric. Kills Pretty was right. The cloth belonged to Blue Eyes. He jerked his gaze away. Blue Eyes had to know women were to stay away from all sacred items during their "bleeds." Even Crow women spent their days in a separate lodge. Did she wish to make his medicine weak? Why? His expression clouded in anger, he glanced over to Blue Eyes, whose gaze was sealed on his. He inhaled deeply and marched over to her.

"Is it true what Kills Pretty has said? Is it true? Do you wish to destroy the powers of my medicine?"

He watched her gaze dart back and forth. It was true.

"I didn't—"

He slapped her face, cutting off her words. Her eyes widened. She drew her hand to her cheek.

A deafening silence enveloped him. Everyone watched. Everyone waited on his words, his next course of action.

"Don't you ever do that again." Her voice although unsteady, held in it a challenge that made his nostrils flare.

"I will do with you as I wish. You belong to me and this warrior is ordering you to walk behind your owner."

"I'll do no such thing!"

"You will follow me, with your eyes to the ground as a proper slave should. Now!" If they stayed before all the others, he feared the anger eating at his gut would take complete control of his actions. Already the stab of guilt he had felt a moment ago when he had hit her was fading as he heard the soft murmuring of those around him.

He swivelled quickly, turning his back on her. He prayed silently that she followed and listened for her footsteps. Hearing nothing, he stopped abruptly and spun on his heels. The look of defiance he saw in her eyes shot at him like a flaming arrow. "You dare disregard my demands?" He reached her before his words had time to penetrate.

"I belong to no one," she spat. "I am not your mother's workhorse and I certainly do not belong to you. If you think I'll follow behind you like some disobedient child, you've got another thing coming."

"You ..." He yanked her off her feet and flung her over his shoulder. "Belong to me."

Everyone followed as he carried her to the river. Her blows to his back, everyone saw. Again she had managed to make him lose face in front of his friends.

A light breeze blew his hair against his face. He spit the strands from his mouth. He was glad his elders did not understand her curses of anger. He knew, however, everything that was happening was being explained to them. Now he could not take part in the ceremonies.

A light breeze blew in from the window drawing Roy's attention back to the man who sat beside him.

Roy handed the whistle back to his host. "Why do you worship the sun?"

"We worship the power behind the sun."

"You mean, what the sun does for the earth," Roy said.

"*Wi*, the sun god, is one of many we give our thanks to; *Hanwi*, the moon, *Maka*, the Earth, our mother, are some of the others. So in what you whites call the Sun Dance, we give back one drop of blood and pain to the mother who did for us."

Maybe it was the accident. Maybe he was getting sick. But it was hard to follow what the old man was saying. Roy ran his finger under his eyes and along his temple, trying to concentrate.

"So. Then the sun turned black and in its center was a hole. A man appeared in that hole. So he spoke to me. He said, '*Tunkashila* heard you. He tells you this land is sacred. Guard it. Protect it. You shall live forever as its keeper.' " He paused for a moment, and took a quick puff on his pipe. "Reflections of your past lives are all around you; they are mirrors in which you can see into and learn."

Roy became instantly awake. "You're talking about reincarnation. Life after death. Is that what you believe? And that hole—a different dimension?"

The old man's brows arched as if expecting him to know the answer. "I told you my story. So now I ask you."

Roy thought a moment. "Nay. Well ..." What about the strange dreams he was having lately? "Nay. I can't say that I do."

"It is late and this old man needs his rest." He rose. "Think deeply about what I have said."

Roy watched as he shuffled out of the room and realized he didn't know his host's name, or where he should sleep for that matter.

"Sleep on the couch, it is comfortable," he answered without turning around. "My name is John Raven Wing."

What? Was the old man a mind reader? Wordlessly Roy stared after him. Had he said Raven Wing? What was it with that bird?

ELEVEN

The cold water seeping through her clothing came as a complete shock. Too startled to do anything but stare at him, Gabrielle sat in the waist-deep river, her words of anger stuck in the back of her throat. Two Moons towered over her, his bronzed chest heaving.

"Your tongue is sharp. Perhaps the coldness of the water will cool it." Not waiting for a response, he spun around.

The crowd parted, allowing him to pass. Then one by one, they followed him.

Gabrielle struggled to her feet and stepped to the river's bank. Water pooled around her, dripping from her clothing, her hair, her soaked moccasins.

"Of all the nerve." God, he infuriated her. "Good riddance." She slammed her hand out in front of her in a gesture of dismissal. Clutched between her fingers, she noticed the small medicine bag Two Moons always wore around his neck. How was it that she now possessed this sacred item? She could recall little of her actions, her embarrassment overshadowing everything that had happened, all but the image of Kills Pretty standing before her holding out that rag and the humiliation she had felt when all eyes were upon her.

And Two Moons ... If he saw her with his pouch ... She must have caught the small bag by accident when she had felt herself slipping from Two Moons' arms.

She tossed her wet hair over her shoulder. Would serve him right he if spent hours searching for the damn thing. Just what was inside anyway? She fingered the small soft leather bag, noticing the two blue and red crescent moons beaded on the front. She bit her lower lip, debating; then cast a glance around, listening for any signs of him. He'd be furious if he knew she had this. Hell, he was furious already. What did she have to lose?

She sat on the river's bank and glanced down at the pouch. Slowly she eased open the drawstring. Her finger brushed against something soft. Her curiosity getting the best of her, she quickly opened the bag and dumped its contents into her lap.

"Huh?" Her mouth dropped.

There nestled among shiny and translucent rocks, what looked like the claw of some kind of bird, a few sage leaves and sweet grass, were the few strands of her hair, which Two Moons had cut off that day in the cave. At least it looked like hers. Why else would it be tied up with a strip of cloth from the red skirt she had worn her first day in the village?

He had her hair! She stared, astonished at the sense of fulfillment she felt. That meant he thought her special. She smiled and fingered the braid. Special enough to carry a part of her by his heart? Several times she had seen desire shine in his eyes, until he blew up over something and left just to cover up his feelings. But maybe there was more to it then just sexual lust. A tiny glow lit, spreading warmth through her chilled body.

A noise like the rustle of branches caught her attention.

Her fingers shook as she quickly placed the contents back into his bag and stood.

"If you wish to gain favor in the eyes of Two Moons, then you must purify that bag you hold." Little Wolf stepped into the clearing.

"What?" she retorted tensely, not sure she had heard correctly.

"Come with me and I will show you what needs to be done." He stood there pointing to the woods behind her.

Gabrielle glanced away. "I'm not going anywhere with you."

"You have caused Two Moons to lose face before his family. You hold in your hand his medicine against those evils that can sneak up upon a man and cut him down when least expected. Do you hate him so much that you wish to see him dead?"

She didn't hate him. How could she? In fact, she couldn't lie to herself any longer. She wasn't sure why, but she was more than just attracted to Two Moons.

Gabrielle shook her head. "No. But you hate him. So why would you care if his medicine is strong? You made your feelings perfectly clear the other day in your lodge. You would have killed him."

"You are wrong." His mouth spread into a thin-lipped smile. "It is like that between Sioux warriors. It is like a game between us."

She stared at the man before her. She didn't trust him; in fact, she loathed him. He was mean looking and dirty. And he was lying.

But Two Moons believed—as all Native Americans did—in the power of his medicine bag and he was mad enough. Maybe when she returned and showed him what she'd done, he'd be in a better mood. Biting her lower lip, she glanced away. Two Moons might forgive her, and if he ever stopped screaming enough to listen, she might get a chance to set things straight between them.

"I don't trust you." Restless, irritable, her gaze bounced from his face to the distance beyond his shoulder, then back at him.

"You have my word that I will not touch you."

"Based on what?"

"My word is good," Little Wolf insisted.

Perhaps her need to please Two Moons overshadowed her reasoning, but somehow she believed him. She sighed. "Tell me what it is that I must do."

Little Wolf grabbed her arm before she could change her mind and turned her back toward the river. They crossed the shallow water. Standing at the edge of the woods, Gabrielle hesitated. Was she making a mistake? It wasn't too late to change her mind.

"I think—"

Little Wolf gave her arm a sharp tug. "Come. We go this way."

Walking in silence through the densely wooded forest, a sense of panic overwhelmed her. She drew in a deep breath and glanced around. A soft breeze rattled the leaves. Slender trees creaked, swaying to and fro. Everything was normal. So why the sudden feeling that something was very wrong? A flock of birds rushed from the trees. She flinched.

Little Wolf glanced around as though he searched for someone.

A horse's whinny broke through the trees. Gabrielle's heart lurched. Little Wolf slammed his hand against her mouth. "Be quiet, or I will kill you." He released her, giving her a shove forward.

The blood drained from her cheeks. Out of nowhere, laced between the trees, a small band of Indians on horseback rode up and stopped before them.

One man, presumably the leader, rode past the others. Walking his horse around her, he completed the circle then stopped before her. "It is good to see you, White Swan. Your father will be happy we have found you."

White Swan? Father? Gabrielle stared up at him, disoriented by his words. His eyes of golden amber showed no anger. His boldly handsome face smiled warmly down at her. His black braided hair bleached by the sun had a rusty hue to it and hung against his lean chest. He wore bangs that stood up straight. Around his shoulders hung a red and white-striped, hooded blanket with the emblem of a thunderbird. Somehow she got the feeling these men were from a different tribe. What would Little Wolf want with them and why? She glanced to Little Wolf.

"There will be time enough later to welcome her back," he remarked, a slight edge of nervousness to his voice. "Give me the white man's whiskey and let me go on my way."

Before she knew what was happening, the stranger's strong arms
lifted her off the ground. Plopped down before him, she struggled
against the arms that held her. "Hey! What the hell—"

"Why do you fight me little one? You are safe with me," her captor
whispered softly in her ear.

Safe? Safer with him or Little Wolf? What a choice. She stared
down at him. Dark squinting eyes examined her with an intense mixture
of lustfulness and anxiety. He fixed his gaze on her face. With a
deliberate slowness he drew his gaze down the length of her. She
reached down and yanked her dress over her thigh.

"She belongs to you now. Take her away." Little Wolf quickly
turned and disappeared into the woods, before she could say another
word.

After what seemed like an eternity of unrelenting travel, Gabrielle
could see over the rise of the hill. A small village of fifteen or so tepees
dotted the landscape. Beyond that, a large fort loomed. Towering
wooden walls pierced the landscape, like some made-up set for a movie.

From up on the watchmen's tower came a cry to open the gates. One
by one the small band of men, with her in the lead, skirted past the
village and paraded through the open doors.

Inside, soldiers in blue uniforms, their glinting swords at their sides,
hurried past her. Women dressed in long billowing skirts of varying
colors, with bonnets on their heads, strolled along the wooden sidewalks.
In the open courtyard, an American flag flew in the warm breeze. Rows
and rows of pillars, standing as erect as the soldiers who marched before
them, supported a low roof of sandy yellow. Beyond, cut every few feet
into the gray flagstone, lead pane windows and doors of sturdy oak lined
the building's front.

Stopping before the massive building, Gabrielle was lifted down off
the horse. She heard the creak of a door opening then slamming shut.
The first thing she noticed when she turned toward the noise was a pair
of polished black boots. Then she noticed the immaculate pressed blue
uniform with its glowing brass buttons and the man's warm smile. His
arms extended, he hurried over and embraced her with tenderness.

"My dear daughter ..." He kissed her cheeks. His long waxed
moustache tickled her jaw. "My heart can at last be calm. When the
snow storm hit, it surprised us all. Please believe me, I wanted to go after
you, but my orders were to stay at the fort. Do you understand that I
couldn't leave?" He looked at her with blue eyes that pooled with guilt

and begged for forgiveness.

Staring into the ruddy pink face of her great-great-grandfather, all she could manage to do was nod. Colonel Jackson Wilfred. She recognized him from the old family albums her mother kept under the coffee table.

"For days I prayed that you lived through that blizzard. It was only when the snows had cleared and we learned from a Sioux brave of your whereabouts, that my prayers were answered."

The man turned and clasped the arm of the handsome brave, who stood tall and proud beside her. "I thank the Almighty that Golden Eagle learned of your whereabouts. I am in your debt my good friend."

"You and your daughter are back together as it should be. I will go now," Golden Eagle answered. With a nod, he walked away.

"Come, my dear. You must be tired. Let us go to my quarters."

His words barely registered on her dizzied senses. She stared, bewildered. He caught her under her arms and held her up before her legs gave way totally.

"Your taxing ordeal has worn on you more than I feared." His voice held a note on concern.

"I'm fine, really. See?" She stepped away from him to prove that she could stand without help. "I'm as strong as an ox."

What a lie. Her knees quivered. Her back ached and her head spun. This man was great-great-grandfather and her father at the same time. Damn, was this weird?

"Still ..." He took her hand in his, tucked his arm under hers and began to walk, guiding her along with him. "It is my duty as your father to worry and protect you."

How she had longed to hear her own father, or her mother for that matter, say those very words. Her throat constricted. She felt as if she had suddenly been set down in the midst of a tornado, with a million unanswered questions swirling across her brain.

"Seeing how I've failed in the past, let me at least try to be a better father in the present." He gave her hand a reassuring tap. "Come let us get inside. There is talk of a battle. We do not have all of our regiment here at the moment."

Battle. The word shot through Gabrielle like a bolt of lightning. "What year is it?" The words slipped from her mouth before she realized how stupid she had sounded.

A quick glint of surprise lit his blue eyes.

Embarrassed, Gabrielle glanced up at the flag as they passed it by, a familiar sight with a lot fewer stars and strips.

"Eighteen hundred and seventy-six, but my dear—"

And it was June. She stopped dead in her tracks and whirled to face him. Custer. Two Moons! Gabrielle's thoughts shifted to the man she had left behind. Would he come for her?

Earlier, when she had seen the village outside the fort, she had slipped his medicine bag between her breasts in fear that the these people, not of Two Moons' tribe, would not understand why she held it; now it weighed heavily against her heart. He would have to come. If any thing happened to him—

"Grand ... Father," she corrected herself. "General Custer—is he here?"

Puzzled by her question, he studied her face. His warm hand rested lightly on her arm. "No. He is not. Are you ill? Should I fetch a doctor?"

She shook her head. "No. I'm fine." Heat dotted her cheeks. What I meant was, I wondered when the general had left the fort."

"Last I heard he left Fort Lincoln on May seventeenth. He should be heading down toward the Little Big Horn River as we speak, but I think Doctor McGarvy should have a look at you."

A wave of relief washed over her, but quickly disappeared, as Gabrielle recalled seeing her grandfather's name listed as having died at the battle site. Confusion crossed her creased brows. Her thoughts scampered, but she smiled with deceptive calmness. "I don't need a doctor. I am perfectly fine."

"Jackson Wilfred, Sir," a voice called out.

Both Jackson and Gabrielle turned toward the voice. A boy of no more than sixteen approached them. A pang of sadness tightened her chest. So many young lives had been lost on the battlefield.

He saluted. "The general wishes yer presence, Sir. Words come that yer regiment is leavin' and yer to dispatch a letter to General Custer, Sir."

The words barely left his mouth, when a realization hit. A letter, a stupid letter would place Grandpa Jackson at the battle site. He was going to die! This man standing beside her was going to die, alongside Custer and the rest of those soldiers, whose bodies would be marked by slabs of cold white stone markers.

She could barely catch her breath. "You can't go! You can't!" Her adrenaline pumped as fast as her words. "Don't you see, you'll die out there! Please!" She grasped his collar tightly.

There was a moment of silence as surprise registered on his face.

"Tell me you won't go. Don't fight with Custer." Custer. The thought barely had time to register.

"Calm down, dear. Calm down." He eased her fingers from his collar and held them tightly in his own. "I will be safe. Don't worry." He glanced over her shoulder. "Tell the general I'll be right there." The soldier turned and walked away.

What could she do? Fate had brought her here. She had to do something to stop him. "Father—"

Grandpa Jackson raised a finger, silencing her. He reached into his breast pocket and pulled out a long gold chain. "Here." He opened her hand, dropped the gold in her palm and closed her fingers around it. "It is a gift for your mother."

Gabrielle uncurled her fingers and stared down at the etched round locket.

"Please. Open it." He gestured to the necklace.

Slowly she opened the cover. Tucked inside, two photographs, one of Col. Jackson, the other of an Indian woman holding a baby girl in her lap, lay nestled between the gold.

Her chest tightened. Other than the color of her skin, the child looked exactly like her own baby picture. "You were so young there," Jackson said.

She snapped the locket shut. Thoughts and speculation gave way to realization. An overwhelming surge of anger, then loss, shot through her. A part of her identity had been ripped away from her—gone, snatched up, just like that, with just a few words. Why had her mother failed to mention Native American blood ran through her veins? Willimina held her English heritage high on who they were and where they had come from. Perhaps that snobbery had prevented her from painting the whole picture. How could Willimina have done this to her?

"When you leave, give it to your mother, for as much as my heart regrets the day that I left her ..."

Left her? What did he mean? Had he left his wife? Was there some family law that said the men in the family had the right to leave when it suited them? Hadn't her own father done the same? It seemed she shared a lot more than just facial structure with White Swan. Gabrielle studied Grandpa Jackson with a cynical eye.

"... I cannot leave my command. Tell your mother I am sorry." His voice cracked. His shoulders hunched. She couldn't stand the look of anguish that darkened his face. She reached out and lightly rested her hand on his arm.

"Whatever has happened in the past is forgotten. I am here now and we have so much to discuss." Had she really said that? Could she really forgive him? Perhaps she would just listen to his explanation, maybe then, she could understand.

"I must go." He pushed open the door that led to his quarters. "Go inside and rest."

"Please, don't go. I—" Her voice broke. Panic echoed in her unspoken words. "Call it a woman's feeling, but something bad will happen to you if you go."

"Don't worry."

She placed a restraining hand over his arm. "Please. Get word to Custer's wife, Libby. She, too, shares this omen of danger."

"Go." He took her hand, urging her into the room. "Go inside and rest."

There was nothing more she could say, yet there were so many words. She watched him walk away; watched as the distance separating them grew farther and farther, as the sadness that weighed on her shoulders grew heavier and heavier. She turned and walked into the building.

Standing alone in the cool, sparse room, her mind, a crazy mixture of sadness, fear and hope, she sighed, trudged over to the lone bed in the corner and sat. The rickety old cot was as welcomed as any thick mattress. Lying across the gray army blanket, she brought the locket to her breast and held it tightly. She couldn't let him die. She couldn't. But what could she do? Was it her place to just change history for her own purpose? Did she want that responsibility? Her head began to pound. She closed her eyes and visions of her new found family swirled across her brain.

Then, moments before she faded off to sleep, a pair of dark brooding eyes and a handsome face filled her thoughts. Thank God, Two Moons and his people were nowhere near the battlefield.

Two Moons' anger blazed like a wild fire out of control. It seemed his medicine bag along with Blue Eyes were nowhere to be found. She was a thief. A thief who had stolen his powers and wanted him dead. He gripped the silver armband in his palm till the edge cut into his skin. Had Blue Eyes planned to run away for a long time? When he found her again, he would stake her hand and foot inside his lodge. She had betrayed his trust. Never again would she make a fool of him. He flung the silver band. The metal cut through the air barely missing Shadow Elks' head as he stepped into Two Moons' lodge.

"Next time I will announce my presence, as I fear I will lose my head." Shadow Elk's bantering words gave way to a relaxed smile.

"I will go this one alone." Two Moons jammed his quiver with arrows and grabbed his bow and shield.

Shadow Elk flipped open the tepee's door. His mouth clamped. His eyes fixed with determination, he watched him pass. Two Moons knew no words would deter his friend from following him in his search for Blue Eyes.

"The horses are ready." Shadow Elk marched up beside him.

"I only go to get back what belongs to me."

"And so you should. She—"

"I only go for my medicine bag. *She*—I can do well without." Two Moons secured a blanket over his horse's back.

"You could no more do without her than a fish could do without water ... than the birds could do without the sky ... than—"

"I hear your words. Cease your talk." Two Moons mounted his war pony. It seemed his friend indeed knew him like no other.

Despite his rage, Blue Eyes' disappearance had left an emptiness in his lodge, one which no amount of anger could fill.

He knew exactly where to look. What surprised him was that she left no tracks to follow. Perhaps Blue Eyes knew more of her people's ways than he had believed. The thought did little to please him as he headed for the Fort, Shadow Elk riding by his side.

They rode hard, stopping once to water the horses.

The moon was high in the sky by the time they reached their destination. Two Moons and Shadow Elk watched the Crow village nestled in the valley before the fort. Blue Eyes was not among her people, which came as no surprise to him. He had always suspected her true heart lay with the people beyond those wooden walls.

With haste, Two Moons and Shadow Elk moved cautiously past the village and made their way to the walled fortress.

Quickly, yet with a quietness that had been taught them since birth, they ran to where the bushes met the wall. Two Moons glanced around, then pushed some branches aside to reveal a small door. Shadow Elk slipped the tip of his arrow through the crack and lifted the lock.

Their senses alert, both men glanced around then ran for cover between two wooden structures. Perhaps now that they were inside, Two Moons would see if Yellow Hair was hiding in this walled village. His gaze fell upon the lodge that flew the white man's battalion flag overhead.

"Not now my friend," Shadow Elk whispered as if he had read his thoughts. "They are too many and we are but two. You will meet Yellow Hair in battle. That is when you will get your revenge."

Her silky voice floated through the air. Two Moons heard her laugh.

He jerked his head toward Blue Eyes. Arm in arm, she walked beside a man with long hair dripping from his mouth. The moon was bright, bright enough even from his hiding place to see the relaxed smile on her face and the way she clung to the soldier's arm.

It had not taken her very long to exchange Chahanpi's leather dress for the garb of the white woman, Two Moons thought with disgust, noticing the long blue cloth Blue Eyes wore. She reached over and kissed the cheek of the man beside her.

Two Moons pulled an arrow from his quiver.

"No." Shadow Elk placed his hand over Two Moons'. He pointed to a group of four men walking toward Blue Eyes and her companion.

Two Moons dropped his hand, making a fist. Again she had lied to him. She had a lover. He glared at the white man with burning reproachful eyes. What could she see in that older man? He could take that Blue Coat down and slit his neck before he even knew what had happened.

His stare intense, his shoulders taut, Two Moons stood in silence watching as Blue Eyes once more placed a kiss on the man's cheek. With a nod to the four men nearby, she turned, walked inside the lodge of wood and closed the door behind her.

If it were not for the group of men who stood around talking, Two Moons would have bolted to that door before it had a chance to close. Instead, he stayed hidden in the shadows, watching and waiting for them to leave. His bow aimed, his finger itching to let the arrow fly, the corded muscles in his arms strained tautly. He had to refrain himself from letting loose the arrow he knew would at least take down Blue Eyes' lover. Finally the group broke up.

He motioned to Shadow Elk to go around to the back. With a nod of understanding Shadow Elk disappeared.

Two Moons' glance darted around him as he ran out into the open, then crouched behind the white man's big-barreled gun on wheels. He heard voices in the distance, the bark of a dog and footsteps over creaking boards. He glanced to the door where Blue Eyes hid, down the long wooden path, then glanced quickly behind him. All was clear.

With the swiftness of the wind and the silence of the gathering clouds, Two Moons crossed the courtyard. He pressed his back to the door. His eyes sharp, his ears alert, he reached behind, slipped his knife between the door frame and lifted the inner latch. He stepped inside; bolted the door behind him.

Except for a dim flicker of light from an adjoining chamber, the room was dark. He heard movement in the next room. Quietly, he slipped behind the open door where Blue Eyes stood a stone's throw away. There was a moment of silence; then he heard the soft beat of her feet against the wooden floor.

She was close.

The muscles in his jaw tightened. Patience, he told himself. Patience.

The knock on the door outside sent his heart on a rampage. He burrowed deeper against the wall. His breath shallow, his eyes riveted, he watched her.

Blue Eyes walked to the table, picked up the glass light and adjusted the flame. The amber glow illuminated her face, giving her skin a golden sheen. Her full lips parted as she drew in a breath. She turned and hurried toward the door.

Through the transparent cloth of her nightdress Two Moons could see the silhouette of her shapely calves and the tops of her thighs. As he studied her, he became aroused. Angry at himself, he pushed all thoughts of desire away. He did not need her in his life. She caused him nothing but trouble.

From his hiding place, through the small crack where the door met the wall, Two Moons watched as she quickly put on another layer of sleep clothes then opened the outer door. He could feel his coiled rage surface as her lover stepped inside the room.

"I know it is late, but I thought I would see if you were in need of anything."

"No. Thank you," Two Moons heard Blue Eyes say.

"Golden Eagle is right. It is safer for you to stay with me tonight. I hope you do not mind my bed."

"No. I assure you it is a welcomed relief."

Her response chilled Two Moons' heart.

She would not share his bed tonight, he thought, satisfied. He gripped the handle of his knife tightly in his hand. He will slice that yellow-bellied Blue Coat from ear to ear, then take his medicine bag and leave her to weep over her lover's dead body!

"Well then, after my rounds I will return for the evening." The Blue Coat nodded curtly.

"I will wait up for you." Blue Eyes' voice was filled with anticipation.

Before the door had time to fully close Two Moons was behind her. He clamped his hand over her mouth. "Did you miss me?" he whispered in her ear.

Her body tensed against his. He heard her quick intake of breath at his words and spun her around. His hand on her mouth, he shoved her back against the wall and leaned into her. "Where is it?"

Her eyes widened in alarm. Then she lowered her gaze.

With a yank, the front of her nightclothes tore beneath his fingers. The light of the moon shining through the window cast a white glow on her naked breasts. There, nestled between her soft full swells, lay what he had come for: The medicine he would need in his battles to come.

He raised his gaze, stared hard into her eyes. His finger slowly trailed over one mound. He encircled the dark round nipple, feeling its tip grow hard and taut beneath his touch. He leaned closer, pressing his own hardness between her thighs; and all the while his eyes studied hers—watching her reaction. He would make her want him. No longer would she desire the white man's arms. It would be his arms, she wanted and his alone. Then, when he felt her become liquid in his hands, he would leave her.

He removed his hand and completely covered her mouth with his. He thrust his tongue between her lips, opening them for his entry. His kiss was angry, meant to punish. Yet despite his fury, he enjoyed the feeling of being inside her mouth. Barely aware that her arms encircled his shoulders, he withdrew his mouth to nibble hungrily along her slender neck. Her soft moan made him want to enter her, to release the ever-growing tension within. She arched closer. He could feel her trembling against him. Her defenses were weakening—or were his?

"Two Moons are you mad?" Shadow Elk's voice was like a splash of cold water.

Two Moons pivoted and glanced to his friend. Crouched outside the window, Shadow Elk motioned that he come. Without so much as a second thought, Two Moons spun on his heels, swept Blue Eyes up off the floor and hurried over to the window. He dumped her into his friend's arms then hauled himself through the opening. Shadow Elk, in turn, tossed her over Two Moons' shoulder and the two men took off into the darkness.

TWELVE

A hawk's haunting cry shattered the stillness. Two Moons kneed Anpo Wie, urging his horse closer to the edge of the forest. Shadow Elk followed close behind. Their senses alert, both men were keenly aware of all that went on around them.

"Let me go you big brute. Do you hear me?" Blue Eyes' screams, like that of the large black bird riding the winds above them, bounced off the mountain tops and echoed across the vast open plains.

"Let me go!" She struggled beneath his hold.

He should have known the minute he threw Blue Eyes upon his horse's back, she would try to flee. He held her squirming backside down with a firm hand. With his free hand he delivered a stinging blow to her buttocks.

"Cease your chatter woman, unless you wish us all dead," he ordered. "Or is that what you had in mind?"

"Is that what you think? Damn you. Stop for a minute and let me—"

"Enough, or I promise I will beat you!" His nerves as thin as a fraying rope, Blue Eyes' constant complaining and struggles to escape from his hold did little to ease his tension. He glanced around. Something wasn't quite right. He sensed a presence that he could not see, but nevertheless, felt.

"My brother, perhaps with the blue-eyed one astride your pony we will make better time? Is it not more trouble to keep her from falling in that position?" Shadow Elk asked from beside him.

"She is as she should be, befitting her position. If we were not in such a hurry to return to our brothers, I would make her walk as any slave of mine should." Two Moons glanced over his friend's shoulder. Someone followed them. He was sure of it.

"Let us cease this discussion. We have many miles to cover before the sun is high in the sky." He jabbed his horses' flanks with his heels and Anpo Wie took off in an easy canter.

Nothing more said, they entered the deep grove of pine and continued their journey toward the village.

It was the dead of morning when Two Moons, now sure no one had followed them, stopped his horse beside a narrow gurgling stream and slid down Anpo Wie's back.

"We will stop here. The horses need their rest."

Shadow Elk nodded, dismounted and led his horse to drink.

Two Moons reached up to Blue Eyes. He placed his hands around her waist and yanked her down off the horse.

Her legs buckled beneath her as her feet touched the ground, but she managed to straighten. She whirled around, facing him. Her hair tangled by the wind, stuck to her lip. She flung the loose strands away from her face. Her eyes blazed. The front of her white sleep clothes, now gray from Anpo Wie's sweat and dust, hung open.

Conscience of his gaze, Blue Eyes gathered the outer layer of cloth across her breasts to shield her nakedness.

"Give it to me," Two Moons demanded, reminded that between those breasts still dangled his medicine pouch.

"What could you have been thinking to drag me away in nothing but—"

He reached out to her chest and covered her clenched hand with his. "If you wish to keep the remainder of your sleep clothes in one piece, you will give me what I want."

She jerked her body away from him, breaking his hold. "God, there's no need for threats." She reached to her neck and lifted his bag over her head.

"Here. I was gonna give it back to you anyway. You don't have to be such a brute about it."

He snatched the pouch from her outstretched hand then grabbed her arm. Dragging her to a large gnarled tree, he forced her down to the ground.

"Stop it! You're hurting me." She tried to twist from his grip. He pinched her wrists together, binding them with the strip of leather he had pulled from his braid.

"Why don't you give me a chance to explain. I—"

"Save your false truths for someone who wishes to hear them." He secured the knot, leaving the leather loose so her wrists would not mar.

"Lies. What lies? If you'd let me talk, I'd—"

Two Moons' lips curled with disgust. He clasped then unclasped his hand. "You will not run away from me again for I will hunt you down and bring you back." He leaned in close to her face. "It will be a dirty game we will play, one I assure you will exhaust you before me."

He stood abruptly then continued loud enough for Shadow Elk's ears. "Get used to those ropes for they will be a part of you from now on."

"I didn't run away, you big jerk!" Her words stopped him dead in his tracks. Two Moons pivoted around to face her.

"Already the game has begun, has it not?" He marched back over and stopped before her. Peering down into her eyes, he searched for the truth of her words.

"Your tongue is sharp and your lies make my blood run hot with anger. Think carefully before you speak to me again." In her gaze he saw not deceit, but a look of confidence. A spark of hope flickered in the back of his mind. Perhaps he had been wrong.

"Two Moons," she began, her voice soft. "Despite your rudeness— wait!" Before he had a chance to open his mouth in protest, she continued. "I had no desire to run from you, or your people. Little Wolf said—"

"Little Wolf?" Doubt and suspicion began to grow in Two Moons' mind. He should have known Little Wolf would somehow be involved.

"He said that I must get your medicine bag—"

"Why did you steal it?"

"Why would I want to go through all the trouble of trying to get the bag purified if I had stolen it? It broke off your neck when you were in such a hurry to dump me in the water." She struggled to her feet. "And as for that little scene with Kills Pretty, to—to have that woman embarrass me like that in front of everyone ... I didn't know my presence was a threat to your powers. And you ..." Rage choked her words. "... you believed her." She took a deep breath then exhaled. "And it didn't improve my day any to be traded for a few bottles of whiskey."

"What talk is this?"

"Little Wolf. He traded me to Golden Eagle for whiskey."

Two Moons rubbed his chin and studied her face carefully. Should he believe her? Her words seemed honest. Now Little Wolf—that he could believe. The man was known to be sweet on the white man's fiery waters.

"I will think on your words."

"Come on." She lifted her bound hands to him.

He ignored her plea. "You will sit. I wish not to hear your talk any longer."

"Damn it, Two Moons! This isn't fair!"

He stomped away, her curses bouncing off his back. No other woman in his camp, or for that matter any other tribe, would dare talk as she did. He wasn't sure if her spirit at this moment pleased him, or made him sorry he had found her. His life had been simpler before.

"Ouch!" Shadow Elk, his brows arched, his eyes wide, curled his hands like claws. "The she-cat hisses. Watch your back. Her nails are sharp, but I suspect her fur is soft. It would be worth the scratches once you tame her."

Two Moons grunted. He strolled past his friend then bent to the water's edge to take a drink.

Shadow Elk knelt beside him and scooped up a handful of water. "A spirited woman is like the angry wind and rain that runs across the land bringing with it, new life." He paused, brought his hands to his lips, drank then continued. "She makes you think and stirs up new feelings deep in here." He pointed to his heart. "Does she not?"

Two Moons stood. Shadow Elk did the same.

"What I feel in here," Two Moons pounded his chest, "is confused by what I feel in here." He tapped his head. "And when I saw her with that Blue Coat, what I felt here ..." He rested his hand over his heart. "... twisted like an angry serpent. I do not like these new thoughts I think."

"Only by listening to her words will you learn the truth. But you must ask her first."

Two Moons glanced over to Blue Eyes who by now had given up her struggles and was sitting, her eyes closed, against the tree.

She had spoken the truth about her feelings for Little Wolf, this he now believed, but what about the Blue Coat? Could he believe that she did not care for him? Did he really want to hear the truth of her words?

Damn his stubborn hide! Gabrielle watched as Two Moons built a small circular fire with rocks and twigs then threw some buffalo dung on top as fuel. She should hate him right now—really, really hate him for the way he treated her, like some insignificant object he could throw around, only she didn't. "You shouldn't have dragged me away from the fort like that," she shouted at him.

Anger, as heated as the flames that hissed and rose into the dark sky, flashed in his eyes. Then, his expression tightened. Gabrielle snapped her head sideways, following his gaze. What had he heard? She squinted, trying to see through the darkness of the woods. The chirping song of the crickets filled the air—and stillness.

Two Moons seemed uneasy as he went back to his task. A deep concern for his safety and that of Shadow Elk welled in her breast. Could it be they had been followed? Was her grandfather out there somewhere searching for her? Grandfather Jackson. A stab of loss assailed her as she thought about him. Her fingers slipped into her pocket and she felt the gold locket she had placed in her robe. Why did Two Moons have to come and interfere just when she was going to learn more about her family? Learn more about herself? This whole time-travel thing had to have a purpose. What if somehow she was supposed to stop Jackson from fighting? How was she ever going to do that if she couldn't get back to the fort? She'd never find her way back alone. She couldn't ask Two Moons to bring her back. He'd never understand.

She watched as he stood, made his way over to his horse and reached into the satchel that hung from the animal's side. She couldn't risk his life. Custer was on the move and that meant only one thing: he was out searching for Indians.

Despair tore at her heart. What a choice, to save the life of her great-great-grandfather or to save Two Moons. She didn't want to lose either one.

"I'm freezing and dirty from that horse of yours. You could have asked for your medicine pouch. You didn't have to destroy my nightgown."

Two Moons pulled a small bundle from his parfleche, ignoring her. Surprised when he walked over and stopped before her, she stared at him in silence. The corded bands in his shoulders flexed as he pulled off his long buckskin shirt. The muscles in his chest contracted. Without a word he dropped his shirt in her lap, then turned and went back to the fire.

"You have caused my friend great concern." Shadow Elk walked over. He sat beside her and untied her hands. "I think that is good for him."

Crouching, Two Moons opened his bag and sprinkled fine shaving over the flames. A strong bitter smell wafted up through the smoke.

"Tobacco and sweet grass. It is through those that *Whope*, the daughter of the sun and moon, transforms her powers and allows Two Moons to ask for the Great Spirit's aid."

Gabrielle slipped the poncho-style tunic over her head. Huge, the garment fell to her mid-thighs and the warmth from his body soothed the goose bumps on her arms. Silently she thanked him.

With an apologetic glance, Shadow Elk rebound her hands. She clamped her mouth shut. Her protests would cause him nothing but trouble.

"The fire represents the sun, the force that allows all living things to prevail upon Mother Earth." He crossed his legs making himself comfortable. "The white sage Two Moons sprinkles over the flames is to drive away the evil forces which your touch has brought to his medicine."

"Look. I didn't mean for him to be haunted by ghosts. The last thing I wanted was for his medicine bag to lose its protective powers. This whole thing isn't really my fault. I—"

"Without the knowledge of our ways you are not at blame." Shadow Elk's kind words and gentle tone comforted her anger.

She glanced at the man beside her. He was quite handsome—in a boyish kind of way.

"You will listen and learn. Aye?" He smiled and his whole face brightened.

Gabrielle nodded.

Shadow Elk continued. "The sun is the all powerful, who reigns over the spirit world, the world itself and the world beneath the world."

World beneath? Her heart leapt. "Are there many worlds?" She took a sharp breath and bit her lip to contain her excitement. Perhaps he would understand. Perhaps he could make her understand how she came to be here?

"Yes. Just as there are many spirits and their powers are many. The powers of the *Sicun*, or powers of good, are greater than those of evil. But the evil spirits are not to be taken lightly. *Iya* is a monster who eats animals and men. His breath can bring disease. *Gnaske* brings insanity. Now *Gica* is the one whom Two Moons is concerned about. He can bring accidents, perhaps even death."

A twig snapped. Shadow Elk silenced. Two Moons froze at his spot before the fire. Both men glanced to the trees. Two Moons began to rise. Shadow Elk raised a hand, stopping him. Lightly he tapped his chest then swiftly rose to his feet.

Gabrielle's heart raced. Her shoulders knotted. All this talk of evil set her nerves on edge.

With the grace of a sleek panther, Shadow Elk disappeared into the wooded darkness.

Two Moons straightened. His gaze followed his friend. She noticed he held his knife in his hand. Was he going to leave her? Struggling, she stood.

He glanced at her.

She raised her bound hands.

His body tense, he hesitated for a moment before he reached her side.

The rope fell to the ground.

Their gazes met.

The snap of a branch brought a demand of silence to his eyes. He spun around, ready for the attack. Nothing happened. Quickly, silently he followed in his friend's footsteps.

Shadow Elk met him at the edge of the woods. "It is just an animal that hunts for food in the night. I have seen nothing else."

With a nod, Two Moons acknowledged his friend's words. He slipped his knife back in its sheath, retraced his steps, and knelt before the fire.

From her place slightly opposite Two Moons and the crackling flames, Gabrielle watched as he began dipping his fingers into the small bowls at his side. He brought his hands to his face. As his fingers left a striped trail across his checks, she listened to Shadow Elk's explanation.

"Red, blue, green and yellow are the colors of the sun, the sky, the earth and the rock. Black is for the evil forces that lurk about."

Smoke wafted in her eyes causing them to water. Her vision blurred. The flames from the fire seemed to come alive, their shadows leaping to the ground like a Disney cartoon.

Two Moons stood and reached upward.

Shadow Elk pointed to him. "Did you know that when you raise your arms to the sky like that it is like touching the face of *Wankan Tanka*, our creator? It is over," he whispered in her ear. "Two Moons' medicine is good." He touched her arm lightly. "Next time you will be more careful. Aye?"

Concern for his friend's well being, touched her deeply. "You are a good friend to him. I hope he realizes that."

Shadow Elk smiled. His gaze rested on Two Moons. Bent over the flames, he removed the medicine bag that hung on a stick in the fire's center. Shadow Elk stood and walked over. After a brief conversation he went to his horse, reached into his satchel and pulled out what even from her distance looked like a can.

Gabrielle's stomach growled. Her mouth salivated. Other than a biscuit and a small bowl of soup, she had been too excited to eat back at the fort and that had been hours ago.

Two Moons glanced at her, a shadow of annoyance crossed his face. She found herself instantly irritated. What was his problem? He wasn't the one who had been kidnapped, tossed about like a bag of beans then dumped, God knew where in the dead of morning. "Go to hell," she snapped then wheeled around.

Her back stiff, she marched back over to the tree and sat. A hand touched her shoulder. She turned with a start.

"Come." Shadow Elk motioned that she rise and go with him to the fire. "Eat."

"I'm not hungry." She jerked her head back to face the tree.

Shadow Elk placed his hand on her shoulder. "You are hungry, no?"

"No." She wouldn't sit and eat with them no matter what. How dare he be annoyed with her. He still thought this whole kidnapping thing was her fault!

"Leave her to her hunger." Two Moons crossed before her, then sat facing her.

She drew her knees to her chest and wrapped her arms around her legs. Big brute. She watched him open the can with his knife.

A frown on his face, Shadow Elk joined his friend.

Gabrielle glanced away, annoyed she didn't understand what the two were saying. Once again her stomach growled. She stole the men a quick glance. A faint smile tipped Shadow Elk's mouth as he nodded in agreement at something Two Moons said.

Very slowly Two Moons stuck his fingers into the can. Leisurely he swirled the can's contents. He looked up. His eyes gleamed like black crystallized rock. Obsidian. That was it, Gabrielle thought, remembering the shiny arrowheads she had seen. A sharp hunger pain attacked her stomach.

"Mmm …" Two Moons' sensuous moan maddening, she grit her teeth. Powerless to resist, she glanced back at him. Peach juice oozed from his lips and dribbled down his chin. A sly smile tipped his mouth as he studied her. He lifted the can, offering it to her.

"No, thank you. I'd rather starve."

With a shrug he turned and offered the can to Shadow Elk, who in turn dipped his fingers into the peaches and drew out a slice. "Such sweetness I have never tasted." Shadow Elk swiped his hand across his mouth. "I must thank the Great Spirits for guiding me to the Blue Coats' food lodge. No?" He winked and jabbed Two Moons in the ribs.

Gabrielle licked her lips. Two Moons took another slice. She detected laughter in his eyes as he brought the peach to his mouth. With deliberate slowness he sucked the wedge between his teeth, then smacked his lips, satisfied.

"It is too bad you are not hungry." He waved the can before her nose then quickly wrenched it away, offering it back to Shadow Elk.

She glanced from one man to the other as they slurped up the peaches like a bunch of hungry hogs. Despite her hunger and annoyance, it took every ounce of her self-control not to laugh. She glanced away, then back.

"You are sure you are not hungry?" Two Moons dark brows arched mischievously. "Smell their sweetness." He waved his hand before the can, blowing imaginary fumes to her.

She bit the inside of her lip, debating. The bum. From the silly smirk on his face, he knew he had her.

Before he had a chance to retract the can, Gabrielle snatched the tin away. She shoved the slices into her mouth two at a time, hungrily devouring the delicacy without even tasting it. She paused, taking a moment to swallow, then glanced up. A grin of triumph pursed his lips. Shadow Elk's smile beamed from ear to ear. Realizing her actions and how she must look, she suppressed a giggle.

Instantaneously, Two Moons threw back his head and burst out laughing. Shadow Elk followed, his laughter rippling through the air, mingling with the chuckles of Two Moons.

"You big brutes." She reached to Two Moons and rapped his arm. Sweet sticky juice dripped from her mouth. She wiped her lips with her fingers. The sound of their contagious laughter filled her ears and shattered the last of her animosity. Unable to suppress the hysterics forming in her chest, she gave in to the moment and joined in.

"I did good, yeah?" Two Moons asked.

"Yeah. You did." She offered the can and a smile to him.

"No. You eat. At last you have made your stomach happy. That is good." He stood.

"Like a sparrow, that one eats," Shadow Elk joked as he, too, stood and took a step behind Two Moons.

Bending forward, Two Moons offered his hand to her.

A swooshing sound like the parting of air passed her ear. A blur of movement whizzed over Two Moons' shoulder from behind her.

The sharp intake of Shadow Elk's breath tore her gaze to the man behind Two Moons. Shock registered on Shadow Elk's face as he clutched the arrow piercing his heart. Blood poured.

A scream tore from her lips.

Shadow Elk stumbled forward.

Two Moons dropped her hand, turned and caught Shadow Elk's slumped body into his arms.

Her mind numb, her legs paralyzed, Gabrielle struggled to her feet as Two Moons gently laid Shadow Elk to the ground. She didn't realize she was screaming until Two Moons grabbed her shoulders and shook them. "Be still."

She swallowed her cry and stared down at Shadow Elk.

His eyes closed, his breathing was shallow.

"It's all my fault." She dropped to her knees. Tears fell uncontrollably. "I'm sorry. I'm so sorry ..." She didn't dare touch him.

She couldn't. Guilt's twisted hand ripped through her mind. If she hadn't gone with Little Wolf ...

"Do not blame yourself, little sparrow." All but Shadow Elk's weak smile blackened before her. He reached out and touched her arm lightly. "You do not know our ways." His dropped his hand to his chest. He closed his eyes. His breathing became shallower.

"My friend do not leave me," Two Moons pleaded. "You must not die. Not now."

Gabrielle peered at Two Moons through a haze of tears. Pain twisted his features—made his cheeks hollow and his face fall. He grabbed Shadow Elks' hand and squeezed. "Hold on my brother." His voice cracked. "I need you. There is much hunting to be done by the two of us."

He reached for the arrow.

Shadow Elk opened his eyes. "Later my brother. She is in danger. You must go. Find the one who has done this ..." He wheezed. His eyes closed for a brief second. "Bring back a piece of his scalp for me." His voice jagged—weak—breathless, he wheezed again.

Two Moons gripped the arrow tighter. "This must come out now. I will not leave you. I—"

"This is a foolish thing. Your blood ..." Shadow Elk paused for a moment catching his breath. " ... and that of hers, I do not wish beside me. You must listen to me." He struggled to rise. A shot of pain clenched his chest. He dropped back, his head to the ground.

Her movements jerky, Gabrielle pulled Two Moons' tunic over her shoulders, then gently lifted Shadow Elk's head and slipped the garment beneath it. His eyes were warm with thanks before he shifted his gaze back to Two Moons.

"My brother. I cannot bring the sunshine, only she can. Only with the knowledge you can give ..."

She couldn't stand seeing his pain. She glanced away, listening to his words and understanding little.

A moment passed before Shadow Elk continued. "... will you share the same path." His voice weak, his breathing shallow, he took an unsteady breath. "Go find him before it is too late."

It looked as if Two Moons would protest; then hesitantly he rose. His gait swift, his steps weightless, he ran into the woods, disappearing into the darkness. But Gabrielle knew his heart was heavy.

THIRTEEN

Two Moons broke through the forest only to stop dead in his tracks at the edge of the camp. He glanced at Shadow Elk, then back at her as though he was afraid   afraid of the outcome.

Nauseating despair churned, rising in Gabrielle's throat. Like a marionette, his movement's stiff and jerky, Two Moons made his way toward her and stopped. He glanced down at Shadow Elk. Disbelief spread across his face.

She swallowed with difficulty. "I'm sorry." Her words faded into the silence.

Two Moons fell to his knees. The despairing anguish contorting his face as he stared down at his friend tore at her heart.

"No. It cannot be so." His words seemed strangled in his throat. Like a madman, his movement's swift, wild, crazed, he grabbed the arrow buried in Shadow Elk's chest.

"I will not let you die ... hold on my brother ... *Kiktá yo*."

Twisting and yanking, he wrenched the deadly weapon free then threw it to the ground. Torment curled his lower lip. Raw pain swelled in his eyes as he began to shake Shadow Elk's limp body. "I will not let you die. You cannot die. *Kiktá yo* ..." His voice cracked.

Blood poured from the wound.

Gabrielle watched in horrifying silence. Helplessness and misery, old familiar friends, circled above her like vultures, their gnawing bite, stronger than anything she had ever felt before.

Words tumbled from his mouth; Lakota words she didn't understand, spoken with tenderness, filled with suffering and despair. Two Moons' broad shoulders heaved as he tried to shake life's breath back into his friend.

"Two Moons! Stop!" She reached out and gripped his arms. He lifted his gaze to hers, a hollow gaze, as lifeless as the man whose body he held in his hands. "It's over. Please. Let him rest," she whispered.

He shuddered, drawing in a sharp breath. Seemingly seeing, yet hearing nothing, he stared at her, his black eyes dull. Then he placed Shadow Elk to the ground.

Her fingers slowly slipped from his arms as he drew away from her and stood. He turned into the shadows, away from the light of the fire. His shoulders slumped. His head bowed and the tears, Gabrielle knew he tried to hide, fell in silence.

Time seemed suspended. The darkness consumed her. She felt his tears in her own eyes. She started to rise, but hesitated. What could she say? That she knew what it was like to lose someone you loved? That she understood his pain? Would he welcome her comfort or shun her?

He turned, his face a mask of apathy. He slipped out his knife. Again, he fell to his knees before Shadow Elk.

Then, before she could anticipate his next move let alone stop him, he began to gouge his arms.

Horrified she jumped up and ran to his side. "Oh, my God! Stop! What are you doing?" She reached out to stop him.

The blade froze on his arm. His eyes riveted, his message was only too clear: *Stay back. Mind your own business.*

She clamped her trembling hand over her mouth, sickened by the blood running down his elbows.

He sliced off the leather fringes that hung from his buckskin pants, the feathers and beads that hung from his hair. To endure the agony of those self-inflicted slashes, to give up all those worldly adornments, that was his way of showing his respect and grief.

The fire crackled. A damp breeze pricked the hair on her arms. Gabrielle shivered, but not from the cold. Death was knocking on her door once again, wrenching at her heart, dredging up memories—so many painful memories. She wrapped her arms around her waist. "Did you find—"

"No."

Stoically he stood and trudged toward the trees to begin the long and tedious labor of preparing a scaffold, where they would lay Shadow Elk's body to rest.

Gabrielle hurried to his side. With open arms, she offered her help. Without a word he cut the branches from the young saplings and placed the slender limbs across her forearms. She worked by his side holding the branches together as he interweaved rope and wood to form the platform. With tears in her eyes, she watched as he prepared Shadow Elk's body, dressing him in his finest clothes—a warrior's clothing, always kept at his side to proudly wear in battle or to meet his maker.

Two Moons dressed his friend's hair with beaded ornaments and wrapped Shadow Elk, along with his knife, bow, arrow and shield in several robes of buffalo hides. He placed him on the platform and with ropes he had slung over the branches of a big tree, he hoisted the body to the high boughs to keep it safe from animals.

With his arms raised to the sky, he began to pray. His heart-piercing cries tore through the early morning's stillness.

For hours Gabrielle sat before the scaffold, listening to Two Moons' prayers. Finally, at the point of voicelessness, he stopped. Exhausted, he lowered his arms, collapsed to his knees and hung his head in silence. Inhaling deeply, his shoulders slumped for a final time; then he straightened. He reached for the fur strip that bound his hair and untied his braids, all but one thin braid that hung to his chest from the nape of his neck.

Gabrielle knew that above all else, a Sioux's pride and joy was his hair. They believed their hair was somehow connected to the mystery of life; it was an extension of their soul and held great power. To give up a part was to weaken their defenses.

He brought the knife to his ear.

Her breath held in her throat. She wanted to reach out and stop him. She clenched her fist by her side. Her fingernails cut into her palm. He knew what he was doing.

The scalp, or lock of hair in the hands of an enemy could cause destruction and allow his adversary supremacy over all.

His braid fell to the ground.

Tears sprang to her eyes as she watched him stiffly walk away and mount his horse.

With just a flick of his wrist, that simple act of total surrender said more about the man than all the bloody slices crisscrossing up and down his arms. Two Moons in a final tribute of his love and devotion, gave up to his friend a part of his own safety—a part of his life.

He beckoned that she come to him, and she did.

With Shadow Elk's horse following slowly behind them, Gabrielle and Two Moons rode away, leaving Shadow Elk alone in respectful solitude, as the pink glow of sunrise spilled over the horizon, welcoming the new day to come.

Despite the bright sunlight shining in through the skylight above him, Roy awoke feeling strangely depressed. He couldn't really find a reason for feeling the way he did. His truck was fixable and he, other than a few bumps and bruises, was alive. He had lived through a lot worse. So why the deep melancholy? The overwhelming sadness swelling in the hollow of his chest felt so familiar. He closed his eyes.

An image of his mother's smiling face filled the darkness. She threw

him a ball and he could see himself swing. He could almost hear her
laughter as she tried in vain to tag him out, allowing him to run to home
base; just another day in a six-year-old's life.

His eyes misted as an image of his mother slumped over a table,
with an empty whiskey bottle in one hand and an empty glass in the
other, replaced his happy memory. Opening his eyes, he came back to
reality.

He sat up.

"You must learn from the past."

The old man's words threw him completely. "What?"

John Raven Wing entered the room, shuffled over and handed him a
cup of tea. "The value of remembering the past is in taking that
knowledge and learning from it."

Roy stared up at him, noticing for the first time that the iris in one of
John's eyes was so dark that it blended with his pupil; while the other
eye, a lighter brown, was flecked with gold.

John turned away without a word and ambled over to a table tucked
in the corner of the room.

Strange eyes, for a very strange man, Roy thought as he watched
him amble away.

"I didn't get a chance last night to use your phone. I need to call a
tow truck."

"There is no need."

Pensively, Roy stared. What was it with this guy? "I really have to
make that call." He clasped then unclasped his hand.

"There is no phone." John took a sip of tea. "So, do not worry, my
friend stops in every day to visit. He will tow your truck."

"Great. OK. I hope he wouldn't mind giving me a lift into town. I
need to get to the reservation, to the headquarters there."

"It is closed."

"For how long?"

"Until it needs to be opened."

Roy shoved his hand into his pocket. He had to get back to work.
This was the last place he wanted to be. Something about this old man
and his knowing smile irked him.

"By any chance, have you seen this woman?" Roy pulled the photo
from his pocket and held out the picture of Gabrielle.

For a minute, he thought he saw a glimpse of recognition in the old
man's eyes.

"You writing a story about her?"

Roy's brows shot up with surprise. "How did you know I was a reporter?" What had he said in his sleep?

John pushed his chair from the table and stood. "Too much thinking." He shook his head as he hobbled away. "Too much. Come." Without looking back, he waved his hand over his shoulder.

The old man seemed to slow his steps as Roy passed by the geometric painting on the wall. Even in the morning's light, he couldn't help but feel a sense of sadness surrounding that picture.

"Some thoughts can't be fully explained with words."

Roy drew his attention away from the painting.

His host continued. "So to fully understand you must explore. There are no such things as accidents or coincidence. Come with me and we will talk."

Roy hesitated a moment before he stepped up beside John. "Are you saying my accident happened on purpose?"

"Everything happens for a reason. Life is a lesson. Learning is a process of remembering the past. So perhaps you are here to learn." With a flick of his wrist a small black bird appeared in the old man's hand.

Roy grinned. "You're a magician."

John opened the front door and the bird flew out. He turned. "Magic. What is magic? A TV or electricity hundreds of years ago would have been thought of as magic. So I ask you: Is magic just a word for something not understood today, which will become a knowing wisdom in years to come?"

The old man stepped outside. Roy followed.

"So what is fate? Is it fate that you happen to be here, your destiny? Or has your life's path already been planned for you by a greater force than you or I?"

"We make our own choices and paths in life. No one knows what the future holds," Roy answered cynically.

"No. But one can travel back through time and walk old paths to learn how to make the future better."

Roy rubbed his chin. If he wasn't confused before, he was now. "When you say travel back through time you mean remembering past experiences, like your childhood or what happened yesterday, right?"

"Your childhood. Yes, and those before."

"Those before meaning ... what? Are we talking about past lives, because I don't believe in reincarnation—".

"Those that are unwilling to even consider the possibility, have allowed their misconceptions to cloud all possible thoughts on the subject."

Roy shook his head. "No. We're here. We live. We die. Maybe there's a heaven, maybe not."

"So, you are smart, but you do not see. The Great Spirit of life is a great mystery like the air." John raised his fingers to the sky. "It is here. You can see it moving the grass and touching the leaves; you can feel it, but you cannot see it. Does that mean it cannot be so?"

"No but—"

"Energy. Can you see it? Do you feel it? So, there are many forms and expressions of energy. Is that not true?"

"Yes."

"Does anyone tell your heart to keep on beating? It is run by energy, innate energy. Your soul is energy. Can it not radiate to a higher level? So who is to say it cannot continue somewhere else in life's circle?"

Roy raked his fingers through his hair and let out a long audible breath. What was he doing here discussing the philosophy of life?

"If we lived before, as you say, why wouldn't we remember this past life?"

"To handle the present and remember the past would be too much for our minds to handle." John shook his head. "Too overwhelming."

Roy rubbed the back of his taut neck. And to think, whenever he couldn't handle something, past or present, the booze usually did the trick. At least it had, then. Nowadays he took one day at a time. Last thing he wanted was to think back to the "good old days." He'd put his past behind him. Getting stuck here with John and drudging up old memories couldn't be a good thing. Roy stood. It was time to leave.

Gabrielle and Two Moons reached the village at dusk. Everyone crowded around them as they rode into the center of camp. The shrieking welcome of the children, the barking dogs scampering around at the horse's feet and the sharp loud chattering of questions thrown, gushed in from all directions, battering her. The tension and anxiety that had been building between them throughout the day, like a bubbling hot volcano, threatened to erupt.

Two Moons gripped the reins tighter. The veins on the top of his hands bulged. The muscles in his arms hardened against her waist and Gabrielle knew without seeing his face, he was just as tense as she was.

Was he thinking her thoughts? Wondering how to get through the day without breaking down, or wishing he had never met her? How could she face Chahanpi? Or look into the faces of Shadow Elk's parents and not feel the guilt at seeing their pain? It was her fault. Her fault he was dead. If only she hadn't gone with Little Wolf, Two Moons wouldn't have followed and Shadow Elk would still be alive.

From her place on horseback, she could see Chahanpi running toward them. She broke through the crowd. Her glance went to Shadow Elk's horse now painted with red mourning blotches. Her smile faded. The spark of excitement and anticipation died, leaving only questions, then anguish in her dark eyes. Her expression was like someone who had been hit in the face, stunned, traumatized. She stifled a sob with the back of her hand.

A woman's bellowing moan tore through the air. Gabrielle recognized Shadow Elk's parents as they stepped through the crowd. Women gathered around She Who Sings, offering their comfort, offering their support.

Two Moons slid down from his horse. His movements strained and unnatural, like a sleepwalker, he stepped up to Standing Bear and handed him the reins of Shadow Elk's horse. Gabrielle could see the silent suffering in the old man's eyes. With a nod, Standing Bear turned and She Who Sings followed behind.

"Get down," Two Moons ordered as the congregation broke apart.

"I—"

"Get down." He clasped his hand then unclasped his hand.

She was afraid of falling, had never gotten down from a horse without help, but the anger she heard in his voice and saw in his eyes kept the words at the bottom of her throat. Cautiously she leaned forward, lowering her upper torso until it rested against the horse's mane. The animal shook his head. She gasped and jerked back up to a sitting position.

"This I cannot believe. You are afraid of a horse?" Rough hands reached up and pulled her down. "I do not know what to think of you." He reached around her, grabbed his horse's reins and pulled.

She stepped out of the beast's way.

"And right now I do not have the desire to think." Two Moons pivoted on his heel.

"It wasn't my fault," she shouted as he began to stalk away. But it was. *It was.* Those two silent words echoed back at her.

He came to an abrupt stop and wheeled around, facing her. "If not for you, who then?" His voice thundered as he came closer. "If we had not come looking for you, Shadow Elk would be alive." He thrust his arm out and pointed to Chahanpi's tepee at the end of camp. "He would right now be sharing his blanket with the woman he loves—would right now be speaking soft words of marriage in her ear. Chahanpi's heart would be light with happiness, not heavy with pain and sorrow."

A deafening stillness grew around her as she became aware of many eyes on her and Two Moons. Without looking she knew supper was cooking and old men sat together with their heads bent in conversation, but ears were listening and voices were quiet. They all blamed her.

"Damn it! Not again. Not this time. I'm not taking all the blame for this. You seem to forget I had your stupid medicine bag because you had a temper tantrum and threw me in the water! If you had listened to me in the first place, none of this would have happened."

A spasm of anger crossed Two Moons' face. He clenched his hand. "And had you left my lodge when you were supposed to, I would not have had to put you in your place. And my bag—"

"You still think I stole it, don't you?"

"I did not say you stole it."

"You didn't have to. I can see it all over your face."

"You do not know my heart," he replied, his voice cold, bitter. "You know nothing."

"That's right. I'm just a stupid squaw with a college education, but hey," she cast her hands into the air, "you're right. What do I know? Why don't you just leave poor little stupid me alone and go fight a battle or whatever it is that you macho men do."

"It is what I shall do, for I have no desire to listen to your words."

"Fine with me," she shouted as he stormed out of sight. She pivoted on her heels. Her insides felt like mush. Her knees beneath her skirt quivered. But she held her shoulders high as she walked past Rattling Blanket and a group of her peers. Heading for her tepee, she prayed to be just left alone.

It wasn't the vibrating snores of Rattling Blanket that kept Gabrielle up all night, or for the next night for that matter; it was her thoughts. Thus far she'd managed to avoid Chahanpi, although that had been easily accomplished since Chahanpi and Shadow Elk's parents had left camp upon the news of Shadow Elk's death. But from the distant bluffs their lamenting cries of utter misery could be heard throughout the camp from morning till dawn.

This morning, however, a chill silence surrounded her. Reluctantly Gabrielle stepped outside her tepee. At the sight of Chahanpi walking toward her, a new anguish seared her heart. Chahanpi's luxurious long hair had been chopped short and hung ragged near her ears. Her face showed lines of sleeplessness and distress. The last thing Gabrielle expected her to do was smile.

"A new day has begun my friend, come and together we will greet it." Chahanpi held out her hand.

"Your hair—"

"It is our way of showing grief. As the pain passes, so will it grow."

"Why would you want to spend time with me? How could you?" Gabrielle glanced away, ashamed, guilt ridden. Her own mother hadn't forgiven her for her brother's death. How could she, in such a short time?

"Do not blame yourself, for I do not."

"How could you not blame me? If I hadn't been stupid enough to follow Little Wolf—"

"There is no blame, as there is no knowing when the Great Spirit calls a person to his home. Just as the winged birds above, my loved one has flown to a higher place and as does the winged ones, he too shall return." Chahanpi's voice was soft. Her words were filled with love and promise.

"I will see him again. He will visit me in my dreams. I will hear his voice in the music of the river where we spent many a day, and the Great Spirit will send his presence to me on the arms of the wind. So do not let your heart be heavy for me."

Gabrielle shook her head. "No. You don't understand. I seem to cause nothing but heartache to those around me."

Hadn't she managed to destroy the life of her tutor, Jeffery? Last time she'd heard, the only job he could get was bussing tables at some greasy spoon somewhere in Iowa. And her brother, Charles. God. He was five years old when he died. What good was traveling back in time, when future actions repeated themselves in the past? She had hoped that things would be different. "Even here I've managed to ruin your life and Two Moons. I'm better off alone. And you'd be better off without me."

Chahanpi placed a warm hand on Gabrielle's shoulder. "I have made you my friend. In Lakota, to make a friend is the hardest. Once you make a friend, a friend never leaves; not when sorrowed, not in anger, not even in death."

With a light squeeze to Gabrielle's shoulder, Chahanpi dropped her hand. "So my friend, do you follow me? Our warriors have gone to fight with Crazy Horse against Gray Fox. Soon they will return and we must welcome them."

"Did you say Gray Fox?" A heart stopping realization hit Gabrielle head on. Gray Fox was the Native American name given to General Crook. "All this time Two Moons has been fighting in the Battle of the

Rosebud." Her words, more a statement than a question, slipped from her mouth. She had told Two Moons to go and fight. She'd read more than thirty warriors died in that battle. Over sixty were badly wounded. She never dreamed ...

"My God. He could be dead." Her voice cracked. She stared down at the ground seeing nothing but a shallow grave.

"Two Moons? No." Chahanpi shook her head. "He is our finest warrior and has strong medicine. Do not fear for him."

Fear for him? She was furious—at herself—at him. Gabrielle snapped her gaze from the ground. He had left without a word. And she hadn't warned him. No. Hadn't begged him not to go. She couldn't lose him. Not now, not when she was just beginning to realize how deeply she cared for him. She needed him, wanted him for reasons that didn't make any sense.

"I know what is in your heart." Chahanpi's words were soft and filled with compassion.

Gabrielle turned her head to find Chahanpi studying her.

"Your path has been joined with Two Moons' for a purpose. He is a lonely man. His spirit is broken. A hurt man is full of anger and revenge. Soften his heart. Make him walk down the path of life with you. You can open his eyes and make him see he is not alone. It is up to you, with your strong medicine to heal his wounds."

A dog howled. The throbbing of the drums boomed throughout the camp. Its pulsating rhythm increased in tempo, pounding like her racing worried heart. She drew her gaze away from the drums and tried to focus her attention back to Chahanpi's words.

"Make him see through your eyes that he cannot and will not survive in this changing land if he does not let go of the demons burning in his heart. Teach him to forgive and to understand. The gods have brought you together. They smile on their angel, do they not?" Chahanpi questioned. "I do not believe they will pull you apart."

Angel. Angel of hell, maybe. Gabrielle wound her fingers through her hair. She knew so much and what could she do? Could she have stopped Two Moons from fighting? Not likely. "Do you know what's in store for your people? They are fighting a battle they cannot win. How can you ask me to make Two Moons forgive and forget when right now, I don't know if I can?" She sighed frustrated. "My people are destroying your way of life and that is something I never could condone. There are no excuses for the way the whites have treated you. What can I say to Two Moons?"

Dark eyes, full of knowing and wisdom met Gabrielle's. "We

cannot change the setting sun. We cannot change our destiny. Though I am saddened, I must survive. We all must survive."

She did see. Gabrielle's heart ached for her. Chahanpi did know where her future lay.

Chahanpi continued, her expression, one of controlled pain, one of tolerance. "We must keep our stories and our ways alive for our children, so that their children and their children's children will learn and understand. This is what will keep my people's breath alive long after you and I are gone."

Rumbling like thunder, a drum resounded, echoing off the distant mountains.

"The sound you hear is the heartbeat of mother earth, the heartbeat of my people. It must continue to be heard."

Chahanpi paused for a moment. Her gaze roamed the village and lifted beyond to the open plains. "The white man may rob us of our home, but he will never take away our pride." She looked back at Gabrielle. "Pride will be our war shield against them. Two Moons, has a lot to teach our children. You must make him see that."

Gabrielle let out a long sigh. "I don't know if I can." She raked her fingers through her hair. "I'll try."

FOURTEEN

The Long Knives were huddled around a smoky fire drinking their coffee when the Sioux and Cheyenne attacked. They descended upon the unaware soldiers like an angry swell of hornets. A wild war whoop pierced the still morning air. Crazy Horse mounted on a buckskin-and-white pinto, was in the lead; Two Moons, was right behind.

"*Hoka hey!*" He screamed the battle cry at the top of his lungs. It felt good to scream. Anger like a raging river coursed through his veins. Revenge tasted sweet upon his lips. If Shadow Elk could not be here to fight by his side, then he would fight for his brother.

Horse and man charged forward as if on wings, racing down the grassy ridges, leaping over rocks and small clusters of yellow flowering cacti.

The soldiers heard their cries and looked up. Startled, they dropped their cups and grabbed their weapons. Man bumped into man as they ran around in confusion. Their shouts of warning could be heard over the gunfire.

Two Moons set his arrow to his bow and let it fly. With a swoosh, the arrow found its mark. The blue-clad soldier fell to the ground. Before the arrow's feathered end barely left his fingertips, he placed another upon the sinew string.

"That one was for you, my brother," he yelled, as he rode up to his kill. He jumped off his horse and hunched over the Crow warrior. With a flick of his wrist he sliced off a piece of the warrior's hair. Two Moons dropped his head back. He clutched the scalp tightly in his palm and raised it to the sky. His shrill cry rose above the roar of gunfire and the buzz of flying arrows. Shadow Elk's name rose to the sky.

He knew not the name of the warrior whose arrow had pierced his friend's heart. His inability to find the one responsible lay heavily on his shoulders. He blamed Blue Eyes, but had no right to. His brother's death had not been her fault, only he had been too angry at the time to see that. Two Moons tucked the scalp under the band of his breechclout then swung himself up onto Anpo Wie's back.

Men swung lances and guns in all directions around him. Horses neighed and ran into each other; some fell then rolled. Panic-stricken men struggled from beneath the heavy animals in fear of being crushed, while others tried to find cover beneath them. Flying dust and gunsmoke as thick as fog darkened the sky, making it difficult to see. Two Moons lost track of all time and feeling as he wielded his club and buried his hatchet. He would not "count coup" today. He had not the need to prove his courage by striking his enemy with his "coup stick". He did not want to leave his enemy alive just for the honor of it. No. He wanted nothing but revenge; revenge for that part of his spirit, which had died beside his brother and could never be replaced. Today many *Upsaroka* warriors would feel the sting of his arrows.

The battle raged around him. Gunfire roared. Smoke wafted in his eyes making it difficult to see.

Roy's arms flailed about him as he fought off his opponent. They struggled back and forth strength against strength. The screams of the dying, the clashing of metal bayonets against metal musket barrels and the buzz of flying arrows filled his head. He looked down at his hands. They were covered in blood. He reached out …

… and gripped the sides of the hammock. Awake and visibly shaken, Roy stared up at the patch of blue sky peeking at him through the thick pines. He swung his legs over the hammock's side and sat up.

What a nightmare. He wiped the sweat from his brow and took a deep calming breath. Damn. He never should have lay down, not with all the talk of the past and Indians. He should have walked to town like he'd wanted to. He should be looking for Gabrielle. He'd never find her stuck here in the middle of the woods. Where the hell was she?

He rotated his stiff neck. At one point in his dream, he'd felt Gabrielle's presence in his thoughts. Hell, lately she was always in his thoughts.

Threading his fingers through his hair, he rubbed his scalp. God. It felt as if he had actually been there. The thirst for blood had felt so strong. The sounds, the sights, the anger …

The hinges on the back door squeaked. John Raven Wing stepped from the house. Roy stood as the old man ambled over.

"I had the most vivid dream."

"The old ones say that dreams are visions into other worlds. So I trust you had a good journey."

Roy rubbed at his chin. Why had he opened his mouth? He didn't want to hear this, not now. For over an hour he'd lain awake debating the question of reincarnation—questions that could only be answered by more questions, nothing factual, nothing proven. And nothing he wanted to believe.

He glanced at his watch. "Look at the time. It's five o'clock! I can't believe I slept the whole day away." Roy glanced back at his host. "Please forgive my rudeness."

John waved his hand before his face. "No need for apologizes, but you have missed your ride. My friend has come and gone."

"What? When? Why didn't you wake me? It's imperative I get into town."

"Tomorrow is another day. So besides, tonight we will have a fire, we will smoke and talk."

The taste of annoyance tipped Roy's tongue. He clenched his jaw. "Look, you've been a gracious host," he said, his words calm, though exasperation splintered his thoughts. "But I'm in the middle of a story. I can't just sit around doing nothing. My boss is expecting a phone call ... my lead could be miles away and—"

"Your lead is that woman, yes? So I have seen her."

Bingo! A moment of triumph brightened his mood. He'd been right all along. He knew the old man had recognized her picture earlier. What else did he know but wasn't saying?

"You are right, the miles that separate you are many, unless you listen to my words."

Oh, he was going to listen all right. He was going to find Gabrielle and go after her. "You know where she is then?"

"I have known all along."

Roy's chest tightened. With a level stare, he studied John's weather-bronzed face. "OK." He clasped his hand on John's shoulder. "You talk and I'll listen."

John paused a moment, pulled out his pipe and lit it. "You are comfortable behind a camera. I sense you are really good at what you do."

"I love my work."

"Yes, you have a fine eye. You get so totally absorbed in your picture you forget all that goes on around you. Is that not so?"

"Concentrating is a big part of taking pictures."

John grinned that knowing smirk that made Roy's mind spin. "So you become a small part of the bird you are photographing or that sunset. So you traveled to a different plane of reality for that moment. Mind projection can be strong medicine."

"Mind projection. Sort of like when you get involved in a good movie, or book and tune everything else out?"

John nodded. "Dèja vu. Has that ever happened to you?"

"Yes."

"Why would a man be afraid of the water if he never waded in it? Could it be he drowned in a past life? Why the feeling that you know someone from somewhere, but you were just meeting them for the first time? So perhaps it is because you knew each other from before this place, this plane of reality."

He took a puff on his pipe. "So by learning from the past you get to do it over, so you can get it right the next time. Only by resolving the past can you move onto your future. So you are a stronger person now?"

"Yeah." He'd been liquor free for years now and more determined then ever to make something out of himself.

"Good. Then you will be ready to meet your soul mate."

"Soul mate?" Roy ran his thumb across his chin. "As in destined to be together, forever?" That was an interesting thought. "I guess I don't get a choice in who that may be, right?" His vote went to Gabrielle.

"Since her life and yours have been joined together in the past, you will know her when you meet her. You will feel the connection. So you will know."

A heavy hot wind blew, fingering Roy's hair as he recalled the strong chemical attraction he'd felt surging between the two of them. Gabrielle had felt it too. Gabrielle, with those crystal blue, topaz eyes and skin like cream. Gabrielle, his soul mate, what a delicious thought.

The sun set low behind the jagged top of the mountain. Shadows crept along the broken ridges, softening the landscape, kissing the cliffs with burning violets, oranges and blues.

Soon darkness would settle in over those woods and without the lights of the city all would be black. Jet black like the color of her hair. He wished Gabrielle would give him a chance. All he really wanted was for her to get to know him better. He wasn't the playboy everyone thought he was. Not anymore. At thirty-two he had finally grown up. Maybe it was time to make room in his life for a soul mate, someone he could spend the rest of his life with. Besides, somehow it just felt right when she was near.

"Where can I find this woman?"

"So love, like a person's soul, is not limited to the physical boundaries of time or space. If a person dies, does your love for them die with them? To love someone else, you must know yourself. So you will open up your eyes and see beyond what is your nose and you will learn to listen to the secrets within you. That is where you will find her."

* * *

The sun sat low in the sky as Two Moons stood on the mountain and prayed. Oranges and yellows spilled over the valley below covering mother earth in a robe of warmth.

The feathers dangling from his lance fluttered in the wind as he raised his arms to the sky and gave thanks to the spirits for another battle won, for the chance to take in their breath one more day. He lowered his arms and placed his lance to the ground. Tonight the victory fires would burn high. The drums would sing, the ground would quake with the pounding of feet and he would be ready.

He strode over to Anpo Wie, reached inside the cylinder rawhide case and pulled out the small buckskin pouch that held his paints. He would cover his face with the black grease of the buffalo and charred ashes, for the fires of revenge, no longer burned in his heart. He clutched the bag in his palm, walked into the shadow of a large pine and began preparing himself for his journey home.

Blue Eyes would be there waiting. He knew now that she had not run away; knew Shadow Elk's death was not her fault. But the emptiness he had felt seared his gut. The pain was so strong, he had let anger cloud his judgment.

Two Moons smeared his face with grease then wiped the black from his hands. He striped his upper arms with the yellow earth he had found beside the yellow-stoned river. Eleven stripes, one for every horse he was bringing back to his lodge. Perhaps he would save the gentle white mare for Blue Eyes. He could carve her a horn-framed saddle from a cottonwood tree. Covered with cloth and softened with the wool from the buffalo, her "seat" would find more comfort. He smiled. A vision of soft round buttocks entered his mind.

He dipped his finger into the crimson-colored paint and dragged it across his forearm.

Blue Eyes had been hot with anger....

He drew in a ragged breath and closed his eyes. The fresh earthy smell of green moss and pine needles filled him. A gentle breeze tickled the leaves.

Like warm honey he would soften Blue Eyes until she melted beneath the fires that inflamed his body.

The touch of his fingers, upon his skin as he blazed a trail of wavy red lines across his chest—down his stomach, down past his hips—made his blood heat. His finger froze above his groin. He wanted her. Wanted her more than any woman he had known.

Again a heavy hot wind blew, fingering his hair, caressing his lips. Desire built like the gathering storm, engulfing his body, engulfing his mind.

He looked to the sky as a ray of sunlight broke through the clouds. A tremor, a hot ache of longing surged through him igniting his soul.

Two Moons could hear Shadow Elk's words drifting through the humid air: *Only she can bring the sunshine....*

He dipped his slick, wet finger into the sacred color of the sky. "Let the dark blue spirit color, the red of the earth and happiness, be as one."

He encircled his one nipple with blue, the other with red. He did not care if Blue Eyes was or was not of the spirit world. He slipped two fingers into the blue paint, then the red. He did not care if she thought like the white man ...

The colors mingled, engulfed his tips like warm, wet sap. He would teach her his ways.

He brought his hand to his chest, feeling the liquid drip down his fingers as he drew a connecting line between his circled nipples.

"Oh, Great Spirit who lives in the sky—forgive my weakness. I am of this earth. I am but a man of flesh and blood, blood that runs hot for the one with the blue eyes. Forgive the weakness of this warrior, for no longer do I seek the woman of my vision. It is of the blue-eyed one I seek."

His eyes and ears to the sky, Two Moons listened for their word, waited for the wrath of the great spirits. All was still, but the creaking of the tall pines overhead and the swishing of Anpo Wie's tail as the animal fought off an occasional fly.

So be it. Two Moons wiped his hands on the grass then stood. With, or without a blessing, fury, or silent, nothing would stop him from claiming her.

The mounted warriors rode into camp like a group of proud peacocks strutting their stuff. Gabrielle stood up on tipped toes, watching, waiting. She chewed her lip. Anxiety flipped somersaults in her stomach. Her head bobbed back and forth as she stretched and swayed, trying to see over the heads of the warriors at the front of the line, trying to catch a glimpse of Two Moons.

One by one, horses adorned with brightly beaded and quilled saddle blankets, carried their owner back into the waiting arms of their loved ones. And there was still no sign of him.

The line seemed endless. The waiting ... torturous.

She dug her fingernails into her palms. Her bottom lip burned from constant chewing.

Finally, she saw him and her heart seemed to leap from her chest. She'd recognize that blackened face anywhere. He wore an eagle feather, like a regal crown upon his head. Straight-backed, he sat tall in his saddle and held his shoulders high. His muscular arms and chest, now striped with paint, bulged as he held his war shield and lance up at his side.

His eyes swept over her face, and uneasiness swept over her mind. What if he was still angry with her? The composed expression on his face did little to tell her of his feelings. Did he still blame her for his friend's death? How the hell was she supposed to help him understand the white world when the blood of their soldiers was still warm upon his hands?

Two Moons got down off his horse, strutted over to Standing Bear and She Who Sings and handed them a fist full of scalps.

Gabrielle cringed. The practice of taking scalps had been a part of the Native American culture as well as the white culture for the era, but she couldn't stop the disgust welling in her throat at the sight of those bloody locks.

She watched him approach her. Had he forgiven her? The question stabbed her heart and tipped her tongue.

"I see you came back in one piece," Gabrielle said, breaking the silence. His firm chest greased and painted, had a sheen to it. Her hands itched to touch his smoothness, to feel his warmth.

He glanced down. A smile tipped his lips. When he looked up, amusement glimmered in his eyes. "One piece? Yes."

"Well, you're lucky."

"Luck had nothing to do with it. I am a warrior. I am the best. My medicine is strong. Luck." He shook his head. "No."

"You sound like a puffed-up rooster, with all your self-praise." And he looked magnificent. Her heart fluttered. The smell of paint and grease brought back memories of her paints and brushes, her work and her home. She could be dropped back there anytime. All desire faded. She was crazy to love him.

"It was a stupid thing for you to go and fight. You could have gotten yourself killed." She turned her face from his glance not wishing to see the anger she knew would ignite in his eyes.

He grabbed her arm. His hold, like an iron clamp, got the message across. He was clearly annoyed and with good reason. He would think her a coward.

"What foolishness is this? Do not look away when I speak. Look at me."

She lazily turned her head.

Anger threaded the lines of his chiseled lips. "Would you have me dishonor my people, my family? If not to fight and earn respect, what then? Your talk is that of a coward."

"I am not a coward. You tell me where it is written that a friend has to die for another. Or that a friend has to suffer for another."

All her anxiety over Shadow Elk's death, Chahanpi's loss and her fear for Two Moons' life, came rushing forth like the uncontrollable waves of an angry sea. "I don't see it written anywhere! All the scalps in the world aren't going to bring Shadow Elk back. All those men killed. What of their families?"

What about hers? Grandpa Jackson had one more week to live. Thanks to Two Moons' interference, she hadn't been at the fort long enough to talk him out of fighting.

Two Moons jerked his hand away and pounded on his chest. "It is written here. It is our way—the way of the people. A man protects the ones he loves, no matter that his life is in danger. The ones with the pale faces rape and steal what is ours. Always there will be hatred between us. But you with your white thinking and talk of cowardice will never understand. I should have left you at the fort."

"You're right. You should have. I didn't ask to leave," she snapped.

"Yes and with good reason. Had I not come when I did, you would be right now sharing his pallet."

"What are you talking about?"

"Do not play games with me. I am only sorry I did not find your lover on the battlefield today with the rest of your precious Blue Coats."

Lover? She stared. What lover?

"It would have been an easy fight for me to win, no contest," he boasted. "Old men belong protecting the women and children, not on the battlefield."

He was talking about Grandfather Jackson and he was jealous. It was almost comical. "He's not that old and he's a good soldier." *Stew on that for a while, why don't you?*

"Next time I see him we will see who is stronger."

"If you kill him, I will never forgive you." What if Two Moons' arrow had caused her grandfather's death? Could she still love him? Could she forgive him? Anxiety churned in her abdomen. It couldn't happen, that would place Two Moons and his people at Custer's Battle Field and there was no talk of going there. She pushed the thought from her head.

Her grandfather, however, was still in danger; she had some unfinished business back at the fort. "If you think me difficult now, just wait. Your life will be a living hell. Take me back. You don't want me here."

"Would you have me risk my life? Was not the death of one man enough?" he spat.

She cringed. What could she say? He was right. She wouldn't let him take that chance. But Grandfather Jackson ...

Two Moons slammed out his arm in a dismissing gesture. "Go. Go back to that old man you call your lover. I want nothing more to do with you."

"Fine! I will." She turned away not waiting for an answer, but got one away.

"Fine." The word hit her back as she stomped away.

FIFTEEN

$\mathcal{T}$ he edgy wind roared, gushing softly, then angry as Gabrielle stomped away from the village. Leaves swirled around her, rattling against the parched ground as she trod her way through a dense cluster of pine and cottonwood trees. It was getting dark. Already steel gray clouds hung heavy in the sky.

She paused to catch her breath then closed her eyes. The wind fanned her hair, blew harshly against her cheeks, cooling her anger. For what seemed like over a half hour she had walked aimlessly through the forest, trying to gather her thoughts, trying to compose herself.

She hadn't meant for it to be this way. The last thing she wanted was to fight. Hell, what she really had wanted to do was run to Two Moons with open arms. He had been jealous. The thought brought a smile to her lips. He thought Jackson was her lover. Good. Let him stew in his jealously.

A light drizzle tickled her nose and kissed her cheeks, mingling with the tears in her eyes. She sniffled and wiped her face with her hand. Hell. Then again, who knew? She might be the one to go first. Did she really know how much time she had here?

Maybe she should go back and apologize. A branch snapped behind her. Startled, she whirled around.

"Curly!" The harshness of her tone surprised the boy. His shoulders jerked. His brows shot up. Then his face puckered and his lips turned into a frown.

She hurried to his side and knelt before him. "It's OK. I'm sorry. It's just that you frightened me."

Perhaps it was the soft gentle tone of her voice that made him relax, but he answered her with a big smile. She gathered his hands in hers. "I don't know what you're doing here, but I'm sure someone's out there looking for you right now. Come." She straightened. "We'd better get back; it's starting to rain."

She pulled Curly after her, but the boy protested by digging his feet into the ground. He broke free and turned from her.

"Curly!"

Curly ran from her just as a bear broke through the trees.

The beast stood up on his short thick hind legs, towering over Curly like a huge monster. Powerful jaws opened as he growled. His loose skin and long shaggy fur, shook as he pawed the air. Curly stopped short.

Gabrielle stared wide-eyed. She swallowed with difficultly then found her voice. "Don't move." Panic tore through her as she realized Curly wouldn't understand.

He stuck out his chest and squared his shoulders. His small voice full of valor, he yelled and feigned an attack.

Straight-backed, her movements slow and stiff, Gabrielle slouched down until her fingers touched dirt. Groping around, her gaze still on the boy, she gathered up a fist full of rocks. Slowly, she drew herself up.

The beast took a step forward.

She drew back her hand. For a brief second she paused. Would her actions aggravate the animal further? Would he attack? Curly was so close she wasn't sure what to do.

The beast's low angry snarl vibrated down the length of her. The downy hairs on the nape of her neck rose. Her breath held. Afraid to move, afraid not to, Gabrielle slowly turned her head and glanced behind her.

Curly's pet wolf stalked past her, advancing toward the bear.

A sigh of relief broke from her lips. The bear shook his large-snouted, black head as he eyed his attacker. The wolf made his way closer. He snapped and snarled; then without warning, the bear slammed out his massive paw hitting Curly's side.

Gabrielle screamed. Seething with fear and hysteria she hurled the rocks with all her might. The rocks pelted the bear's face; the rain began to pelt hers. The wolf attacked. As he bit and pulled at the bear's front legs, Gabrielle ran to Curly. He lay silent, his eyes closed. Angry red welts and blood covered the side of his face and shoulder. She stifled a cry and gathered him up in her arms.

It started to pour.

She struggled to her feet barely aware of the sounds of snapping teeth and angry growls.

Finally, be it the pouring rain teaming down upon them, or the fierce attack of the wolf's unrelenting fight, the bear had enough. Gabrielle watched with relief as the beast turned his heavy-set body around. She held her breath—held her glance—until the short stumpy tail disappeared into the darkness of the trees. Only then did she dare to move.

Gabrielle ran with the wolf by her side. She had no idea where she was going; had no idea what she was going to do. Curly lay limp in her arms. Neither the rain plummeting down upon his face, or her pleas to waken, stimulated a response. Her leather dress stuck to her legs as she ran. Her moccasins sank into the muddy ground.

Visions of her father trudging through the pouring rain carrying her brother, struck her thoughts. She fought her tears and continued her onslaught past branches and fallen logs.

Several times she hesitated, glancing left, then right, searching in vain for something, anything that looked familiar.

Nothing did.

She heard the wolf's bark before she saw the small opening. The hole in the curve of the slope looked no bigger than a few feet wide and God knew what was inside, but she didn't care. With difficulty, she struggled to her knees and crawled in after the wolf. Dark and damp, the smell of wet dirt assaulted her nostrils. Her head hit the ceiling as she raised up on her haunches and twisted onto her backside.

Cradling Curly in her arms, she crossed her legs before her and tried to make herself comfortable. The wolf nudged his way to her side and slid his head under her arm.

Memories came flooding back—memories of her brother falling, of her screams; hours of waiting, of wondering if he was alive as she lay on the cavern's floor, peering into the dark hole below, praying her younger brother lived. He hadn't.

The memory of that day still haunted her. She'd been eight years old; her brother, Charles, five. It had been her fault then, as it was now. Charles had followed her into that cave so many years ago.

And now, Curly had followed her into the woods.

Tears fell, mingling with the droplets of water streaming from her hair. Rain slashed down hammering the ground outside. She hated the rain. It had been raining that day when her tutor, Jeffery, following after her father, had carried her from the cave. She could still hear her mother's screams above the thunder. And the tears—so many tears.

A suffocating sensation tightened her throat. The walls around her seemed to close in from all sides. Curly's limp body felt so cold against her arms. She hunched forward and wrapped her arms tighter around him.

"I'm sorry." The words choked her. "So very sorry."

Empty words said so many years ago. Words that couldn't bring her brother back from the dead, or erase the guilt burning in her gut.

Her mother had never forgiven her for that day. So many lives had been ruined because of her. Jeffery had been fired. She never saw him again. Then the fights started. Her brother's death drove a wedge between her parents that no amount of therapy could tear down. Her father left in the midst of a raging battle between the two. That was the last she had seen of him. And her mother ... hated her.

"Dear God, please let him live. I'm begging you. Listen to me. Please listen ... this time." She rolled her head forward and opened her eyes. Tears blurred her vision as she stared down at the small child cradled in her lap. "Please listen ... this time."

She began to rock back and forth. Her teeth chattered as she prayed and begged and rocked. Uncontrollable tears fell. Tears shed for a brother whom she'd barely known—tears of guilt, tears for forgiveness and tears shed for the child in her arms. "Don't die ..."

From the distance, she heard a voice calling. The wolf ran outside.

She jerked her head up. "We're in here!" She sniffled and wiped her cheeks with the back of her hand. Thank God. They had been found. She glanced back at Curly, at the shallow rhythm of his chest. There was hope....

She heard the footsteps moving closer. "Over here," she called out once again. She uncrossed her stiff legs. "We're—"

Little Wolf's body filled the space before her. His gaze rested on Curly then shifted to her.

A moment of panic swept over her. Little Wolf's betrayal still tasted sour upon her lips. "Are you alone?"

"Yes."

"Go get Two Moons."

"Give the boy to me." He made a small gesture with his right hand. "Or he will die."

"No."

"You must trust me." Little Wolf knelt down before her. "Two Moons and I were not always enemies. The coldness in our heart was not always there. I wanted to marry his sister."

"What happened between the two of you?"

He held out his hands. "Give him to me and I will tell you."

Though hesitant, she placed Curly in Little Wolf's open arms then crawled outside. She got to her feet.

A frown etched Little Wolf's brow. "We were young. Two Moons was my best friend, like a brother." A twig snapped beneath Little Wolf's weight as he stomped upon the ground. His dark bony face set in a malicious expression, he continued. "Always he had to be better than I—a better hunter. His arrows flew further and faster than my own. He was the stronger one; the one who won every game, the one who won the hearts of the women." Little Wolf's voice held a heavy note of bitterness. "The one whom my father wished was his own."

Gabrielle stared. No wonder he hated Two Moons. Thanks to his father, he thought himself inferior. "You shouldn't hate Two Moons for your father's blindness."

"Two Moons could have done differently, for my sake."

"No." She shook her head. "He couldn't. It isn't his way to be what he is not. To pretend to be a weaker man would be in his eyes, a lie." Being the best warrior, fighting his battles and protecting his people made him who he was. What Chahanpi had asked of her, was a losing battle. Two Moons would fight against the whites and never accept their ways. To do any different would kill him.

"Enough. I have said enough. I wish to no longer hear Two Moons' name."

"What about my name?"

Two Moons broke through the clearing. Fear. It wasn't something he let himself feel—until today. When Blue Eyes hadn't returned, the thought of her lying hurt, or worse, had terrified him. Throughout his search he cursed his foolishness. Guilt at letting her go off alone, ate away at him like a gnawing worm. Now, seeing her walking to him made his heart soar.

She crumbled into his arms when he reached her side. He heard the word "bear" but all he saw was her tear-smudged face; all he felt was her shivering against him as he scooped her up in his arms.

"It's my fault—" She hiccupped. "I'm sorry. Curly—he tried to protect me. I threw some rocks ..." She started to cry. "I don't know if he's going to live."

"Shh." He placed his temple against her cheek. "He is not going to die. It is because of you that he will finally start to live." The boy was a fighter. Gentle Fawn's words came back to him. *My son has breath. Go find them. Bring me back my child.* He never knew whether or not to believe in his sister's sight. Her words at times confused him. Her acknowledgment of Curly had been unexpected. Never before had she spoken of him.

Two Moons watched the steady rise and fall of Curly's chest. He would live to see tomorrow. Curly's fight was the spirit's way of bringing Gentle Fawn and her son together. Gabrielle was the spirits way of lifting his own blindness toward that part of them he could not change. "He is in good strong hands."

"You can put me down." Blue Eyes unwrapped her arms from his neck.

"You are fine where you are."

"No. Really. I'm not hurt."

"Cease your talk woman," he commanded sternly. He grinned. "You will not win this battle." A jolt of happiness shot through him as she placed her arms around him once more and rested her head on his shoulder.

"You're my guardian angel, aren't you?" She sighed.

"I do not understand this word."

"You're always looking out for me, like one of your gods."

"I am not a god," he protested. "I am just a man like any other." He stepped over a gnarled tree stump, brushed aside the needled pines with his shoulder as he passed through the heavy wet branches.

"No." She lifted her head and stared into his eyes. "You're not. You are the most extraordinary man I have ever met." Desire shone in her eyes.

His heart pounded against her side. "You showed great courage." His feet were light upon the ground as he walked; his spirit light within his chest.

"I was frightened to death."

"When you stand up to your fears, you show even greater courage."

"So, I'm not a coward anymore?" Her airy, teasing voice drifted between them.

He paused for a moment and studied her carefully, realizing what a fool he had been. She was by far, the strongest spirited woman he had ever known. "I never thought you were."

After what seemed like hours of endless pacing and nail biting, Curly regained consciousness to the sounds of rattles raised in prayers and the pounding drums of the victory dance.

Everyone came to the center of the village to celebrate in their success at the Battle of the Rosebud. But to Gabrielle, it was a celebration of life—for Curly and for herself. For the first time in years, she felt alive. It was still hard to admit and it scared the hell out of her, but the truth was, she was in love. The thought sent her heels spinning in dance, sent her head to the clouds.

And better yet, he loved her. She had seen it in his eyes; she had felt it in his strong embrace, in the way his heart had pounded with hers—he was in love with her.

Caught by the elbow, she was spun around. Strong hands circled her waist drawing her body closer to his. "Soon they will dance in your honor." Two Moons' warm breath fanned her face. Pride glistened in his dark eyes.

"But why? I did nothing."

"It is no small feat to meet up with a bear and to live to tell of it."

The pressure of his strong hand on her shoulder made her heart pound. "Two Moons we need to talk."

"Yes, there are many thoughts in my head."

"I'm sorry I called you a fool. I—I was afraid you weren't coming back and then when I saw you—"

"I am here now. Do not fear for me." He ran his finger along her cheek.

The air around them seemed charged. The deep chanting voices and the hollow shaking of a rattle keeping rhythm with the drums, echoed in her ears.

"About your medicine pouch—"

"I know you are not a thief."

"Then you believe me? So you admit that you were wrong?"

His eyes lifted. "You are not a thief."

Not exactly an apology, but close.

The pounding of the drums and singing voices stopped.

Over his shoulder she could see a dancer step through the circle of people. A bear skin, complete with head and claws covered the man's body, making his face difficult to see. Around his neck and ankles were a band of bear claws. A single drum began to beat.

Two Moons stepped to her side. "Come, it is for you he dances."

The flames of the fire crackled. Two Moons slipped his arm around her, resting his hand at her waist. He ran his free hand up and down her thigh. His gentle fingers slowly traced sensual trails against her body. The heat increased, coursing under her skin, a flush of sexual desire she hadn't felt in years, and never, never so intense. His thumb poised below her breast, he stretched his finger and stroked. Her groin throbbed.

The drum beat. Voices accelerated, pounding, pulsating. Smoldering waves of rhythm came faster and faster, louder and louder. The fevered pitch grew higher and higher until Two Moons' thumb caressed the tip of her breast.

Gabrielle's breath caught in her throat. God, she wanted this, had waited so long. She had believed she'd never again allow herself to feel this kind of magic and now ...

Rock hard, her nipple throbbed beneath his touch. He nibbled her ear. She pressed her back deeper against his chest. She could feel his hardness jutting, straining tightly, swollen against her buttocks. The intense music echoed in her brain, swirling, rising. His closeness, his hot breath and teasing fingers, flooded her with dewy moistness. Her heart pounded as a torrent surge of passion shook; and the rattles shook; and the ground beneath her feet vibrated with the rhythm of music and desire.

Then abruptly the drums stopped. But her heart kept on beating in the pin-dropping silence surrounding them. A woman appeared before the glowing fire. With the grace of a seductress she moved ever so slowly around her partner and he, around her. Again the music sounded slow and easy as both dancers moved around each other like in a game of cat and mouse. The man raised his arms above his head then came down upon the woman, covering her with his massive paws, but to Gabrielle, the dance, more a seduction than an attack, made her limbs quiver and her knees weak.

"You have gained respect in the eyes of my people." Two Moons ran his fingers gently across her cheek. "And you have mine." His voice was husky, low, seductive. "Today you are no longer my slave," Two Moons whispered in her ear.

But she was, more than he knew.

He thought himself incapable of jealousy. Had thought no woman could hold such strong medicine over him but, as Two Moons watched Little Wolf step into the circle, old feelings surfaced.

What of Blue Eyes' lover back at the white man's fort?

He glanced at the woman beside him. He could still see the desire in her eyes; had felt her melt like warm honey in his hands. She wanted him, was ready for him.

He forced away his desire. Fought the urge to run his hands across her body once more, to caress and feel her beneath his fingertips. He wanted more. More than just a willing body lush for the taking, he wanted her thoughts, her mind; for her to understand his way of thinking. So, he would wait. And he would teach her. He was a patient man.

"Little Wolf dances the hoop dance." Little Wolf stepped in and around different willow hoops.

"Each hoop represents part of the family: father, mother, all relations."

Little Wolf wrapped two hoops around his knees, two around his ankles, arms, waist and head. He swung them quickly, twisting and turning, circling the hoops around his body. Then he removed them, drew them together and one by one tossed a hoop out before him.

They watched as one after the other, the hoops returned to Little Wolf. "Each member of the family is their own person, can go their own way," Two Moons whispered, "but only when they are united will they find strength and fulfillment. The old ones say that only when the family is one, can the circle of life be complete."

Tucking himself through each hoop, Little Wolf intertwined and connected the hoops. He looked like a prisoner in a cage; which is where he would personally put him, Two Moons thought with venom, if he ever tried to harm his woman again. His palms were itching for a fight. His blood pumped. Soon he would get some answers, soon, when the dance was over.

He drew his attention to the woman beside him. "Little Wolf holds Mother Earth around him, as all men are one with the forces around them." He studied Blue Eyes' face, lit by the crackling fires throughout the camp, happy to see the deep interest in his words.

"There are many worlds, those above and those below. Many levels, many roads. As Little Wolf steps from one hoop to the other, as he brings each hoop over his head, he is traveling, passing and leaving behind a part of his being in one sphere, moving on through the next, until he steps into the fourth world. The world of the Great Mystery ..."

"*Hambeday*, means 'mysterious feeling'—a consciousness of the divine. So when you are dreaming you are in another place, no?" John asked.

Roy scratched his itchy palm and stared over the blazing campfire, listening as John continued.

"It is said my people possess a great occult power. Our spirit is tuned into a higher level, to the vibes not commonly felt by others. So perhaps it is because we are one with the world around us that we not only live with nature, but are one and the same." John, with a theatrical gesture, placed his hand to his heart. His eyes closed briefly. "So perhaps that is what keeps our spirit sensitive."

Roy shifted his position. Sensitive. That was a word that described how he felt. For the last hour his thoughts had been of Gabrielle. The darkness of the sky reminded him of her hair, the fire flaming before him—of her spirit. He had to find her.

He picked up a rock and hurled it into the fire. Ashes flew and sparks of amber crackled.

"So there are many songs out there. The fire sings, the rocks. Each has a language of its own. The earth sings and you must listen," John stressed, nodding in his direction. "So, only then will you come to know the truth."

A powerful wind from the east swept across Roy's body and with it came a foreboding sense of the unexplained. "I'm not sure what you mean."

"When the spirit comes we don't ask questions. If you don't understand, hold onto it, the answer will follow." The old man's voice was so low, he had to strain to hear him.

"The fire is energy. The flame, like a pulsing heartbeat is spreading energy and awareness within and around you. Let it fill you. Let its warmth, bring comfort ..."

John's voice was quiet, hypnotic, lulling, and an unexplainable weighted down feeling seemed to surround Roy, taking hold. His eyes felt anchored, glued to the golden blaze.

"When you are remembering the past you can only feel the emotions, but can't feel the scene. When you are reliving it, you become completely absorbed. So hear, see, touch, taste and smell the sights and sounds around you."

Roy's thoughts began to spin. The sweet smell of what he could only guess was marijuana, seeped up into his nostrils. Yes, that would explain this feeling of weightlessness, of expansiveness, a disconnection to his body, of floating.

His throat dry, he swallowed then swallowed again. The light of the fire seemed to dart back and forth. Muted flames leapt at him from all directions. He closed his eyes.

A buzzing sensation like a million swarming bees, hovered above—around—beneath him. Vibrations of energy cloaked its warmth over and throughout, in every muscle, every bone, every tissue and every organ of his body. What was real, or seemed to be real, slipped into a crack in time.

"What do you see?" John asked.

Trance-like, Roy answered. "A man—a warrior."

"What is he doing?"

"Staring, watching. There's a ceremony." Peering into his eyes was like looking into the warrior's soul.

"You share the same spirit."

Roy felt the man's longings, frustrations and love, yes love. They shared the same love. And he saw her, through this man's eyes; and the need to wrap his own arms around Gabrielle was so great his heart seemed to tighten and swell like a balloon that only she could burst.

"Gabrielle!" He reached out his arms, seeing her in the distance.

Only she could quell his growing need for her. Only she could make him feel whole. And this he knew, without a doubt.

"So. Where are you now?"

"In a village." He heard himself say. "Surrounded by tepees. I hear drums—music." Droning voices of chants filled his head. Rattles shook. He could taste the smoky fire on his tongue, could feel the night breeze ruffle through his hair.

And a wind from the west took him—took him up to stand above the clouds, looking down over the battlefield, Custer's Battlefield. And there below, where once white slabs of stone had marked the dead, the ground ran red with blood; and the screams of men and the cries of the women filled his head. And then he saw her lying beneath the tree....

"Oh, my god!" Roy gasped, feeling like the air had been knocked from his lungs. "Gabrielle!" The shouted word echoed in his ears. "N— ooo ..."

White lights flashed under the darkness of his lids like popping light bulbs, blinding him. In his reverie Roy felt himself catapulted through space and time. His body jerked. He began to shake. Broken images swirled around like bits of fractured glass. Blending, unrecognizable sounds roared in his ears like a passing speeding train, leaving only the ringing wind and then echoing silence in its wake. He felt himself being sucked down; then a familiar heaviness settled in.

He opened his eyes and stared into the flames.

Something deep, dark and unsettling, embedded itself in his heart.

John's droning voice seemed miles away. "So, she is your semantic link, which has brought the two worlds together."

Physically and mentally drained, Roy slumped back in his chair and let the world of darkness as he knew it, embrace him in slumber.

SIXTEEN

O ther worlds. Traveling through time. In a way that could be what Two Moons was saying. A breeze blew. Gabrielle shivered. He might believe her, if she told him. He might. Maybe he wouldn't think her strange, not if his people believed in more than just a heaven and hell. He had said many worlds. The music came to an abrupt stop.

"Come. Soon the morning will be upon us. You must leave and get some sleep." Gabrielle could hear the controlled tautness in Two Moons' tone. His firm grip on her arm seemed possessive, his manner anxious.

A twinge of disappointment squeezed. Sleep? That was the last thing she wanted. Why the sudden change in attitude? "What's wrong?"

He cupped her chin in his hand, brushed a gentle finger across her jaw. "Nothing. Do not let your heart be heavy. It is not of your concern."

Was he kidding? He wanted her out of there. Why? Even now, seeing his attention focused on her, she got the feeling his thoughts were somewhere else. "Two Moons—"

"Go," he commanded.

"Fine. I'll go." *For now.* She swivelled slowly, teasingly, knowing only too well his gaze rested upon her back. With a voluptuous sway, she headed to his tepee. She reached his tent in a matter of minutes. Without hesitating she stepped behind the hide structure, then quickly doubled back to the dance site.

Peeking from behind still another tepee, she saw Two Moons silhouetted by the fire talking with Kills Pretty.

The sharp knife of jealousy prodded Gabrielle to take a faltering step from her hiding place. She caught herself and held back. She strained to listen to their words, annoyed to hear voices raised in Lakota. Damn! She swore beneath clenched teeth. She wished she understood what they whispered in the shadows.

Kills Pretty pressed her body seductively against his. She locked her arms around his neck.

Shock held Gabrielle rooted. Doubts aroused old feelings and uncertainties. She couldn't be wrong about him. She couldn't. He loved her, not Kills Pretty. So why? Why would he seek Kills Pretty out, when his desire for her had been so apparent? There had to be an explanation.

He'd said she was no longer his slave. What did that mean, that he no longer wanted her? That she wasn't his responsibility? No, there had to be an explanation. She couldn't believe—didn't want to believe—all men were the same cheating ...

Two Moons withdrew Kills Pretty's arm from his neck and turned away with an abrupt twist. Gabrielle could see by his quick steps, by the tautness of his straight-backed body, his clenched hands and tight jaw, that he was mad—gloriously mad. A triumphant smile slid across her face as she watched him walk away, leaving Kills Pretty to sulk in the shadows.

Quickly, Gabrielle followed him, ducking past tepees, darting behind people and bushes. Her gaze glued, her mind congested with questions, she watched him stop before Little Wolf's home. An angry scowl crossed his face. Two Moons wasn't paying a welcoming visit.

"My son goes to fight in your honor."

Gabrielle spun around, startled by Rattling Blanket's voice. "What do you mean, my honor? How do you know that?"

"You belong to my son and thievery is punishable by death."

His possession. God, she hated that. She made it sound like she was a piece of store-bought goods.

"My son calls to Little Wolf. He is telling him to come out and face him like a man. To meet his challenge."

Little Wolf stepped from his tepee. His bare chest barred, his shoulders arched back, he glared at Two Moons as if saying, *I'm not afraid of you.*

"My son says Little Wolf had no right to sell you to the Long Knives. He is challenging him to a fight. Little Wolf has accepted. He has waited many moons for this night to come. He says the ground will grow red ..." Rattling Blanket paused, as if stabbed by sudden grief and despair; then she lifted her chin and continued, "... with my son's blood."

"You must stop them," Gabrielle demanded, her voice shrill.

"It cannot be stopped."

Guilt hammered her brain. Rattling Blanket was right. She did bring Two Moons nothing but trouble. "Please believe me. I didn't mean for this to happen."

Without replying, Rattling Blanket drew her gaze away.

Gabrielle watched as Little Wolf and Two Moons stripped themselves of their leggings. She watched Little Wolf slip his beaded breastplate over his neck; watched as Two Moons removed the silver bands from his bulging forearms. But Little Wolf's arms were just as muscular; his chest was just as solid.

Wearing nothing but their breechclouts and moccasins, both men moved into the clearing to stand beside the fire.

Gabrielle started toward them. Rattling Blanket placed a restraining hand on her arm.

"You must not. My son is a proud man. Do not shame him in front of the others."

They threw both men a knife and a tomahawk. Gabrielle noticed the gleam of light that bounce off the weapon Little Wolf held in his hand.

She guessed it was inevitable, seeing the hatred burning between the two, but she didn't want them to fight over her. No matter what they portrayed in storybooks and on TV, she wasn't thrilled, or honored—not in the least. She was petrified.

Two Moons' attention seemed calmly focused. His brow appeared dry, his composure cool. Hers was about to crumble. She clasped her clammy palms tightly. Sweat dotted her brow.

Kills Pretty stood across from her, her face swathed in uneasiness, her jaw clenched. Gabrielle could feel her pain. They both stood to lose the man they loved. And no one should have to feel this terrorizing fear. No one.

"You will die tonight my brother. Do you not feel the hand of death squeezing your throat?" Two Moons asked.

Circling Little Wolf, he focused on his opponent's face. He stared deeply into his eyes, reading into his thoughts, guessing at his next move.

"Blue Eyes belongs to me. You had no right to decide her fate," Two Moons continued, his voice edged with hostility. "No one steals what is mine."

Little Wolf plunged.

Two Moons jumped back as Little Wolf's tomahawk swooshed through the air, missing him.

"Your blue-eyed one is not worth this." Little Wolf spit.

Two Moons could feel the spittle on his cheek.

"I wish I had ridden her first, before I gave her away." Little Wolf's nostrils flared. His eyes narrowed. "Do not be mistaken my friend. I do not fight over her—"

Again he plunged.

Two Moons swerved to the right.

Swoosh. The blade sliced the air.

"I fight to prove once and for all, which of the two of us is the stronger one," Little Wolf snarled.

They circled like vultures around one another. Each one watching the other; each one waiting for the right moment, in which, to bury his hatchet.

From the corner of his eye Two Moons could see Blue Eyes standing alongside his mother. The fear touching her face cut as deeply as if Little Wolf's blade had pierced his skin. He wanted to shield her from this fight, had tried to keep her away—

He felt the sting upon his shoulder before he saw the blood.

A sneer of triumph twisted up the corners of Little Wolf's mouth.

Two Moons forced a smile above his pain. "Come, try again. See how my blood runs." He gestured Little Wolf closer.

"Come …"

Wheeling his tomahawk above his head, Little Wolf charged.

Two Moons dodged aside as the blade made a long high arc to fall beside him. Little Wolf stumbled forward. Dust swirled up around his feet as he caught himself. He whirled around, only to find Two Moons' tomahawk count coup on his shoulder. Realizing the bravery of his action, anger blazed in Little Wolf Eyes.

"Has the white man's fire water made you slow?" Two Moons asked.

"You fight like an old woman," Little Wolf replied.

The two men stalked each other, each close enough to touch the other. The veins in Little Wolf's neck bulged. "My blade will make you a woman."

They grappled in a fierce, well-matched struggle, but Two Moons thrust his leg behind Little Wolf's knee and sent him crashing to the ground

The knife flew from his grasp.

With a quick dash, Two Moons kicked the weapon from Little Wolf's reach; then threw himself on top of him. Before Little Wolf could rise, Two Moons locked his knees around his hips. His hand pressed deeply into Little Wolf's throat. His knife raised above Little Wolf's chest, Two Moons felt him shudder beneath him. Little Wolf's lips trembled with fear. His eyes squinted shut. His head tilted to one side, he cringed as he awaited the final blow. Disgusted by what he saw Two Moons dislodged his hand from Little Wolf's neck.

"*Henala*," Two Moons shouted. Enough. "You will live, for I do not wish the blood of a coward on my hands." He leaped to his feet and watched in disgust as Little Wolf crawled away, then stood at a distance.

"Leave this place and never show your face among our people again, for you can no longer call yourself a Sioux warrior. And take Kills Pretty Enemy with you."

Two Moons could hear the surprise of murmuring voices, rising around him. "I began to wonder what, other than your hatred of me, would make you do such a foolish deed. Other than a few bottles of whiskey, what, Little Wolf, would you gain by kidnapping Blue Eyes?"

A dead silence hung, as all eyes watched and all ears listened.

"You want my sister and everyone knows how my mother has no love for you. So now I look to Kills Pretty, whom my mother treats as one of her own. Did she promise to convince Rattling Blanket to change my mind about the marriage? And Kills Pretty ..." He turned, directing his words to her. "How your anger must have risen when Blue Eyes reappeared in our village. It was your idea to return her to the fort."

"No!"

"It is true. A moment ago before the fight when we spoke, your words told me of your deceit. When I told you of my displeasure with Blue Eyes, you suggested we give her back to Golden Eagle. *Back.* Only the one who had arranged her abduction with the Crow warrior would call him by name and know they had been together. Did you think I would not search for her? Did you think without her presence I could care for you?" Two Moons shook his head. "Never. So go." He pointed toward the woods. "Both of you. Jealousy and hate are good comrades."

Kills Pretty hung her head in shame. A dull twinge of pity settled in his chest. She had been a good woman. A moment's sadness darkened his soul, but he pushed the feeling aside. Blue Eyes was not safe when she was around.

"Watch your step and look behind you." Little Wolf brushed the dirt from his face and chest. "For I will be following close behind." He spun around and walked stiffly toward the elders, who glanced away as he passed. Women turned their backs on him. Children called him names as they flung pebbles and rocks his way.

Kills Pretty slunk back into the shadows and disappeared.

"Two Moons." Blue Eyes flung her arms around his neck. "Thank God—thank God!"

Her body melted against his and his thoughts reveled in her closeness. He wrapped his arms around her. Her voice trembling, she murmured incoherent words into the hollow of his chest. He could feel her warm lips, her warm tears, against his skin.

"To whose god, do you thank?" he teased.

She drew away. Staring up into his eyes, she smiled. "To yours."

Her words pleased him. Soon she would no longer think in the white man's world.

Her glance dropped to his shoulder and her smile fell. "You're hurt." Lightly she touched his wound.

He grabbed her hand; brought her fingers to his lips and kissed her warm flesh. "I am fine. It is nothing but a scratch."

She slipped her hand from his. "It is not and you'd better let me clean it if you don't want an infection."

"I do not know this word 'infection' but cleaning me ..."

He paused and lightly ran the back of his fingers against her jaw. Her beauty was like the sunlit blossoms of the flowered covered prairies. His shoulder throbbed, as did his groin. He grinned. "Cleaning me makes me think all kinds of interesting thoughts."

A sharp pain shot through his shoulder. Roy awoke with a jerk. He winced. Sweating profusely despite the coolness of the evening's air, he glanced around disoriented. A bright moon shone, illuminating a fire that had long ago burnt out leaving charred gray ashes. He rubbed his eyes then stretched his legs working out the kinks. It seemed his host once again had failed to wake him, choosing instead to find the comfort of his own bed.

What had happened to him before he had fallen asleep? Had he completely lost his sanity? To believe he had lived before as some Indian warrior was absurd.

Old fears swept over him. A picture of his mother back at the institution flashed across his thoughts. His stomach clenched. It had to have been another dream, but he had been awake. No. It was impossible—

He took a step forward. His toe hit a metallic object. He glanced to the ground. It was impossible, wasn't it? He bent over and picked up the flashlight

Then why this nagging feeling he'd shared some kind of karma with this warrior? Why the connection he felt he shared with this stranger from a past century? It didn't make any sense; yet it did. It explained, in part, why he knew Lakota words when he'd never studied their language. And why the sudden interest, fascination for Native American jewelry, when in the past he had stayed away from anything having to do with Indians? And while he thought about it, why had he always felt apprehensive about covering stories about the local natives? Whenever there had been a powwow or a tribal gathering, an unexplainable resistance fell like a barring wall before him. Why? Fear? Fear of what? Knowledge? Fear of the past? Nay.

He flipped on the flashlight and made his way to the house.

The door swung open. A stream of light guided him through the dark as he made his way into the living room. An excruciating pain attacked the left side his chest.

"Damn it!" He stopped short and leaned against the wall. He needed to go a hospital. Maybe he had hurt himself a little more than he'd thought. He took a deep breath, pressed into the pain and straightened.

The beam of the flashlight illuminated the picture hanging on the wall. A chill blasted through him, pricking the hair on his arms. Of all the pictures, this one of the warrior shot through the heart, had a strong effect on him. Fact was he didn't like it. It was way too modern for his taste. He rubbed the sore sport at his breast.

Death. The feeling hit him so strongly. It was as if that picture sent off some strange sense of weird energy.

With an abrupt turn, he quickly moved away to find his way to the couch. The old man had said that portrait represented death and rebirth.

The nagging feeling that Gabrielle was in danger grew with each minute he now paced the floor. He had to get out of here. He jumped up, reached to the table beside him and turned on the switch. If he had to walk to the nearest town to find a phone, he would. To hell with his truck. When the sun came up, he'd be on his way.

A stack of books caught his attention. Restless, he ambled over and scanned the titles. *Reincarnation: We have walked here before,* caught his eye. He picked the book up and began thumbing through the pages.

> *Everything in your life has happened to you before and will happen again. People who have a deep bond in this lifetime have been close to you in a previous lifetime. Love is the most powerful force in the universe and once two souls are united in love, they will always be as one.*

OK, he thought as he moved to a chair and sat. Convince me....

Two Moons slipped his warm calloused fingers between Gabrielle's, and they walked hand in hand back to his tepee.

The soft, amber flicker of the fire's light cast a warm glow around the inside of his lodge. The heat kissed her cheeks.

Their gazes met. She studied his chiseled, dark face. The strong line of his jaw, the rugged proud tilt of his head and the bronzed skin stretched over high cheekbones, sculpted the face of an extremely handsome man. He reached out and gently cradled her cheek in his palm.

"I am proud to call you mine." His low, sensuous, throaty voice quickened her pulse.

She closed her eyes, feeling the silent strength of his comforting touch. He ran his thumb back and forth, caressing her jaw, then his fingers shifted to rest beneath her chin as he raised her face to his. His kiss was gentle, yet left her mouth burning—begging for more. Crushing her to his chest, his fingers caressed her back. He pressed his lips deeper, hungrily tasting hers; then his mouth descended to nibble on her neck. Her knees weakened. A surge of heat pumped through her veins. She dropped her head back. His breath was warm as he ran his tongue along the rim of her ear. The soft moist tip darted in and out, playfully. She heard herself groan as his strong arms lifted her from her feet.

Cradled in his arms he carried her to his fur blanket and gently laid her down. Kneeling over her, his one arm resting at the base of her head, he drew his face closer.

"Your wound. We must—"

He kissed her. "It is nothing but a scratch I barely feel," he whispered softly before he reclaimed her lips once more.

His tender kiss left her breathless. She wrapped her arms around his neck, pulling him closer, needing to feel his driving heat and possessive strength. Her lips parted as he thrust his tongue in her mouth. Consumed by the stroking, velvety moistness of his tongue, her head whirled.

She watched him stretch out beside her and the jagged gash marring his shoulder caused her concern. She stroked him lightly. "I promised I'd clean this—"

"And the thought of your touch upon my skin sets my heart a flame, but it is not a bath I need right now." Again he kissed her. "The flame that burns ..." He nibbled her neck. His fingers played with her hair. "... is not of my shoulder. The fire that burns is much, much lower."

Lost in his intoxicating kisses and the feel of his exploring hands upon her skin, the loud cough from behind them came as a jarring bolt, splintering their passion.

She turned her head to stare into Rattling Blanket's eyes. Her cheeks burning, Gabrielle glanced away. With a tug on her dress, she raised her body from Two Moons' in a desperate attempt to break away from his embrace. But he held her pinned to his chest. His face showed no emotion as he addressed Rattling Blanket in his native language. She could just imagine what his mother was saying. The word *hussy* came to mind.

Finally after what seemed like an eternity Gabrielle watched Rattling Blanket turn and duck outside, leaving the tepee flap open behind her.

"My mother says you must leave my lodge." He planted a kiss on her nose. The dismissive kiss made her feel empty, disappointed by his sudden change of heart.

"I don't understand?"

Gently he urged her off and he sat up.

"Your heart is heavy, is it not?" Lovingly he ran his finger against her cheek. "There is no need. This is a good thing, my mother asking that you leave."

Gabrielle crossed her arms across her chest, already missing his warmth, then glanced away, confused.

Gently, he tilted her chin toward him. "Rattling Blanket says since you are now free to walk among us, you are now accepted as one of my people. And an unmarried maiden does not sleep in an unmarried man's lodge, unless they are family. I do not like this rule, especially now when I ache so deeply for you."

Rattling Blanket was actually concerned about her virtue? Gabrielle bit her lip and stared outside, watching Rattling Blanket's departing steps.

"Do not be mistaken, my blue-eyed one." Two Moons' voice broke with huskiness. "This is not finished between us."

SEVENTEEN

*T*he next day the camp caller rode through the village announcing that they were to pack up and move. Within minutes every tepee was rolled, every cooking utensil packed, every horse loaded down with huge bundles; and every man, woman and child was ready to leave. As usual Gabrielle took her place in line. Two Moons rode up beside her leading a white horse by the reins.

"You will not walk today." He looked down at her. "Come, see what a fine animal I bring you."

He slid from his mount and handed her the reins. "Here. He is yours—a gift. There is no need to fear him. He is gentle."

Hesitant, she reached out her hand.

"I have made sure of this." Two Moons insisted. "You will be safe. I will ride beside you."

She patted the horse's velvety nose and thought for sure the beast would snort or react in some way, but true to his words, the animal stood placid.

"Does he have a name?"

"A name should be given by the one who rides him. You must decide."

She thought a moment, studying the white horse before her.

"Beast. What is your word for beast?"

Two Moons brows rose. Then realizing her thoughts, he grinned. "*Wamakaskan.*"

She nodded. "Wah-mah-`kahs-kahn. I like that. Thank you." *I think.* She stared up at her new gift.

"Come, I will help you up." He lifted her onto Wamakaskan's back.

Gabrielle held the reins tightly, afraid the animal would kick or run, but it didn't. She sighed a breath of relief.

Seeing the anxiety on her face, Two Moons reached over and grabbed the bridle.

It took her a while, but finally she relaxed. At one point Two Moons let go and she managed to steer the animal in the right direction. Pleased with herself and by his thoughtfulness, she smiled. "She is beautiful. Thank you."

"I will bring you many fine horses."

"No. Please. One is more than enough. Thanks. Really."

He laughed and nodded with understanding.

"Look. There." He pointed to a cluster of trees. A herd of elk stood erect. Their antler's held high as if mesmerized by some silent music, they watched with curiosity as the procession passed by. "We call them *unpan*. And there." He pointed toward the sky. An eagle soared above them. "*Wanbli*. What name do your people call them by?"

"Two Moons, I ..." Did he expect her to know the word in Crow? She sighed and shrugged her shoulders. "Eagle." He must be wondering why she didn't speak the language. Maybe she should just tell him who she really was and where she came from. But then what? Have him think her a crazy fool again? No. Not yet. Not when things were going so right between them.

"My father—he is a soldier. I was very little when he brought me to live with him. I don't speak the Crow language."

"This soldier—your father, was he at the fort where I found you?"

"Yes."

"And did he have ..." He waved his hand under his nose. "Hair here?"

She suppressed a smile, realizing where his questions were leading. "Yes."

He grunted.

"His hair is red, like a fire." She lied.

Two Moons' brows creased. A frown tipped his lips. The way he had acted the other day, it would serve him right if he thought Grandpa Jackson was her lover.

"I demand to know his name." Two Moons frowned.

"Who? My father?" Her voice trailed, teasingly.

"You know of whom I speak."

"You're cute when you're jealous."

"I am not jealous." His broad chest expanded as he straightened.

"No? Good. Then I wouldn't tell you that the man you saw me kiss was my father."

"I do not understand. Your words said—"

"I was kidding. My father has brown hair, not red. That was my father you saw."

He looked confused; then a grin slid across his lips. "I think you play with me."

She smiled. "Yes. I play with you."

"That is good. I will tell you that I play with you when I say I blame you for my friend's death."

"No. You meant that. You weren't joking."

"I do not blame you. I am sorry if I caused you any sadness. My heart was also laid upon the ground; my words were said in anger."

She pulled on her reins, reached out and lightly touched his arm. "We both said things we didn't mean. Guilt has a way of doing that."

"You do not have guilt. His death was not your fault. I take the blame."

"Why. You didn't force Shadow Elk to go with you. If I hadn't gone with Little Wolf, he'd still be alive."

"This is not good, this talk. Many words come back and beat me. I wish not to speak of this."

He nudged his horse forward. Following his lead, she studied him. She got the impression Two Moons wasn't just talking about his friend. It seemed they both had a skeleton or two from their past, haunting them.

The thunderous sound of horses hooves and a loud roar of bellowing voices, echoed across the valley. Gabrielle lifted her gaze. Before her was a sight beyond anything she'd ever seen.

Racing over the hills, leaping over low lying bushes, a swarm of Indians merged with Two Moons' people. Riding a gleaming blue-black stallion, Sitting Bull was in the lead, followed by a band of some twenty or so warriors.

Momentarily stunned, she stared, letting the image of him register. He wore a fringed smoke-tanned buckskin shirt, decorated with green porcupine quill work and tassels of hair locks. His leggings matched the dark color of his shirt. His long breechclout of deep red was a striking contrast. Rows and rows of black and white eagle feathers forming a headdress, cascaded down his back and that of his horse's. Picture perfect, in all his stately splendor, she knew the sight of that man would be etched in her memory for the rest of her life.

All feelings of elation over Sitting Bulls' appearance dissipated like a puff of smoke, however, when Gabrielle realized what his presence meant. She jerked her gaze back to Two Moons.

"Where are we headed?"

"We join our brothers at the banks of the Greasy Grass."

The Greasy Grass? That was what the Indians called the Little Big Horn River. All her suspicions of the past few days were right. They were heading for Custer's Battlefield.

"No!" She pulled back on her reins. Her horse stopped. "You can't go there."

"Your words cloud my head. The river is good. There are fine cottonwood trees for firewood and the children look forward to the sweets we make from the trees' bark. I must admit I find myself a bit of a child also, for I feel as they do. I like the sweet juices that run from the trees. It is my weakness. But do not tell my friends." He winked. "I have no weaknesses, aye?"

Despite the radiant smile beaming on his face that made her insides flip-flop, anxiety churned like a gnawing lawnmower. She shook her head. "You don't understand." Exasperated, her voice rose an octave. "In a week, maybe less your people will fight against Custer and an entire army."

In his dark eyes she could see the blunt stare of disbelief. How could she make him understand? What could she say? He was looking at her as if he thought she'd lost her mind. The words were at the tip of her tongue, but she couldn't spit them out.

She flung her hand out in despair. "Do not ask me how I know this. I just do."

"I believe you and your words make my heart light, for I have waited many nights to meet with Yellow Hair again."

"Two Moons, please ... please tell your chiefs it is not a good place to go."

He shook his head. "No. Now your words are foolish. *Tatonka Iyotake*, Sitting Bull, leads us to the rest of his people and we go with him. This is a good thing. Our women wish to meet men, our old ones to share stories with others. It will be a time for games and much dancing. *Hiya*, no, we go. I have much to show you."

Gabrielle knew by the tight-lipped, closed expression on his face she would just anger him if she persisted. He made his thoughts perfectly clear; the conversation was over.

That night she sat cross-legged, outside the tepee she shared with Chahanpi. Staring up at the sky, listening and feeling the space around her, she tried to force the image of Sitting Bull and her anxiety over the future from her mind.

It was at times like this, in the stillness of the night, when a million stars, like diamonds on black velvet filled the sky, when above the chirping crickets she could hear the distant drum and droning song of a single voice in prayer, when she felt totally at peace with her surroundings.

And yet, she felt so torn between both worlds. Knowing the outcome of the battle, the fulfillment of history, knowing what lay ahead for Two Moons people, frustrated her. She was afraid to tell anyone. Perhaps for their sake it was better that no one knew.

She missed the comforts of her own century. Yet found the simple way of life, the openness, the honesty, the almost church-like quality of this world, a comfort. Meeting Two Moons and being in love was the best thing that ever happened to her. Yet, she felt saddened. Who knew when fate would pluck her away again.

All Two Moons talk of family life made her miss her mother for the first time in a very long time. Maybe all these years her mother felt just as lonely.

She glanced toward a group of old men sitting in front of a tepee glowing like a huge golden cone from the small firelight within. She could hear their hushed, murmured voices, see their animated expressions and exaggerated hand gestures as they each took turns telling their stories. She bet her mother had a few stories to tell.

Gabrielle sighed and stared up into the vast endless darkness.

Her world was so far away. She was here as White Swan, walking in footsteps that weren't hers. Every step she took, every word she said, had the power to change the course of history. An awesome responsibility she fought against every day, she managed to push these thoughts from her mind. But seeing Sitting Bull ...

She wondered for a moment if she and White Swan shared the same feelings and fears as well as their bodies. And if she was White Swan incarnate, then where was White Swan's soul, back in 2000? A jarring realization hit. That woman could be causing all kinds of havoc back home; hadn't she done the same?

She closed her eyes. An image of Shadow Elk's cold body flashed before her. Her presence had sealed his coffin.

At the sound of footsteps walking up beside her, she jerked open her eyes.

Rattling Blanket handed her a woven blanket. "It is cool."

"Thank you."

"I have not offered my gratefulness to you. You brought my daughter's child back when I feared his danger. It is I who should thank you." Rattling Blanket sat. "There is a sadness in your eyes. They tell me you think of another. It is not my son you think of, for he brings the brightness to your eyes. Who then?"

In the distance the light melodious song of a flute danced upon the wind, like a sweet voice calling.

"I was just thinking about my mother."

"You miss her?"

"Well ... yes."

"I will tell my son to bring you to her."

I'd like to see him do that, Gabrielle thought with cynicism "He can't."

"She is far from this place?"

"Yes, very far."

"My son should never have brought you to us. It is not right. Your mother's heart must be heavy with sadness."

Would Willimina be worried? Probably. At least she hoped so. Gabrielle sighed. "Do not be angry at Two Moons. It is not his fault that I am here."

"You care deeply for my son and he for you. He is a changed man. His footsteps are lighter. The anger that once clouded his vision is fading. When we talked about his father this night, his words were not as heavy with guilt and sadness." Rattling Blanket, placed her hand, over Gabrielle' wrist. "It is because of you." Her eyes were misty with gratitude. "I think you may be good for him."

Her acknowledgment brought a lump to Gabrielle's throat.

"It is hard for a mother to watch her child struggle, we want to protect and shield our children from hurt." Rattling Blanket chuckled. "It is like that for mothers. It is in our blood. One day you will know of what I speak." She patted her hand.

Her gentle sign of affection touched Gabrielle.

She wondered if her mother felt the same way as Rattling Blanket. All these years she thought her mother hated her, blamed her for Charles' death. Maybe she didn't. Willimina wasn't the warmest person in the world, but maybe that had nothing to do with her. "I only hope I can be as good a mother as you."

"You will do good." Rattling Blanket stood. "Come. Soon the sun will awake and we leave. It is a shorter walk to our next camp, but you will need some sleep."

Their next camp! Gabrielle scrambled to her feet. For a moment she'd forgotten their destination.

"Rattling Blanket ... Thanks for talking with me. I was feeling a little homesick."

Rattling Blanket nodded then stepped into the tepee.

Gabrielle sighed. She didn't know if she felt better after their talk, or worse. Added to her list of growing concerns and confused emotions was the need to talk to her mother and learn once and for all just want Willimina's true thoughts were; only that would mean she would have to leave; and that thought grabbed her heart and squeezed.

All morning, Two Moons thought hard on Blue Eye's words. He had seen the fear in her eyes when she had spoken about their new camp. How did she know there was to be a fight? Had she heard those words at the white man's walled village? Before he spoke his thoughts with the elders, he would need to learn more. Yellow Hair. To meet him again, that would be good.

He fingered the knife at his side then let his hand drop. For the first time, he wished not to think on the Yellow Hair. Last night he had gone to see Black Hawk. He had a flute made for her. Far from their camp and for most of the night, he had learned the courting song he wished to play to her.

He turned and glanced to Chahanpi's lodge where he knew Blue Eyes would be resting. He should go to her, tell her how he felt, tell her of his growing need for her and of his growing love. It had to be love.

He glanced down at the neckband he held in his hand, the one he had made her from the claws of the bear he killed; the same bear she had fought against. He hoped his gift would bring a smile to her lips. She was so beautiful when she smiled.

Two Moons clenched the claw band in his palm. He would return to his lodge and wait. That was where she would find him; that was where he would present her with his offering of love.

His steps hurried, he made his way back to his lodge.

A soft, light voice, raised in song, coming from his place of shelter stopped him dead in his tracks.

That voice. He had heard that voice before, in his vision. He took a step closer, half in anticipation, half in dread. His body stiffened. It was the song sung by his Spirit Woman. A voice he longed to hear. But where that song once offered comfort, it now ripped his soul.

Two Moons' thoughts scattered like the falling leaves. He should just leave, pretend he heard nothing and perhaps she would be gone, for he had no desire to meet this woman of his dreams.

Deep down in his heart he knew he could not walk away. This was the woman *Tunkashila* had chosen for him. And although his heart was heavy, he could seek her out. He tucked the neckband at his waist.

Slowly, with feet that seemed rooted to the ground he pushed himself forward. His fingertips touched the front of his lodge. He hesitated. He closed his eyes, took a deep breath, mustering the will to take a step forward—a step that would forever change the path he was to walk.

With a flick of his wrist he threw open the flap and glanced inside.

Caught off guard by the sight before him, he stared wordlessly. There, before him, sitting cross-legged on his blanket of fur, braiding her long black hair and completely naked, was Blue Eyes.

Their gazes met.

Her hair, kissed by the rays above, shone blue-black. Her skin glistened like honey under the sun.

The unexpected, like a flash of light lashing through the sky, slapped him, and a flood of relief broke throughout. He rushed to her side and dropped to his knees before her.

"It is you." His words seemed lodged in his throat.

"Two Moons are you all right?" Confusion and concern touched her brows and clouded her eyes.

He glanced to her breasts where a circle of gold lay snuggled between her soft mounds. Could it be? His heart raced. He reached out his fingers then stopped. His eyes rose. "Tell me of this gold you wear. From where did it come? I have never seen it before."

She glanced down and lifted the gold, fingering it lightly. "This locket? My grand—my father gave it to me. It is a present for my mother." She brought her other hand over and cracked open the metal. "See, it is a picture of my family."

Two Moons' spirit lifted. A four-sided piece of gold. He grabbed her shoulders and squeezed gently. "Do you know what this means, this gold rope you wear around your neck?"

Happiness made his chest swell—made his heart sing—for the song she had sung only moments ago, now echoed in its chambers.

Gabrielle raised herself from her sitting position to kneel as he did. "What? What does it mean?" She stared at him, startled by his reaction.

Two Moons held the locket between his fingers. A smile lit his face. "I have seen this in my visions. You are the one who brings sunshine to my face, the one that makes my heart sing. It is you, my chosen one whom I love."

Love. Tears sprang to her eyes. Her chest constricted. He said he loved her. She rested her cheek in his hand and closed her eyes feeling his comforting touch, letting that word register in her mind. Cradled against his open hand the veins in her neck pulsated wildly against his caressing thumb.

"*Wiwasteka*, my beautiful woman ..."

She opened her eyes and gazed deeply into his. He thought her beautiful. She had wanted this, to see his desire. She had waited patiently for him, knowing what would happen once he saw her. She had scrubbed her skin until it tingled and then dried herself with fur. A mixture of pulverized columbine seeds and water perfumed her entire body. For what had seemed like an eternity she'd brushed her hair until it shone. She'd waited, letting the warmth of the sun shining from the opening above finger her naked body, preparing herself for his return.

His voice soft, deep and sensual, licked her skin like the heat of a flame. "I burn hot for you," he whispered against her ear.

"And I for you."

"Listen to the language of my heart." He placed her hand against his bare chest. She could feel its rapid thumping.

"My heart, too, speaks your language." She brought his hand to her breast.

Slowly, seductively, his gaze slid downward over her body—a gaze as soft as a caress. The air around them seemed electrified. She drew in a shuddering breath. The fresh scent of pine and mountain mahogany leaves that lay scattered around them, filled her lungs.

He leaned closer, wrapped his arms around her waist and drew her near. She encircled his neck with her arms. His leather loincloth pressed against her hips. His chest crushed her breasts.

"*Winyan. Tanyán yahí yélo.*"

Their lips only inches apart, she could taste his hot, hypnotic whispers upon her mouth. The need to touch him, to feel him touch her was insatiable.

She stared deeply into his eyes, magnificent dark eyes, warm with desire. "I do not understand your words."

"Woman," he repeated. "I am glad you came."

His musky scent intoxicated her. "I love the way you speak. Tell me more."

"You wish to speak my tongue?" His brows rose and he smiled. "That is good. There are many words I would like to say; much I would like to teach you." He leaned forward and kissed her forehead. His long black hair tickled her collarbone.

"This is *ituhu* and this ..." His lips were warm upon her nose. "*Poge.*" He ran his finger lightly across her cheek, then down, trailing a blaze of heat to her mouth. "*Wicai.*" The word was a bare whisper that fanned her face. "And one such as yours was made to be kissed."

His moist, firm lips pressed against hers. His tongue gently coaxed her to let him in—and she did. He tasted of tobacco and sweet grass.

Clinging together they fell back against the fur. On his side and facing her, his broad chest felt smooth against her breast, his flat stomach pressed into her hip.

His kiss grew hungry, urgent and she returned that kiss with the same wild intensity. Breathless, they parted. Up on his elbows he gazed into her eyes, studying her; then he leaned down and kissed the pulsating hollow at the base of her throat. "*Tahu,*" she heard him say before he moved to her earlobe and sucked.

Between each whispered, erotic word describing her body, he planted kisses on her shoulders and neck, down her arm and kissed her knees. His large hands explored her body. His tongue darted in and out of her mouth. She breathed quickly between parted lips. He eased himself lower and playfully planted kisses around the outer part of her breast then worked his way in a circular motion, coming closer and closer to her nipple. She could feel her tips grow hard. "*Azepinkpa ...*" He swallowed the word in his throat. His mouth descended covering her breast.

She closed her eyes allowing herself to be swept up by the rapturous feelings he aroused. Her head lobbed back and she could feel the veins in her neck stretch tautly.

His wet hot tongue stroked and licked her aroused, swollen tip. She writhed beside him. Lifted to a height of passion she'd never known before, a primitive groan escaped her lips.

One hand slid down her stomach to the swell of her hips, then ever so slowly moved lower, skimming her body to her inner thighs. The light stroking of his fingers made her quiver.

When he slipped his thumb up into her moistness exploring her inner folds, she gasped and arched her hips.

"Your body's voice tells me you like this." In and out he teased her, rubbing around in her wetness.

"Yes—oh, yes." Pleasant spasmodic jolts shot through her.

He pressed his palm flat against her groin and thrust his finger forward. "And what does your body say now?"

From deep within warmth spread, pumping her blood, igniting her groin. Her legs fell open. "Don't stop," she murmured. Her hips began to rock.

He leaned over and captured her mouth in his in a kiss that left her lips throbbing.

Wanting to please him as he did her, she reached over and slipped her hand beneath his breechclout. Soft yet hard against her palm, she felt him lengthen under her stroking thumb. God, he felt so big. So hard. So warm.

His fingers stopped their playful onslaught and she watched him untie the strings of his breechclout and slip it off his hips. Staring into his compelling dark eyes she could see the desire igniting their deep endless depths.

He hooked his leg over her thighs, pressing his naked body against hers. His one hip rested on top of hers. His heated erection rested between her thighs. The warmth of his flesh intoxicated her. He nibbled on her neck, cupped her breast in his hand and fondled her taut nipple.

As his fingers worked their magic, she writhed beneath him, eager to feel him inside her. As he roused her passion, his own grew stronger. His rigid tip nudged her, seeking entry and she welcomed it. He hesitated, studying her face. She arched closer. Then with a driving need that matched her own, he bore down, his pulsating hardness filling her.

A quick sharp pain tore through her. She gasped as her body stretched to welcome his enlarged rigid flesh. The burning pain quickly disappeared, leaving only a consuming need to feel him even deeper.

Abruptly he withdrew. "I have hurt you."

Like a slap of cold air, the emptiness she felt startled her. "No."

She was a virgin. The thought floated through her feathery mind then rocketed through her semi-consciousness. The shock hit her full force. Her eyes widened in astonishment as feelings of elation soared.

"You could never hurt me." Her second chance at love! It was like being born all over again. Never had she felt this way when she'd made love with her fiancé.

Not believing her, Two Moons' face clouded with concern. "Perhaps you are not ready for me again."

She wrapped her arm around his neck and drew his closer. "I am ready. I've always been ready."

A devilish smile tipped his lips. "Good." He kissed her nose then rolled off her. "For there is much I wish to bestow upon your beautiful body." He stood then turned. Her gaze followed his lean athletic body; studied the sinewy muscles of his legs and the way his smooth bronzed buttocks pulsated as he walked. He reached for his headdress, which hung over his chair and plucked a single feather from the cloth band. His stride quick, he was back and kneeing by her side.

He brushed the downy feather along her arm. The hair on her arms rose. Its velvety tip caressed the hollow of her stomach. Feverish waves of liquid delight flushed her body. He ran the soft feather up and down her legs, back and forth between her thighs, teasing, tickling her ever so slightly between the soft folds of her womanhood. Her legs quivered. An outcry of delight broke from her lips in a fevered pitch.

Happiness shone in his eyes.

"Please. Please," she pleaded as she stretched out her arms to welcome him closer.

He grabbed her hand and kissed her open palm. "Patience my blue-eyed one. Patience."

He ran the silken feather across her forehead, slowly, sensuously to the tip of her nose. The tickling sensation left by his invisible trail lingered as he brushed her lips. She nipped at the feather, ran her tongue over the satiny plumage then sucked the tip in her mouth. He watched her, his eyes widening. The feather dropped from his hand. The veins in his neck throbbed. His breathing raced.

Unable to hold back the desire she saw coursing through his taut body, he mounted her, his knees bent, his legs between her open thighs. His hands rested by her shoulders. He held his upper torso up so that her taut breasts touched his chest ever so slightly. His elongated shaft positioned close to her groin, made her heart pound. She reached down and grabbed him, ran her hand up and down the length of him, pressing firmly near his root, fondling his stiffness. He groaned and she urged him closer and closer till his swollen tip rubbed against her moistness.

He raised to a sitting position, slipped his hand beneath her buttocks and yanked her to his hardness. She wrapped her legs around his back as he thrust himself deep within her ready flesh.

Waves of ecstasy throbbed, engulfing her as he pumped and rocked against her. She met him thrust for thrust, arching up to take him in. Her hands clenched at her sides. His, cupped the meaty flesh on her buttocks. And as the hot tide of passion raged, rocketing them higher and higher, the world seemed to spin around her, swallowing her up once more.

EIGHTEEN

O ver the next couple days, Two Moons became her world. He was the air that she breathed, the sunshine that filled her life.

He courted her by day, showering her with presents, a silver comb, a spray of flowers. At night, he'd serenade her with his flute.

He taught her the names of the animals and birds. Which plants were good to eat, which were poisonous. He recited Sioux legends about the sky and the stars and how his people came to be upon this earth. He never lost his patience when she failed at a task he tried to teach her.

Yet ...

With each mile traveled Gabrielle's heart felt heavier. One moment she felt cheered by his love; then she would sink to uncontrollable depths of despair, knowing the terrible blight of his people. Knowing the fulfillment of history and the battle that was to come, was like a curse overshadowing their love. Many times she had tried to tell him the secret burning in her chest, but each time she tried they were interrupted by something needing to be done, or someone needing their help.

She heard his husky voice and glanced up. If he was trying to impress her by his appearance, it worked. He looked magnificent. Her breath caught as she stared at him. The long, fringed mustard-colored shirt hanging a foot or so below his waistline shimmered as he walked. The sun's rays played with the multicolored beads and silver hanging disks, creating different light patterns with every turn of his body. The elk's teeth hanging across the yolk of his shirt struck the broad expanse of his clavicle as he stopped before her.

A spiraling rush of anxiety began churning throughout. She had to tell him everything. "Two Moons, we need to talk."

"There is a sadness in your eyes. From where does this pain come?"

"I ..." She hesitated, drew in a deep breath then exhaled rapidly. "There is something you need to know. Something about me I've failed to mention."

He studied her for a moment, shook out the blanket he held then wrapped it around both their shoulders. "Talk is good. We will share this blanket and talk."

She had seen men and women around the camp standing huddled

together under their "talking blankets." A form of courtship and a means in which to escape from the eyes of all those around them, this was their way of having a little privacy; something this village sorely lacked.

A magical moment meant to talk of love and of dreams to be shared, her words might surprise him, but it was time.

"I don't know where to start."

"All that is around us has a beginning." He held her hand in his and stared deeply. "Your words will not change what I feel in here." He placed her hand against his heart.

Biting her lip, she lowered her gaze.

"Nothing," he empathized. "There is nothing that can change my love. Look at me and tell me."

She saw his concern and felt the truth of his words. "I—I come from a very far away place—"

"If you miss your home, I will take you there."

"No." She shook her head. "You can't. It is not of this world."

The lines of concentration deepened along his brows and under his eyes as he studied her quietly. Then he smiled. "Your words do not surprise me. The Great Spirit sent you to me. I saw your coming. You are the woman who fell from the sky. My *winyan wangai*, woman of my visions."

"You saw me in a vision?" He thought she was his vision woman? That's why he held her hair in his medicine bag, as a medicine charm. A couple of time she'd been tempted to ask him about the significance of the items in his bag, but then he'd know she'd looked inside. And that would be as bad as reading someone's diary.

"Yes. I have seen you." He rested his forehead against her. He breathed evenly against her face. Then he drew back and ran gentle fingers against her cheek. "I have been waiting many moons for you. You are my chosen one. I have been a fool not to have seen this before. I saw you coming, but until I saw the gold around your neck, I did not know."

"Why didn't you say something? You saw that locket two days ago. Why didn't you tell me then?"

He smiled a lazy grin. "It was not talk I had on my mind then." He nuzzled her neck with his face then nibbled on her ear.

"Two Moons stop." She crunched her shoulder up then edged herself away. "Not now. We need—"

He straightened. "Fine. Speak."

"What else have you seen in your visions?"

"I saw a man with hair the color of the sun, but he is not the one called Yellow Hair. I have seen him often this man of my visions. I think his thoughts. I feel what he feels. It is through his eyes I see. We are one and the same. This I know; the spirits have shown me."

A moment's silence lingered between them.

"What name do your people call you by?"

"Gabrielle."

Two Moons grunted. "I shall always call you Blue Eyes."

"What do you mean you are the same?" Blue Eyes frowned. "Who is this man? Is he here among us?"

"No. He is not of my world. He is a man who sees the world through a hole in a small black box. He is a man who makes the papers talk."

Two Moons saw the cloud of confusion veil her face.

He ran a gentle finger across her brow. "Your mind is heavy with concern. I am sorry."

"No. I'm fine. I—I just don't understand."

"Many of my people believe as I, that one may be born more than once."

He brought his medicine bag away from his neck and showed her the two crescent moons beaded into the leather. "Although this man and I do not share the same face, he wears my totem and shares my heart."

"But what does all this mean. Why am I here? What's the purpose?"

"I do not have all the answers. We must be patient, the spirits will tell us when they wish." He nodded. "Now it is your turn to speak what is in your heart. You spoke of a battle that is to come. Tell me of this."

She looked hesitant.

He wondered what she was afraid to tell him.

She took a deep breath. "I, too, have seen a vision. I know that in a few days your people will fight with Sitting Bull against General Custer and his army. Many will die, including my father. I have seen this, it is from my world, the future of which I speak. I know I cannot stop this battle, but I beg you to talk to your people. Do not follow Sitting Bull. Perhaps you can spare the lives of those you love so dearly."

"Do you think me a coward that I would hide from a fight?"

"No, but fighting does not always mean you will be victorious." Quickly she rose and came to his side. "To be able to talk and understand other people, is the only way to win. By learning their ways and beliefs, like I have tried to learn yours, that is the only way to victory."

Rubbing his chin, he thought a moment. Perhaps he, too, was to die. Perhaps his family ... "Who will live and who will die?"

She shook her head. "I don't know, but more soldiers will die."

"Good. Then if I should walk the path to the land above I will be happy. It will be a good day to die."

A tear sprang to her eye and twisted deeply in his gut. He reached over to wipe it away.

"Do not lay your heart on the ground for me. This is a good thing. It is an honor to die among those who fight against evil. It is the only way to die. That is the way a warrior gains even stronger medicine for his next life. It is the way I shall die."

"Two Moons please don't talk of death." Her tears began to fall like the rains from above. Each drop running down her cheek was like a knife cutting into his flesh. "I don't want you to leave me alone. They all leave, don't you see ... they all leave."

He brought her head to his chest and wrapped his arm around her, cradling her body to his in comfort. "Shh—I will not leave you," he whispered against her ear.

"I will never leave you," he promised.

"But I was torn from my world without any notice. How do I know it won't happen here?"

"We cannot change the sunset. We cannot change a vision or the path chosen for us. The Great Spirit says this is so. If you must walk the pathway to the skies from which you came, you will but have to look into the eyes of the one with the yellow hair and you will see me there." He kissed the top of her head. "Know this to be true. I will be with you until forever."

They reached the Little Big Horn River—or as Two Moons and his people called it, the Greasy Grass—when the sun was high in the sky.

Gabrielle, her mind congested with thoughts and unanswered questions, walked back and forth like a zombie, from the river with the rest of the women as they hauled the leather sacks back and forth to camp.

How could Custer have missed all this commotion? It just seemed impossible to miss the hundreds of tanned buffalo-hide tepees pitched in seven huge circles, each section over a half a mile in diameter.

She glanced around at the vast open plains that stretched for miles and miles all around her. This was where it had all started. She'd completed the circle. Was this where it would end? White Swan died here. Would she? Had her presence changed anything? If it had and she lived the rest of her days as White Swan, what would happen to Gabrielle? She didn't want to die, but she didn't want to never exist. It was all so very bizarre. And still the question haunted her as to why she was sent here in the first place.

"You are here because of them." Gentle Fawn walked up beside her.

"Who?"

"My brother and the man with the yellow hair."

Stunned, Gabrielle stared, speechless. Was she some kind of psychic mind reader?

"You passed him by many times, but it is here that you will find him." Like a small child her voice was light and playful. "I have seen him many times," she teased. She shook her head. "You never gave him a chance."

Who was she talking about? It couldn't be Two Moons, so who? Roy? She'd never found the time for him, though there was some kind of spark between them. A heaviness centered in her chest, aching like an old wound on a rainy day.

"You will know him when you see him." With a twist of her head, Gentle Fawn walked away as if the conversation between them was over. Gabrielle stared after her, open-mouthed.

"I have been looking for you." Two Moons strolled over and grabbed her hand. "Your work is finished here, for I believe I could use your assistance elsewhere." His deep, smooth voice blew warmly against her ear. "And I believe you will find your new task more to your liking."

NINETEEN

*T*heir eyes met and Two Moons saw the love shining. "Come with me."

Blue Eyes slipped her warm fingers into his outstretched ones and they walked past a group of women making their way to the outskirts of the village to dig up turnips.

As Anpo Wie drank at the river's edge, they rubbed the animal down splashing water both on the horse and themselves. Blue Eyes' laughter like the sun dancing off the sparkling surface, filled him with warmth.

He grabbed her hands and pulled her to his chest. "I am hot and in need of some relief." Slowly, seductively his gaze traveled over her face searing every feature to his heart and soul. Her face he would see forever in every dream, in every sunrise and sunset.

"Maybe you should go for a swim and let the water cool you off."

Like a feather, her lips brushed his ear. He grinned. "The fire that burns is not of my skin, but beneath it."

She pressed her body closer to meet his lips as he brought his mouth down upon hers. Hungrily he drank in her sweetness like a man whose parched soul had at last found quenching nourishment. He kissed her eyes, her cheeks, her neck. He heard her moan. As he aroused her passion, so his grew with every touch, every kiss, every quivering breath between parted lips.

Gently she pushed herself away. "I think ..." She undid the beaded rope around her waist and let it drop to the ground. "... we both need to cool down."

He watched as she slowly pulled the white leather sheath from her body and stood before him naked. Then she reached to his breechclout and untied the string. Silently it fell at his feet. His heart thundered in his ears. Blood shot to his groin like a flaming arrow. He reached for her and she grabbed his hands pulling him after her.

The cool water swirled around his knees. She released her hold and he watched her dive beneath the surface. Quickly he dove after her. He could see her swimming before him. He kicked his feet, hurrying to her side. As he resurfaced, water splashed his face. She laughed. He splashed her back. Again she dove beneath the water. Again he followed her. Reaching out, he caught her arm. She wiggled like a fighting fish. Together they broke through the water to catch their breath. He grasped her tightly under her arms. Sparkling blue eyes held his before her lashes lowered and she dropped her head back. Water glistened on her skin. Droplets traveled down between her firm breasts to taste the sweetness of her golden aroused tips.

He felt himself growing thick and hard beneath the water, felt his need for her squeezing. A mounting tightness of desire consumed him. He lifted her closer, sliding her down against him, skin to skin, wetness to wetness. Trailing kisses up and down her taut, warm neck, she shivered. And the air, water, sun and space around him seemed to come together, as Mother Earth reached out embracing them in her open arms.

She heard herself groan as he entered her, felt the cool water rushing between their legs as their bodies slapped together. Calloused strong hands slid across her buttocks, squeezing, pumping, urging her closer, inviting her to open herself to him, to welcome his jutting hardness into her throbbing, moist folds. Her mind and body seemed consumed by the blazing sun, and the heat of his skin pressing up against hers.

Abruptly he withdrew from her and ducked beneath the water. Probing fingers sought that from which only moments ago had been filled with his thickness. She gasped at the feel of his tongue darting in and around, teasingly. With parted legs she dug her heels into the river's soft bottom and tried to hold her balance as her knees shook and her body trembled. She closed her eyes. His lips slid up her belly. She felt the quick intake of his breath against her as he resurfaced only to plant more intoxicating kisses upon her skin.

Strong arms scooped her off her feet; and she watched the riverbank grow closer as he carried her from the water.

He laid her down upon the soft grass then stretched out beside her. His exploring hand traveled over her thigh, skimming its way inward to seek that part of her pulsating moistness. She gasped in sweet ecstasy. Feather-light kisses along her neck, her face, her eyes, sent tingling waves through her entire body. He shifted his position. Chest to chest, she could feel his aroused shaft against her inner thighs. His eyes gazed down at her, burning with desire. Then, ever so slowly he eased himself lower....

And there under the branches of a big cottonwood tree their bodies intertwining, they became one, to the melodious chirping of the birds above and the soothing gurgle of the swift flowing river.

In the afterglow of their lovemaking they lay in peaceful contentment. Gabrielle, cradled in Two Moons' arms, stared up at the blue sky. He fingered a lock of her hair between his fingers and chewed on a blade of sweet grass.

Suddenly the serenity of the moment shattered with the exploding sounds of gunfire.

Startled, they jerked themselves up to a sitting position and glanced around, confused.

In the distance a big dust cloud rose to the sky. Galloping across the river, a warrior on horseback rode with urgency toward them. *"Oka hey! Oka hey!* The chargers are coming. *Nutskaveho!* The white soldiers come!"

Two Moons grabbed his breechclout. Gabrielle reached for her dress. As they struggled with tense and hurried fingers back into their clothing, the warrior plunged through the river without paying them any notice and continued on his mission of warning.

More shots pierced the air. The loud roar of voices raised with panic, echoed with the booming guns.

"Hurry." Two Moons grabbed her hand. They dashed to his horse. With one swift leap he was on Anpo Wie's back. He snatched her up then pivoted his mount. At a full gallop they charged back to his village.

Chaos and confusion met her every glance. Old men shouted advice at the top of their lungs. Women with no time to strike down their lodges ran in and out trying to gather their belongings. Younger men grabbed their rifles, bows and stone-headed clubs.

Two Moons jumped down off his horse, then reached up to catch her. "You must go with the other women. Gather the children and head for the hills."

His gait shift, his word's rapid, she could barely keep up with him. "No. I wouldn't leave you." She grabbed his arm.

Men, women and children tore passed her, some on horseback, some on foot. An old woman knocked into Gabrielle's side as she stumbled past them.

Two Moons reached over and caught her. "Do not fight me on this."

"Two Moons please—"

Stray horses ran wildly about them. Dust flew into her face, stinging her eyes. Children screamed. Dogs scurried around getting in the way of the rushing hordes.

"I must see to my mother and sister." Two Moons' fingers bit into her wrist as he dragged her with him. "You must go with them."

Suddenly he stopped short. Gabrielle nearly tripped over her own feet. She glanced up. Her gaze darted around searching for the reason why they had stopped so abruptly.

Between the stumbling old men and women who barely hobbled away, between the screams of anguished mothers searching for their loved ones, between the roar of gunfire, a young girl trembled—frozen to her spot, clutching a blanket over her head.

Gabrielle jerked her gaze to Two Moons. The expression of torment etched in his face tore through her heart as she realized, that in that little child, he saw himself.

Simultaneously they jolted forward. Two Moons reached the child first. With one arm he jerked her off her feet. She struggled against him, kicking and wiggling. Gabrielle, realizing the reason for the child's fear, pulled the blanket off the little girl's head, so she could see that it was Two Moons' strong arms that held her safe.

Battle cries echoed through camp. Roaring gunfire grew louder. Hell nipped at her feet as they ran to the edge of the village. She glanced to Two Moons. Silent remorse, dark and vivid, hovered in his hawk-like eyes and she felt his self-condemnation. She knew his torment.

"Give her to me," Gabrielle ordered above the deafening firecracker blasts and clamoring roar. Without stopping she drove her hands under the child's body and wrenched her from Two Moons' arms. "Go back for your family. We will be safe."

He hesitated a moment, studying her face, then nodded, swung on his heels and headed back to the village.

Ducking and dodging, Gabrielle made her way past warriors who leapt onto their skittish mounts as women waving shawls and sticks tired to keep the terrified horses close enough for their men to catch. A clod of dirt hit her arm; one slapped her calf. She ran past a group of women hurling clumps of earth at the charging animals. She bolted up a hill, scurried down the other side and dashed toward a clump of trees where the others hid.

Glancing at the silent faces around her, it saddened her to see not so much the terror furrowed in the lines of their dark faces, but the knowing acceptance of reality dulling their eyes—the sense that this was just another day in a changing, torn-apart world.

Feeling helpless, knowing she couldn't bring hope to their anguished faces, she leapt to her feet and ran from her hiding place to the edge of battlefield below.

The sun glared with exhausting heat. Sagebrush and thorny cactus scratched her ankles and calves as she ran. The air thick with dust being kicked up from horse hooves and gray with the sulfuric odor of fired gunpowder, made it difficult to see. Her eyes teared. She covered her nose and mouth with her hand.

At a fast clipped gallop, a warrior rode toward her. His arrow pointed toward her, she ducked. The shaft flew over her head. She heard the yelp of a man. Pivoting around she saw the soldier fall from his horse, the arrow piercing his chest. She spun around again, pushing forward past fallen horses and dying men. The stench of blood made her gag.

Quickly she glanced to the river where only a short time ago, beneath its cooling swirling currents, she and Two Moons had made love. Now it ran red with blood as man fought man and horses plunged through the broken torrent water.

Frantically she glanced around searching through all the chaos for him. A bugle blared on a ridge. The earth thundered with horse hooves. Warriors galloped up and down the hillocks, their carbines cocked and ready, their lances and clubs raised; while blue uniformed soldiers so encased in dust they seemed as ashen as the gray horses they rode, fired and reloaded their pistols.

Panic stricken, she threw herself into a cluster of nearby bushes. Afraid to close her burning, dust-inflicted eyes she lay there and did the only thing she could: she prayed.

TWENTY

Sunlight filtered in through the skylight, illuminating the page in Roy's hand. He glanced at his watch: 6 a.m. Hours had passed. Hours of reading numerous documented case studies of past life experiences left him intrigued, yet skeptical. Perhaps it was possible. Hell all those people couldn't be crazy storytellers. Achy from reading so long he rubbed the back of his neck and yawned. As soon as he found Gabrielle he was taking a way overdue vacation and perhaps a visit to his neighborhood psychologist.

It was 8 a.m. by the time John awoke and 10 a.m. by the time they had finished eating their breakfast.

"A watch will do that." John pushed himself from the table. "It becomes your master. You become a slave to time."

"Sorry. I hadn't meant to keep glancing at my watch. It's just that I'm a little anxious to get into town." Roy picked up his plate, helping to clear the table.

John placed the dishes in the sink and turned to face him. One dark eye studied him, while the other lighter one seemed to being looking the other way. "Yes. You should go to the hospital."

"I don't need a hospital." Roy handed him his dish. "Do you have any idea when your friend will stop by?"

A crunch of gravel and halting sound of tires screeched in through the open window. John glanced outside then shifted his gaze back. "So it seems he is here now."

He placed the dish in the sink, turned and walked through the back door.

Roy spun on his heels, moving quickly to the living room. He retrieved his camera, swung it around his neck and headed outside.

John was talking to his friend, a young man of the same nationality. He extended his hand to Roy as he walked over. "Meet my friend, Dean, also known as Red Bird. So he will be happy to drive you into town."

Roy shook Dean's hand. "Thanks, I appreciate it."

"No problem. Got your truck in my shop. Engine's working fine and I replaced the hood, but it'll need some more bodywork and a paint job. Could have it ready by the end of the week."

Roy shook his head. "No. It's fine the way it is. Thanks. I'm kind of in a hurry to get back to work. Let me pay you what I owe you. I can get it fixed later." He reached into his pocket.

"Hey, no problem." Dean waved his hand. "Pay me later. Promised John here I'd drive you to the hospital."

Roy glanced up, puzzled. "I'm fine. I've got to—"

"Said you didn't want to feel responsible for any injuries, right John?"

John nodded. "So you must go."

"I'm fine, really."

Dean walked over to his car, got inside and started the engine.

"I'm not in any pain," Roy insisted as he focused his attention back to his host.

John placed his hand over his arm. "So humor an old man. Go to the hospital. Don't be a slave to that time again."

Roy took a deep breath then exhaled. He wasn't going to get anywhere arguing. "All right. It's the least I can do."

A dog's bark drew his attention to Dean's car. A familiar white hairy beast hung his head out the window. Blue eyes stared at him. Dean waved indicating he was ready to leave.

"Well, I guess this is it. Time ..." Roy turned to address John. "... to ..." Confused, he glanced around. John was nowhere to be found.

A black hawk sat on the fence watching him. Its yellow-flecked eyes peering intensely, the bird cocked its head as if studying him. There was a weird sense of familiarity in those strange eyes that made him increasingly uneasy. Roy glanced away, hastily. "John?" he called out hoping his host would reappear. "I'm leaving."

The hawk cawed. Startled, Roy's shoulders jerked. The hair on the nape of his neck rose. With a whoosh the large bird lifted its wings and took to the sky. In disquieting solitude and wonderment, he stared as the large black bird soared higher and higher and disappeared into the clouds. And John Raven Wing's words seemed to flow through the warm air. *Magic, what is magic ...*

A hot dusty breeze blew, and from the bush in which she hid, Gabrielle could see that some women had begun walking out onto the field in search of their loved ones. It seemed the battle was over, although sporadic fighting still occurred in the distance.

Cautiously she stood and glanced around. Sheer black fright twisted around her heart as she stared at the multitudes of dead bodies strewn across the open plains before her. Where was Two Moons? She didn't want to look down as she ran past the dying. But she did. The putrid stench of blood made her gag. The frozen expressions of terror and pain on the faces of the dead tore at her insides.

Warriors crazy with excitement stripped the soldiers of their clothing and possessions. A vast flood of women ascended from the hills. Their tremolo voices raised in song, tore at her ears.

She glanced to the ridge, praying silently she would see Two Moons standing there. But with all the confusion it was difficult to distinguish him from the other warriors. Mounted Indians with lances rode around jabbing their spears into the fallen men. Others at close range fired into the heads of those still standing. Death and chaos circled her as she ran, not knowing in which direction to go.

She saw Chahanpi moving across the field. A cry of relief broke from Gabrielle's lips. Running toward her friend, she watched as Chahanpi bent down to examine a fallen warrior. Then out of the corner of her eye, Gabrielle caught a glimpse of a soldier hiding in the thick timber nearby. She saw him raise his rifle, saw his aim . . .

"Chahanpi! Watch out!" Gabrielle ran. Her friend's life depended on it. She jumped over bloody, mutilated bodies, pushing away the horror and fear eating at her gut. The moans of the wounded fused with the lamenting screams of the women and crying, confused children. Again she cried out, this time getting her friend's attention. Chahanpi looked up and waved.

"Nooo ..." Gabrielle frantically waved her arms.

Chahanpi began to rise.

"Don't get up," Gabrielle screamed, shaking her head and pointing to her right, over her friend's shoulders.

Gabrielle reached Chahanpi before she had a chance to straighten and smashed into her. A searing hot sting bit Gabrielle's back. They hit the ground with a thud that knocked the air from her lungs and sent an excruciating pain to her chest. She pushed the feeling away. Her eyes closed, her breath held, Gabrielle, too terrified to move, lay paralyzed.

"My friend, I, too, am filled with joy that once again we are together," Chahanpi said softly.

Gabrielle opened her eyes. Her fear subsided with Chahanpi's smile. Her friend was all right. Thank God.

Chahanpi chuckled. "But you are not as light as you look."

"Oh. Right." Her brain numb, her movements jerky, Gabrielle slowly peeled her body off her friend.

"You are hurt!"

Before the words had barely left Chahanpi's mouth, before she felt the wet blood soak her skin and felt the searing pain attack, Gabrielle knew her time upon this earth—her time spent with these people, with the ones she had grown to love, had come to an end. And the thought was more painful than the fire-burning spasm consuming her.

Chahanpi jumped up and thrust her arms beneath Gabrielle's in an effort to help her rise. "We must get you back to the village."

"Two Moons—please ..." Gabrielle's voice broke as a wave of excruciating pain flared like an inferno, engulfing her entire body. Her legs numb, the effort to stand too great, she slumped back to the ground. "I can't—"

"No," Chahanpi said sternly. "You must come with me. Black Hawk's medicine is strong. He will heal your wound." Frantically she glanced around.

Saddened by the fear on her friend's face, the same fear she had seen on Two Moons' the night Shadow Elk had died, Gabrielle reached out to touch her arm. "Chahanpi, look at me ..." She squeezed gently. "Look at me."

Tears spilled from Chahanpi's eyes.

"Until I came here, I didn't know ..." Gabrielle took a deep breath. Exhaling the sharp pain, she continued, "... what it was like to have a real friend—"

"We will have many long talks about our being friends." Again Chahanpi glanced around.

"Yes. You will hear my voice in the wind—"

"No." Chahanpi jerked her gaze back and shook her head. "You will not walk the path to the land above—"

"Alone." Two Moons' shadow loomed before her. He knelt by her side. His hands were warm against her cool ones.

"Two Moons, I—"

"Hush my blue-eyed one. I am here now and will never leave you again." Gently, he scooped her up in his arms. Gabrielle laid her head against his shoulder and closed her eyes. Despite the fear throbbing, she felt so safe cradled against him. His strength, his heat, his closeness like a protective shroud, comforted her.

She heard him talking to Chahanpi, felt her friend's gentle fingers brush her hair and lightly touch her arm. When she glanced up, Chahanpi turned away.

"Chahanpi wait." Gabrielle reached over her head and struggled to remove the gold chain hanging between her breasts. A spasm of pain shot across her shoulder blades.

"Please," she wheezed and held out the locket. "See that my mother gets this."

Chahanpi nodded, took the chain and hurried away.

Gabrielle glanced to Two Moons.

"Could you take me to our river, to the river where we made love?"

She heard his intake of breath, could feel the muscles in his arm grow taut with tension. Her chest burned with pain. Light headed her lids fluttered.

Without a word he carried her to the tree beside the river and gently laid her down beneath its boughs.

His jaw quivered as he gazed down at her.

She shivered. "I am so cold."

Lying by her side, he wrapped his arms around her and brought her close to his chest. "Take my heat, it saved you once let it do so again. All my strength, all my life, take it, it is yours." He kissed her head. The pain in his voice was as heavy as the torturing pain racking through her body. He knew ...

"This isn't fair." She began to cry. "I don't want to die. Not now, not when I just found you." She saw her tears mirrored in his.

"You are not going to die. It is a long journey you will take. The spirits are calling you back to the land from which you came."

She shook her head. Pain exploded. She cringed. The bravado of his words were meant as comfort, but in his eyes she saw the sadness he tried so hard to hide. "I—I don't want to go ... there is so much ... talk ... it's too difficult ... to breathe. I don't' want to lose you." Pain erupted simultaneously through her chest and back.

"You will not lose me." A tear slipped from his clouded eyes. She reached up and wiped it away.

"I show my weakness. I am sorry." He glanced away.

"You are not weak. You could never be weak. You are my warrior, my ..." She drew in a shallow rapid breath. "... brave, handsome warrior."

Two Moons' heart tore, crumbling bit by bit with every shallow breath she took. He bit the inside of his lip to keep his jaw from quivering. She would die and so would he, for to walk this land without her by his side would not be living.

"My heart is laid upon the ground, for had I listened to your words and chose not to fight, perhaps—"

His strangled words seemed to echo in his ears.

"No." Weakly she reached up and touched his cheek. "This is foolish talk. You had to fight. You would have died on those reservations." Her eyes closed.

He brought his hand to her wrist and kissed her fingertips. "To spare your life, I would gladly go." A sharp ache stabbed his chest.

"Now who is talking fool ... ishly?" She turned her head.

His gaze followed hers to the battlefield. Wounded warriors, dragged their weary bodies back to camp, leaving wailing women and crying children behind searching for their loved ones. Dulled by their keening cries, feeling nothing but his own pain, he glanced away. He, too, wished to scream like the women; would like to take his anger out on any soldiers who still lived, but he had not the strength or will to fight.

"Open your eyes to me, my blue-eyed one. Let me see the summer sky once more."

She turned toward him, her eyes brimming with tears. "The fighting is over?" she asked in a whisper.

"Yes. The one you call Custer and his men no longer walk this earth. My sister's shame has been revenged."

She took a shallow breath. "It was by your arrow?"

"Yes." He felt as though he couldn't breathe.

"I always wondered...." Her voice faded. Her head dropped.

And as the darkness reached out to cover her, it seemed to pull him down as well, leaving a lonely warrior to weep beside his loved one—his life.

Two Moons' tormented scream echoed across the plains. He wanted to die. On bended knees he stared down at her, his blue-eyed one, his love. Cottonwood flowers fell, covering her with white petals, fulfilling his vision of a woman surrounded in white; and he recalled, when he had found her in the snow. He brushed her hair lightly. "What a fool I have been. So many moons wasted in questions and doubts ..." With gentle fingers he touched her lips. "We could have spent those days together."

Dead in spirit to all but the woman who lay before him, Two Moons leaned back on his haunches and slowly drew out his knife.

He barely felt his blade as it sliced through his hair; barely felt it nick his ear, as he sheared off his locks. "Soon," he promised. He bent over and kissed her. "Soon I will travel to the land above, where we shall be together." A promise had been made—a promise that he would never leave her.

His words strangled in the back of his throat, he kissed her closed eyes. "*Ohinniya*, always, forever ..." He brushed his lips against hers.

"*Nimitawa ktelo*, you will be mine."

Gathering his strength, he stood and raised his arms to the sky. "*Tunkashila* forgive me. I wish not to dishonor you or my people. I shame myself, this I know. There is no honor in what I am about to do. Forgive me." To take his own life was the only way; the only way to give up his soul to the one Blue Eyes was destined to be with.

A black hawk floated lazily on the wind. Two Moons closed his eyes and prayed, thanking the great ones above for sending one of his animal spirits to guide him. It seemed they understood that he could not wait until his bones were weak with age to see Blue Eyes again. That he had made her a promise he could not break. "It is a good day to die."

With a downward motion he arched his knife. But before its tip found its mark upon his skin, a sharp stabbing pain cut into his flesh. Two Moons' eyes flashed open, to stare in disbelief at the arrow piercing his chest.

"At last, my brother, it seems I have won the final battle."

He glanced up to see Little Wolf strutting toward him.

"Yes, it is my arrow you wear upon your breast." He spat the word into Two Moons' face. "Mine. Not like your friend, Shadow Elk, who died from a stolen Crow arrow."

Pain attacked. Two Moons doubled over. His knife fell from his hand.

"You look surprised." Little Wolf grinned. "Your feeble attempts at finding me that night only proved once and for all which of the two of us is the better warrior."

Two Moons reached out to grab Little Wolf's neck. "I should have killed you when I had the chance." The ground beneath him blurred. Clutching the arrow, he shook his head, hearing Little Wolf's laughter.

Little Wolf poked Two Moons' chest, causing him to stumble.

He caught his footing then glanced up. "I must thank you ... my brother ..." His shoulders heavy, his chest on fire, he wavered in his spot. "You have made my heart light. Now I can travel on my journey with honor."

Through the hazy cloudiness of his eyes, he could see the confusion on Little Wolf's face.

"What talk is this? This is the talk of a crazy man who is afraid to admit he has been beaten."

The pain too great, no longer able to stand, Two Moons sank to his knees. "Before your arrow pierced my heart ..." He coughed. Blood bubbled up into his throat. He swallowed with difficulty. "I sought death by my own hands." Short winded, he continued. "So it seems by friend, because of you ..." He coughed again. He could feel the blood now seeping from the corner of his mouth. "I shall die as a warrior should."

Anger exploded on Little Wolf's face. "No! This cannot be so." Like a man bitten by a mad animal, he began to stamp the ground and pull at his skin.

Knowing Little Wolf would forever walk the ground tormented by losing this final battle, Two Moons closed his eyes. No longer hearing Mother Earth's voice around him or feeling any pain, he gave himself up to his animal spirit, who led him down his path—a path that lead to Blue Eyes.

On a high butte, in the far off distance, a lone wolf stood with his head raised to the sky. And throughout death's silence one could hear his haunting cry floating in the wind like a beacon in the darkness, leading two destined lovers to their promised land....

TWENTY-ONE

A nother coincidence? He doubted it. After Dean had dropped him off at the hospital he had considered leaving, but first there was that phone call. And that was why he now found himself standing over a hospital bed, his search for Gabrielle at an end.

Roy glanced at Mrs. Camden, who stood out in the hall talking to a nurse. He still couldn't get over their being at the phone at the same time. When he had heard her mention Gabrielle's name to whomever was at the end of her line, he had thought he'd heard incorrectly. Then his boss confirmed it. Gabrielle Camden had been found at the site, in a coma and had been in the hospital for three days.

Needless to say, he'd felt like a fool. It didn't matter. He'd made a decision. He was going to open a gallery, fill it with art and his photographs. Any money made he would donate to the Native American Children's fund. This was his dream—a dream he hoped to share with Gabrielle.

He glanced to the cold stark white walls of her hospital room. He'd do any thing to make her happy—make her want him, and he was going to make her see that.

His gaze settled on her sleeping form. Did she sense his presence? He brought her warm hand to his lips. Would she feel his kiss? The deep cutting ache in his chest was from no accident. It was from the fear that she would send him away without getting to know him.

"Gabrielle. Wake up. Do you hear me?" he whispered. "Give us a chance. I realize now that I've had feelings for you for such a long time, only I couldn't tell you. Probably thought it was a one-man paper, what with me hanging around so much." He laughed. "Fact was, I asked to be assigned to you." His throat felt like an old document, dry, dusty.

"You felt it, didn't you, the connection? There's something there between us. I know there is." He raked his hand through his hair. "Hiding wherever it is that you are right now, isn't gonna stop me from visiting you every day till you open up those beautiful blue eyes of yours."

He shook her gently. "Do you hear me?"

Gently he placed her hand by her side then ran his fingers along her brow. "Come back to me. Please. You owe me that dance."

"Welcome back Blue Eyes." In the hazy dreamlike state of her mind, Gabrielle heard him call her name. Two Moons! He hadn't left her. Her heart soared—only to crash like a comet hurtling to earth. Roy's face materialized before her. It was his voice she'd heard.

She struggled to sit, disoriented. "I don't understand?" She glanced around the room.

"You've been in a coma."

A wild flash of grief ripped through her. "No." Just her imagination? Images formed in a coma? It couldn't be. Two Moons, Chahanpi, Shadow Elk—they all seemed so real. It couldn't be.

"How long have I—"

"A couple of days. Your co-workers found you at the site."

She dropped back against the pillow, turned her face from Roy's questioning gaze and closed her eyes. How could she explain the pain she felt slicing through her and the loneliness that brought tears to her eyes.

Gentle fingers stroked her temple. "Gabrielle?" His touch sent tingles across her neck.

"I'll go if you want. But I'll not give up on you. This is one battle you will not win so easily."

There was a vague familiarity in his words that made her heart swell with feelings of desire she thought dead. She turned to face him, noticed how he clasped and unclasped his hand as though tense.

He started to rise from her bed and she grabbed the collar of his opened shirt. "Wait. Don't go."

Her glance dropped to his smooth bare chest and she tried to ignore the pulsating surge of blood throbbing at the base of her throat.

He tugged his shirt closed. "Sorry, the air conditioning's broken."

She brushed aside his hand and pointed to a set of marks near his left breast. "What's that?" She bit her lip, fought to calm her racing pulse and swirling emotions. Two Moons said Roy would wear his totem. Could it really be? She knew from the very beginning there was something special about Roy. That unknown spark. That connection.

He glanced down at his chest. "A birthmark."

Gabrielle's spirit lifted. "They look like two crescent moons."

"Yeah." He rubbed his chin. "I guess. I never saw it that way."

"A good likeness, no?" A deep voice asked from the hallway.

A good likeness? Yes. Roy and Two Moons' mannerisms were so

similar. Gabrielle turned, but out of the corner of her eye she saw the astonishment on Roy's face.

"John? You're ... How?"

The doctor ambled over to her bed and Gabrielle took a quick breath of utter astonishment. The Shaman of the village had two different colored eyes. The thought froze in her brain. Had she dreamt the entire thing up?

Her mind reeled splintering off in a million different directions. Could it be? Had she really? Had she seen the doctor in her coma? Had her befuddled mind played tricks on her, sending her to a place that hadn't existed, merging those around her, with those made up in a comatose state?

"So how are you feeling?" The doctor picked up her chart, studying the paper.

She stared. Screams of frustration welled in the back of her throat. What of little Curly? George had curly hair and Two Moons' sister had George's mentally. Was Rattling Blanket the mother she wished she'd had? Was Shadow Elk just a reminder of the guilt she'd felt over her brother's death? And Roy wearing that Native American neckband, wearing Two Moons' mark. God, she felt like Dorothy in the *Wizard of Oz*.

"In answer to your question. I did my rounds as you slept." The doctor flipped the chart closed. "Today I took the shorter route here."

She noticed how Roy's brows fell; noticed how a ray of sunlight kissed his light blonde hair.

"All this time you had a car?" Roy asked, his voice tense.

"Car? No." The doctor shook his head. "A motorcycle—no place to sit an injured man."

"Injured?" Her gaze shot back to Roy. "What—"

"I'm fine. I'll tell you later." He flashed her a smile, a familiar smile that brightened his face and lit up his eyes. And as she stared into those dark brown pupils she felt a stirring in her breast—a spark of hope.

"So you two have much to talk about." The doctor turned and placed his hand on Roy's shoulder. "Take good care of her. I release her into your hands."

As quickly has he had come, the doctor left and she was alone once again with Roy.

"Roy—"

He turned. Their gaze met and she remembered Two Moons' words. *You but have to look into the eyes of the one with the yellow hair and you will see me there.*

"What is it that you see when you look at me?" Roy asked, his voice tender.

A man from another century who stole her heart. A man she grieved for, but who could have been a dream.

"Do you see a man who cares deeply for you, or just that pain in the neck reporter you wished so desperately to run from?"

His hand felt warm in hers. His beautiful long fingers, strongly interweaving through hers, sent a familiar tingling to the pit of her stomach. Run? No. She was through with running.

Gently she brushed her fingers along his cheek. This man was her reality.

Hope glistened in his eyes. He leaned closer.

His kiss drew her breath away. An intense euphoria exploded around her as though at that moment, two souls instantaneously met, fusing. The dreamy familiar intimacy of his warm, moist lips pressed against hers made her senses reel. She inhaled his musky male scent. Two Moons' scent? Roy's? And his touch upon her chin, so familiar, so comforting. There was no denying the strong magnetism between them. The sense of completeness she felt. No denying the desire igniting her soul. Dream or magic—the impossible—the hope of loving someone again, suddenly became a reality. She loved him. The admission dredged from a place beyond logic, beyond reason, made her heart thump erratically.

She drew away, staring deeply into Roy's eyes. "I need to tell you what happened to me. I—"

He placed a warm finger upon her lip. "Hush. Lie back." Gently he eased her shoulders back against the pillow. "There'll be plenty of time for swapping stories later. And boy do I have a doozy for you. But right now I demand that you get some rest."

She smiled. "And if I refuse?"

"Refuse? You refuse me? No. I think not. I'll have that dance and your heart." He grinned and took her hand in his. "Take all the time you need. I'll wait for you." He leaned forward.

His dark warm eyes gazed deeply into hers, eyes that brought her back to another time, another place.

"We lost each other once. This time if you'll have me," he said softly. He rubbed his cheek against the back of her hand. "I'll not be so easy to get rid of." His mouth covered hers.

"Gabrielle!" Their kiss broken by the sound of Willimina's voice, he leaned back. The smile on his face, like a ray of sunshine, warmed her soul.

Her mother hurried over and threw her arms around her neck. Gabrielle stiffened. Disappointment mingled with anxiety.

Roy stood and backed away. Over Willimina's shoulder Gabrielle saw him discreetly leave the room.

Teary-eyed, Willimina fiddled with Gabrielle's collar and hair. "Thank God. Thank God," she mumbled. "I was so frightened I had lost you. What would I have done without you?" She brought Gabrielle to her chest and hugged tightly. "I love you."

"You love me?" Gabrielle sat back, momentarily baffled. "How can you love me when I caused you so much grief? Dad and Charles they'd—"

"Of course, I love you." Surprise arched Willimina's eyes. "I don't blame you. I never did. Charles' death was an accident. You weren't to blame."

"It drove daddy away—I drove him away."

"No." she said, her voice hard. "Your father was having affairs on and off for years long before I even had you. It was a mutual agreement, his leaving." She reached out and stroked Gabrielle's cheek. "I'm so sorry you blamed yourself."

Weariness began to settle in and guilt. "I'm sorry." Tears clouded Gabrielle's vision. "I've been so distant. All this time I thought you hated me, blamed me—"

"Have I been that cold?" A sad tired look settled on Willimina's face.

Gabrielle sighed. "I think we both were."

An uncomfortable silence hung over them; a silence that undeniably brought with it the truth. If she had learned one thing from Rattle Blanket, it was that she needed her mother.

"Do you think we can start over?" Gabrielle asked somewhat hesitate. "Maybe be friends?"

Willimina nodded. "Friends." She smiled weakly.

She reached into her pocket. The locket dangling from her fingers caught Gabrielle off guard. A sudden jolt of shock flew through her.

"Here. I want you to have this." Willimina reached over and slipped the chain around Gabrielle's neck. "I was up in the attic going through some old things and found that locket. It belonged to your great-great-grandmother and was handed down through the generations. Open it."

Gabrielle's heart raced. "The colonel lived?"

A look of bewilderment crossed her mother's face. "You know Jackson died at the battle."

A twinge of pain tightened Gabrielle's chest. Her fingers shook as she opened the locket.

"Her name was Woman-Who-Walks-With-The-Stars and this ..." Willimina pointed to the woman she knew more intimately than her mother would ever guess. "This is her daughter, White Swan."

Gabrielle blinked, confused. She ran her fingertip over the picture. A warm glow flowed gently through her as she shared a moment back in time with a man who had called her daughter. Dream or reality? Had she seen this picture at some other point in time? Had the image been hiding in the recesses of her mind? "What happened to them?"

"White Swan died during the Battle of Little Big Horn. Woman-Who-Walks-With-The-Stars lived on a Crow reservation until she died." Her mother leaned back and sighed. "I should have told you this a long time ago. I just—"

Gabrielle placed her hand over her mother's. "It's all right, really. Tell me more."

A pensive shimmer in the shadow of her eyes, Willimina's lips pursed; then she continued. "Her oldest daughter, Bright Star—"

"White Swan had a sister?" Gabrielle asked, amazed at the thrill that news brought.

"Yes, born a year before her, the daughter of the colonel. She is your great-grandmother. You know her as Anna. Anyway," Willimina waved her hand dismissively, "she married an American soldier and had two children. Their daughter—your grandmother—eventually met an Englishmen who took her away to London where they raised their family. By now no trace of their red blood showed on their face." Willimina frowned. "And don't give me that disgusted look. Times were different. They accepted only those of blue-blooded heritage into society."

"You should have told me. I had a right to know."

Her mother sighed. "I know. I'm sorry."

"I think I'm tired."

Willimina leaned forward, planted a kiss on Gabrielle's forehead then stood up. "I'll be back tomorrow to take you home."

"OK."

"And Gabrielle?"

"Yes."

Willimina hesitated. "When you feel up to it ... I'd like to have you over for dinner."

"I'd love to come, only ..." Gabrielle glanced to the hall where Roy stood patiently, the man she had traveled a long and winding road to meet—the love she no longer needed to search for....

Disappointment clouded her mother's face.

Gabrielle smiled. "There's someone I'd like to invite."

Over the next couple months, Roy became her world. He was the air she breathed and the sunshine that filled her life. He courted her by day, taking her on picnics in the park, or for long walks in the woods. They visited the excavating site where a white marker bore White Swan's name.

At night he'd take her dancing.

He taught her the names of the birds he was photographing, about camera lights and angles. They recited case studies on reincarnation and soul mates. And by spending time with him came the realization that she had been given a great gift. The love of her life was two men, two men who were one in the same.

"Let me make love to you here and now beneath the sky." Roy's deep voice, sensual, warm, blew against her ear.

The sweet fragrance of cut grass wafted in the air.

Gabrielle, ran her fingers through his hair, across the smooth expanse of his bronzed hairless chest. She leaned forward and kissed his well-developed peck muscles, kissed the crescent birthmarks nestled in the hollow of his chest. His breathing quickened as her lips trailed a path down to his belly, to the top of his groin.

He grabbed her shoulders, lifted her chin and pressed his hot mouth against hers. Gently his tongue coaxed her open and she urgently welcomed him.

The soft grass met her back as they fell upon the earth. Their gaze met. Their fingers blended as they reached for the buttons on her blue silk blouse. Quickly together the blouse came undone. Ever so slowly he slipped the straps of her bra from her shoulders, and blazed a path of warm kisses that left her breathless. She heard herself groan.

"So soft..." His voice trailed. He kissed the swell of her breasts. "Like satin against my lips."

The cool air, his eager fingers, touched her hardening nipples.

"Wait." Roy reached over for the picnic basket and pulled out a bottle of honey. A mischievous grin tugged at his lips as he squeezed the bottle over her breast. The warm, thick, sticky liquid dropped, hitting its mark.

She closed her eyes. As he sucked and gently tugged on her nipple, a fire began to build deep down in the pit of her belly. A fire so right she knew without a doubt that this man at her breast was the missing link in her life. Now she understood where her jaunt into the past had been leading to. It led to this man.

Lying in his arms, with the afterglow of love still clinging to their bodies, Roy nuzzled the back of her neck. He ran his finger between her shoulder blades.

"How did you get this scar?"

She glanced over her shoulder, baffled. "What scar?"

"This small round one in the middle of your back."

Dazed she sat up. The bullet. She had taken a bullet in the back. Tears welled in her eyes.

"Gabrielle?" He reached out and gathered her into the circle of his arms. "What's wrong?"

She closed her eyes for a brief second and Chahanpi's face emerged in the darkness, only to evaporate by an onrushing wind.

As the sun set over the ridge, Gabrielle spoke of the battle and how she died. And with this newfound knowledge, a peacefulness settled over the valley and over her heart.

And as the silhouette of a crescent moon began to rise over Mother Earth merging the two worlds together once more, Roy and Gabrielle thanked the Great Spirits above, for leading them down the path to a deeper understanding of the great mystery of life, where love waited for them at the end of the road—and their find through time.

Author notes:

Legend has it that no warrior came forward to say he was the slayer of Custer. Rodman Wanamaker of Philadelphia gathered the eleven tribes together that took part in the battle and offered a sizable reward for the warrior who could prove himself the slayer. Not knowing for sure which warrior had done the killing, it was decided amongst the tribes that an elder, Chief Brave Bear, be elected to assume the honorary distinction since he had been at the great fight.

Curly is fictitious, however my research indicates that several Cheyenne's believed Custer did father a Cheyenne child named Yellow Bird.

Although Gabrielle in Two Moons' eyes was his to do with as he pleased, which included sharing her, women captives were for the most part fairly treated and commonly adopted through marriage to their captor. If they rejected this proposal they could be returned to their people. The removal of the protective rope from a Native American woman, made a man subject to death at the hands of the girl's relatives.

Sioux religion demanded self-denial to a high degree. Men kept constant vigil on themselves. Not only did the religion provide lessons and penalties for those who would disregard the precept of self-control, but it seemed to add further danger in the form of evil forces which tested man's courage. With this in mind, for the purpose of my story, Two Moons believes that by taking his own life he is shaming himself and his gods.

To my readers:

Although I live in the state of New York, which is so different from the vast open prairies of Montana and Wyoming where my story A FIND THROUGH TIME takes place, I have always loved the West and the people whose struggles and perseverance has had such a great impact on our lives today. If not for those pioneers who traveled across our great continent in search of a new life, if not for the people who fought for what they believed in, who struggled to preserve their way of life and sacrificed everything in the name of progress, we would not have moved on to become the society we are today. It is from their blood, sweat accomplishments and sometimes their deaths that we have learned and grown.

I have always felt a connection to the Native American people that I cannot explain. I once had a reader ask me if I was Native American. What a wonderful complimenting question! Although my answer was no, as a believer of reincarnation, I believe Two Moons and I share the same soul, for his voice was so clear in my mind and his story had to be told.

As for soul mates ...

I knew I was going to marry my husband before we even fell in love!

I hope you enjoy reading A FIND THROUGH TIME as much as I enjoyed living it through the eyes of Two Moons, Roy and Gabrielle.

Marianne Petit

Marianne Petit is vice president of the Long Island Chapter of the Romance Writers of America and is a member of the New York City RWA Chapter. Her love of writing stems back to high school. She spent hours reading Nancy Drew, Alfred Hitchcock and poetry. Her love of history stems from her father, Roger, a Frenchman whose love of American history greatly influenced her.

When she is not writing, Marianne works with her husband in his Chiropractic office. She loves to ski, raft, horseback ride, and enjoys the theater. Marianne lives on Long Island with her husband and two teenage sons. She has been happily married for 21 years.

Readers may write to Marianne via e-mail at born2rite1@aol.com or visit her Web site at http://cordovainc.com/~marianne/.

Printed in the United States
52183LVS00001B/7-15

9 781930 076181